I've travelled the world twice over,
Met the famous: saints and sinners,
Poets and artists, kings and queens,
Old stars and hopeful beginners,
I've been where no-one's been before,
Learned secrets from writers and cooks
All with one library ticket
To the wonderful world of books.

© JANICE JAMES.

A CURE FOR DYING

Chief Superintendent Charmian Daniels decided to make her roots in Windsor, but the pleasantness of the local community was disturbed when someone tried to attack her. On the same night, another attack is made — this time on a horse. Then the body of a woman is found, her throat cut, just like the horse's. The elusive connection between the killings taunts Charmian as she is drawn into the enquiries on a personal and professional level. Charmian has another worry: the deaths seem to be Ripper-style killings. Could a woman be a serial killer?

JENNIE MELVILLE

◆

A CURE
FOR DYING

Complete and Unabridged

ULVERSCROFT
Leicester

First published in Great Britain in 1989 by
Macmillan London Limited
London

First Large Print Edition
published June 1992
by arrangement with
Macmillan London Limited
London

British Library CIP Data

Melville, Jennie
A cure for dying.—Large print ed.—
Ulverscroft large print series: mystery
I. Title
823.914 [F]

ISBN 0–7089–2667–3

Published by
F. A. Thorpe (Publishing) Ltd.
Anstey, Leicestershire
Set by Words & Graphics Ltd.
Anstey, Leicestershire
Printed and bound in Great Britain by
T. J. Press (Padstow) Ltd., Padstow, Cornwall

Author's Note

I have to thank Mrs Henry Forbes for the information she so generously provided about polo, polo ponies, and the size and style of their shoes, all of which I used. But with even greater generosity and trust she lent me a valuable and informative book, *An Introduction to Polo* by Marco, a pseudonym of the young Lord Mountbatten. I owe a lot to this book and to Mrs Forbes.

In addition to this help from a friend, I received a great deal of help from another quarter. Anne Holdsworth of the Forensic Science Society responded to my appeals for advice by suggesting the names of several psychologists who were knowledgeable about the sort of crime I was writing about.

On the telephone Eric Ward and Dr Gisli Hannes Gudjonsson were kind and helpful.

But my greatest debt here is to Dr Tom Pitt-Aikens, and I want to thank him for all the help he gave me. He was informative, instructive and stimulating. He showed me things I might never have seen for myself. He opened doors in my mind.

Of course, any errors I have fallen into on polo or psychology are entirely and absolutely my own, I must make that very clear.

All people, places and institutions are completely fictional.

J.M.

1

THE first body was already in place and waiting before Charmian Daniels, or the local police in that small but royal Berkshire town, knew anything about the case. Before there was a case to speak of.

This first body had four legs and a tail and was quite unlike all the other bodies that were to follow. Nevertheless, it marked the beginning. It was not the worst death, nor the most violent, nor the bloodiest of those that followed, but it was the one that counted.

Every sequence of murders has a beginning, a significant death, and for the murders that marked that royal summer, this was it.

As Madame de Sévigné said of the lady who was reported to have walked after having had her head cut off, "In matters of this sort, it is the first step that counts." This was the first step.

Three other steps, at least, followed.

There may have been others, unknown, unburied. The bodies were never buried, that was not their point. They were for display.

Charmian Daniels, a high-ranking woman police detective, would always wonder how much she made happen.

When she first arrived in Windsor, a woman throwing herself into a new part of her life, taking a sabbatical year and working on a thesis in a nearby university, she had rented a flat above a friend's. She had enjoyed it, and living close to Anny Cooper, old companion and ally from college days had been fun. Now the thesis was finished, the diploma won, and she had gone back to work as a policewoman. She could have stayed living where she was, but Anny's marriage was breaking up noisily, and that was less fun. Better to keep a distance. And then there was the cat.

Charmian had a lean and muscular tabby called Muff who had let her know in unmistakable ways that cats and flats are not compatible. So she had found a small Victorian house in a terrace near the railway station and was in the process of moving in. Muff liked it.

She was enjoying a new house, a new and important job in the Metropolitan police, a new way of life. She could live here and travel to London every day to work. There was the motorway and the railway, the travelling was simple. If she had to stay the night in London, there was the university women's club near Piccadilly where she could have a room for the night. She was learning to make things easy for herself.

Kate, who was Anny Cooper's only child, and Charmian's god-daughter was going to lodge in the house. A wayward girl, she was (for entirely personal and impractical reasons) homeless. She was glad of the room, Charmian was glad of the rent. This was the first house she had tried to own, all her other homes had been possessed in different ways, and the mortgage was formidable.

She had been surprised at the price of a tiny period house in the town. There was something about the near presence of majesty that put a premium on property.

"You can see the castle from the bedroom windows," the estate agent had pointed out. "And look at the name of the street. That's good for a thou' or more." The terrace was called Maid of Honour Row.

"Sounds like a kind of cake," Charmian had said, as she signed the contract. But she enjoyed writing it as her address. For a woman who had been born of sound working-class stock and been educated in Dundee University, she was getting very middle class. South of England tastes, she told herself.

The moving in was easy. Anny and Kate helped her repaint the house. Anny, an artist of distinction, could do anything with her hands, and Kate was training to be an architect. She did the hard bits, like altering the wiring and checking the plumbing.

"You have got a circle of sorts in the electric wiring," she reported, "you won't blow up." And there would be enough power to support without danger all the electric gadgets that came with her like the necessities of life: her computer, her printer, her video and her very very

4

special music player that she set up herself with such loving precision that there was barely room for her bed. "These little Victorian houses are built better than you'd think."

"Thank you, god-daughter."

"Don't mention it, godmother. Let me know if there's anything I can do. Like redesigning the kitchen, say. You might need me there. I'd call that sink an antique if it was any newer. As it is, I think fossil might be the better word."

"I like it," said Charmian, to whom her kitchen was not of great importance, and who had spent all she could afford on new curtains and broadloom for the floor.

"You won't see much of me, Char'. I won't be in the way. I'm out most of the time."

"Don't you believe it," said her mother. "You'll know she's there, I can promise."

Kate kissed her mother, banged Charmian affectionately on the shoulder, hoisted the huge bolster bag that was always with her over her shoulder, and prepared to depart.

"Know who the kids are next door?" she said as she left.

"No." There had not been time to think about neighbours.

"Find out. They interest me. There are four of them, and they come back at night in the same old car and looking knackered. I don't know when they leave. I've never been up that early." Kate had been camping out in the house for a week.

"All girls?"

"Three girls and one chap. He's the one I'm interested in."

"You do your own work."

"Oh I will. But you could do the background investigation. You're the detective."

When Anny and Kate had both left, and Charmian was alone for the first time in her own house, she went to the bedroom window and looked out. Yes, there was the castle. You could see the top of Tom Tower, and beyond that the Royal Standard fluttering.

She looked down into the street. There was Muff slowly crossing the road. She would have to explain to her about traffic. And there were her neighbours returning, somewhat earlier than Kate had suggested, but certainly looking tired and kind of exercised.

Three girls, wearing jeans and sweaters, and the lad on whom Kate had her eye.

He was certainly attractive. Fair curly hair, a sun-tanned face, and a body that looked at once light yet muscular. He was like a sophisticated cheerful cherub. Also a lad that knew his way around. He and Kate might fight on equal weights.

Three girls, two tall above average, and one short with light auburn hair, and the boy. These were her neighbours, a nice lot, she decided. Perhaps they were a pop group. They looked as though they worked as well as lived together.

As they went into the house, one of the girls, the short one, bent down and patted Muff.

Muff did not respond, such was not her way, but without doubt it registered. Muff came from a long line of cats with sound coats and good memories. A friend was a friend and not forgotten. Likewise enemies, and she had a few of those, too. Charmian had seen to her alarm

7

that there was already definite hostility between her cat and a small dog who lived down the road.

She returned to tidying her books and papers. She had notes to check on a case of child murder that was going up to the Crown Prosecution Service, an institution which, like most police of her generation she regarded with caution. Action would be taken there, she hoped, but with juries so difficult now, you never knew who would get away with what. Then she had to collect her own mind for a talk she had promised to give to a local self-help for women group in a club building on the Slough Road. That was a few weeks off, but she needed to think about it.

Women and murder was her business. Murdered women, murderous women, and women innocently involved in murder, this was her work. She knew that it was against the current feminist thinking that no crime was special to women, but lately she had come to wonder.

Her friend Anny was hostile to her work. "You complete an investigation, arrest someone and then that's it. You leave someone else to pick up the pieces."

"I do my job."

"Is that all you believe in?" Anny herself was sufficiently rich and talented to maintain high standards. Being poor on sixpence a year had never been part of her life.

"I believe in evil. And so would you, Anny dear, if you'd seen what I've seen."

Their arguments usually ended this way.

Charmian finished her work for the evening. She made a cup of coffee and took it to the window to drink. She was enjoying the pleasures of ownership.

As she looked out she saw the group from next door leave the house. One girl, the short one who had patted Muff, got on a cycle and pedalled down the road, while the other three linked arms and strolled off in the direction of the Duke of Wellington pub on the corner. Or the Buzz Disco and Nightclub which was also in that direction. They saw her at the window and gave a friendly wave, she waved back.

After that, Charmian got no further in knowing them. They waved when they met and she waved back.

True to her word, Kate was not in the way. In fact, after a few days she did not appear at all, causing Charmian to wonder if she had done one of her disappearing acts. Kate was given to taking off and had done so more than once before. Very often without notice. This time, however, Kate telephoned from an airport to say she was flying to Venice to study the architecture. She had an affinity with airports that only the child of rich and self-absorbed parents could have. Sometimes they must have seemed more like home to her than her parents' house.

A week or so passed. Charmian did not get home every evening, but when back she was amused to see how often the same evening ritual was performed next door. Off went the three to wherever they did go, but judging by the sounds she heard as they came back it was the Duke of Wellington; and off on her bike went the other girl.

One evening she was watering the newly planted shrubs in her front garden and keeping an eye on Muff at the same time (she too gardened in her way, but her motives were different) when the performance took place.

The boy saw her watching as the girl on the bike sped away. Perhaps Charmian looked interested because he smiled at her.

"She keeps to a routine."

"Oh yes. Old Les," he continued to look amused. "Every night she goes off to feed her horse and see her father. Or is it feed the father and see the horse? It could be either."

"Les?"

"Lesley. I'm Johnny and the others are Freda and Gillian." No surnames were offered, but she guessed there was no blood relationship between them.

"Evening, Miss Daniels," he gave a wave of the hand and was gone.

So he knew her name while she did not know his, knew more about her in short than she knew about him. This was an unusual position for Charmian to be in and she thought about it with some concentration.

She went back inside, fed the cat, washed her hair, noted without surprise

11

that several grey hairs were appearing among the red, and decided she must find a new hairdresser.

When she decoded this thought, which she guessed not entirely what it appeared to be on the surface, she decided it meant she was regretting the man with whom she had once been more than half in love. He had been good about hair.

Since he had been a murderer, this regret was most unwise and must be banished.

She picked up a letter which had come by the afternoon post and which was from a man with whom she was not in love, but who had for her some feeling (what exactly she was never quite sure, Humphrey having been professionally trained not to let his right hand know what his left hand was up to) and for whom, in a way, she had once worked, and to whom she certainly owed her promotion.

A card fell out of the letter. A very elegant and beautiful thick creamy card, nobly embossed and engraved.

An invitation to luncheon in a pavilion on Smith's Field, The Great Park, and then to watch the match between this illustrious side and that distinguished team for the Duke's Diamond Cup, sponsored by Marco Polo Industries, plc.

In the presence of HRH, who would be handing over the cup.

"Polo," she said to herself. "What do I know about polo?"

As if he had anticipated her thoughts, Humphrey had scribbled underneath, "If you are going to continue to live where you do, then this is something you have to learn about."

And that was it. No words such as "It would be lovely to see you." Or, "I do hope you can come, I shall look forward to it."

Just a kind of royal command.

"I shan't accept."

Charmian threw the card to the floor. The childish gesture pleased her. Then, because it was so childish, she picked up the card and replaced it in the envelope. That was more dignified. You had to hang on to your dignity with Humphrey, and your sense of humour, or he won all down the line.

Muff's face was pressed against the window, demanding entrance. Since the house move she had won herself enormous freedom of movement and knew every exit and entrance to the house, roaming dangerously free and wide.

Charmian drew the window up. She could see the tree-lined street in the moonlight. Les was just cycling up.

There was a figure across the road under the lamplight that seemed to be trying to catch her attention. Charmian looked.

"Damn it, a flasher."

He had placed himself with a quiet skill that suggested he knew the area, had been here before looking around. There was always any number of young people passing up and down this road at night either from the Duke of Wellington or the Buzz Disco. He would not lack for an audience.

There were two things she could do: she could go out and make an arrest, or she could ring up the local police.

But the man was already moving off. It was likely that he was a known figure, already observed by the local

14

mob. They might have a record for him and an address. They could certainly start looking.

She used the telephone.

She knew precisely the extension to demand.

The group of women to whom Charmian was booked to give a talk had mixed feelings about her.

"We want her to speak on women and self-help in violence, whereas it seems to me she is going to talk on violent women and women who provoke upon themselves violence," said Miriam Miller who had been on the telephone to Charmian.

"It's her job, she is a police officer." Flora Trust was sitting at the table typing up the minutes of the last meeting. She always left them until the last minute and many a good argument as to accuracy and what had actually been said had been provoked at committee meetings on account of this habit. "And after all we have our Karate Club so we do tackle that side of it."

The two were founder-members and

chairperson and secretary respectively of the Sesame Women's Club which met once a month in Merrywick, the rich suburb on the outskirts of Eton and Windsor. The club hired a room in the public Library in Crescent Street off the busy Slough Road. Miriam worked there as a librarian.

"She's a great draw." Flora went on writing as she spoke. "We've got twice the usual number of people coming, including some new faces. We are lucky to get her, she is very distinguished."

"Oh you're such a hero-worshipper."

"And she's a very good speaker. Anny Cooper says so. And we aren't always so lucky. Remember the woman who couldn't be heard beyond the front row? A real whisperer. About the most celebrated woman scientist we've got in the country, and no one could hear her."

Miriam was not mollified. "I hope we don't regret it. Anny does not always give good advice. I think we would have done better to show that Chinese film again. A lot of people said they were sorry they missed it."

16

"They were lying. They missed it on purpose. They planned to miss it. I would have missed it myself if I wasn't secretary. I think we've had enough of films about women working in factories. Especially when they are badly dubbed and you can't see what on earth they are making in the factory."

"We could have the doctor who talks on women and madness."

Flora put down her pen. "You know what? I think we should have a talk on women and cheerfulness, women and how to enjoy yourself, women without pain."

"But that's not what we are about," cried Miriam.

They always bickered like this. It was part of the fun for them. There was not much fun otherwise for these two hard-working women. Miriam looked after her elderly and infirm parents while Flora had the strange burden of a twin sister who, as Flora put it, had given Flora all the brain they had between them and kept only too little for herself. "Not that there was all that much to start with for us," she said sadly. Emmy, her sister, came to every meeting, indeed was there now, sitting quietly in a corner apparently happy. She could not function without Flora's presence. No one knew if Flora could function without her.

"I hope that man won't come," said Flora uneasily. "That's my only worry. I don't like the way he looks at Emmy." Or the way Emmy looks at him, she might have added.

"I don't think we should admit men."

"We are open to all sexes."

"There are only two."

Flora turned upon her. "That's where you are wrong. I reckon there are about six. As soon as we admit there is a broad spectrum on either side of the divide, a lot of problems will disappear."

"Oh you do talk rubbish."

"It's my fixed belief."

"All right. Which sex are you?"

"About one and half to the left. I'm a betwixt and between." But Emmy was not. Emmy was definitely one sex. She had all the sex in their unit while Flora had what there was of brains. "Thank goodness we're only identical twins and not Siamese," flashed through

Flora's mind. "What would I have had to witness?"

In the corner, Emmy stirred. She did not always direct her gaze at her sister, sometimes she looked up at the ceiling. She very rarely looked at Miriam for which Miriam was both grateful and yet irritated.

Flora was still worrying away. "He's quite an ordinary man. Not bad looking in his way. I don't know why I don't like him." But she did know: it was his intense interest in Emmy.

"He's only come twice. He may not come again."

"I think he will."

"There is something odd about him," agreed Miriam. "I can't put my finger on it, but it's there. Does anyone know his name or where he comes from?"

"We could try and find out."

"Let our speaker get a look at him for us. She ought to know a wrong 'un when she sees one." They both knew that clubs such as theirs attracted the strange ones.

"We could do that. But I don't suppose she can." He was so average, so anonymous, it was hard to believe the police knew him. "Still, we could offer her a look. What's she like herself?"

"You've got a photograph."

Flora shrugged.

"Anny says she's tall, well dressed and with red hair." Miriam and Anny Cooper were old friends, but did not always see eye to eye on all subjects.

"You couldn't tell size or colour from that photograph and to tell the truth, she didn't look too good in it." Flora had got together a small publicity display which she would set out in the entrance hall on the night in question. She liked to do things properly. Afterwards there would be coffee. Real coffee, she told herself, and not powdered. "Not pretty at all."

"Anny didn't say pretty. Attractive."

"But of course, the photo I cut out of the paper was very small and didn't show her hair." It had been taken as Charmian had emerged from an inquest on a murder victim and was far from flattering to her.

"How's she getting here? Have you arranged?"

"I have arranged."

"So?"

"Anny's bringing her. Your friend Anny. Walking."

"You can't park round here, that's for sure." The lack of any parking-space outside their meeting-place was an old grievance, especially to Miriam.

Flora had been thinking, going back to her old worry which might have nothing in it at all. "Tell you what: I'll get names and addresses at the door. He'd have to put something down."

"Even if it's a lie?"

"Lies can be helpful."

She looked up and caught Emmy's gaze. And don't you know it, my girl, she thought. Emmy could lie in her own way when it suited her. Flora wondered sometimes if Emmy's whole life was not a lie, in spite of what all the doctors said, and that inside her was a perfectly normal silent person conducting life in her own way. Flora felt suddenly tired. It was no fun being the front one in their tandem. For that was what she was and had been all her life.

Charmian surveyed the crowded room in the Merrywick library as she began

21

to come to the end of her talk. She had the enviable gift of being able to count her audience as she talked. Forty souls, not a bad total for a club like this. There were one or two hiding behind a massive row of potted plants, and she thought that someone had left during her slides. Either to start making the coffee or because of the nature of the pictures she was showing. They were a bit rough, especially the rape in the wood one. She just hoped she had got the level right. From a seat tactfully in the back row she saw Anny give her an imperceptible wink. Good, so she had got it right.

She was on her last few words now and was already drawing her notes together.

There was the man whom Anny had suggested she take a look at. No mistaking him. He was where Anny had told her he would be. He was sitting at the end of a row which contained Emmy. And Emmy, from her marked resemblance to Flora, they even wore identical clothes, she had no difficulty in locating. Both were dressed in pine green jersey suits of fine cashmere with neat little blue bows at the neck. Emmy wore pearls and Flora a set of amber earrings and necklace. Emmy was a sturdier, less pretty version of Flora, but with the same large pale grey eyes and soft fair hair. Interestingly, while Flora looked her full age of thirty, Emmy appeared to be at least ten years younger. Perhaps she would always look girlish.

The man could have been anyone, but he was older than the two women. Middle-aged, spectacled, with greying hair that seemed to match his dark tweed suit, he looked like a business man. He had a bag at his feet as if he had dropped in on his way home from work. Perhaps he had.

There were other men in the audience, but they were firmly anchored to wives or girl friends. He might be a journalist looking for a story, but as Miriam's and Flora's worry was that he always sat near to Emmy this did not seem likely.

Unless Emmy was the story. Flora and Emmy together might be a story, they were quite a pair.

Miriam stood up and made a speech thanking Charmian. She was a good speaker and enjoyed the task. Then she invited questions.

After the questions, there was coffee, and finally Charmian and Anny walked home through the summer night.

The roof of the Eton College Chapel was profiled against the sky on the one hand, and on the other they could see the solid mass of the castle. Then the path dipped and houses and trees crowded in. It could have been any town, anywhere in southern England.

"I couldn't make anything of the man," Charmian said to Anny.

"Did you say so?"

"Found an opportunity. I said I'd go on thinking. But I don't suppose I'll dredge anything up. He might be worth keeping an eye on."

She thought the club was the sort that might attract odd types.

"He didn't look dangerous."

"You can never tell."

"No." Anny accepted the judgement without argument. If anyone had cause to know this, then Charmian did. "Miriam has his name now. Did she tell you? She took all names and addresses at the door this time."

"She wrote it down for me. He's called Edward Pilgrim. Or says he is. And he has an address in Slough. Or says he does."

"You don't believe him?"

"Let me just say it will be interesting if he doesn't."

"And if he does? If he's genuine?"

"He might be quite genuine, as you put it," said Charmian slowly, "and the more dangerous for it."

They crossed Eton bridge, still crowded with visitors. There was never a day, not even Christmas Day in the rain, when this town was not crowded. On that day the Japanese tourists crowded in.

"They're a nice little outfit, doing a good job, and I wouldn't want to see them run into trouble." Anny swerved to avoid two young men eating ice-cream. Large cornets topped with whipped cream and nuts. Her mouth watered. She would take one home and share it with Jack. Then she remembered her husband was no longer there: she had thrown him out a week ago. We're not careful enough with husbands, Charmian and I, she told herself sadly, they're an endangered species with us.

"Flora and Emmy are an interesting case themselves." Charmian too had seen the ice-cream eaters, but was not drawn to them or what they were eating.

"I know. I'm never sure if they are one person or two. I don't think they know themselves."

"Mr Pilgrim might help them sort that out."

"You think so?"

Sex would come into it somewhere, Charmian felt sure. At this point, their ways diverged. Anny turning the corner which would lead her to Wellington Yard where she had her studio, and Charmian taking a right-hand turn to her cosy little street named after the Maids of Honour of Victoria, Queen and Empress.

"Heard from Kate?" she asked, as they parted.

"Picture postcard of St Mark's Square saying she was drinking coffee in Florian's. What about you?"

"The same." Except it had been a card of a severely intellectual Bellini Madonna holding an elderly looking baby.

"And Humphrey?" Anny pursued the subject of Humphrey with the interest of one who was not herself happy in that sphere. When her marriage was intact, although shaky, she had been able to ignore him.

"Oh he wants me to go to a polo match. I shan't, of course."

"I believe the champagne is very good," said Anny, who had always been rich enough and sufficiently well born to know that sort of thing.

Charmian walked on alone following a path that crossed a small park. She could have continued on the road, but this way was shorter. Pleasant too, beneath the trees on this summer evening. They were lime trees and their sweet, sticky breath floated down to her.

It was darker than she had expected, crowded in here by the trees, but she walked confidently on.

Behind her, she heard footsteps. She could see the street lamps in the road ahead. The feet came closer, moving fast.

She was alerted, but not alarmed. Then a hand came round her throat

27

and she was dragged back against a body. She could smell sweat. She dug her heels into the ground, simultaneously delivering sharp blows with her elbows into somebody's ribs. She heard somebody draw in a sharp breath.

"That'll teach you," she thought. The grip on her neck had loosened so that she could jerk herself free. A fist hit her head hard, knocking her against a tree trunk. She was just conscious of a body, head hooded, dressed in dark clothes.

Charmian was a strong, muscular woman, and she had been trained in self-defence. But this called for attack. She was angry. She gathered herself together. She stuck her hand with two forefingers extended into her attacker's face. Then with all her force, she jammed her knee into him. She got a scream in return.

Then she turned and ran towards the lighted street. She ran until she reached Maid of Honour Row.

Les was just wheeling her cycle into the garden next door. She stopped at once.

"Miss Daniels, what's happened?"

"Someone tried to grab me in the park."

Lesley looked at her in horror. "Your face!" She was dabbing at Charmian with a piece of tissue, making noises of sympathy.

"I hit a tree."

"I'm afraid you're going to have a black eye."

"I'd like to think he feels worse than I do," said Charmian with satisfaction. "But thanks for the help. I've been giving a talk."

"Yes, I know I was there."

"I didn't see you."

"I was behind a potted plant stand. I know Miriam. I use the library. You were great." Her voice trailed away, her face whitening.

"What is it?"

Les swallowed. "It's all this blood." She held out her hands, patchy with red stuff. "It's on you, too. Are you sure you're all right?"

Charmian examined herself. Yes, she had blood all down her pale shirt and on her arms. "It must be from him." She must have hit his nose.

Les leaned against the garden railing, her eyes closing. Charmian put an arm round her. "Come on in."

Inside her house, pushing aside an interested cat, she poured some brandy for the girl and took some herself. While she drank, she reported the incident to the local police.

Her name was known, she got action and efficiency. All the details were taken at once. The incident was not brushed over.

"I'd like to have brought him in myself, but I don't think I could have done it." She was remembering the strength of that dark figure.

"You did the right thing. Could you identify him?"

"He was masked. But he smelt."

"If anything occurs to you, just let me know. Every little helps."

"Could be the flasher I reported the other night. They do turn to action in the end." Not always but sometimes. Should she give them Mr Pilgrim's name? She decided not to at the moment.

"Agreed." The CID officer on duty that night was making notes. "I'll pop in and see you tomorrow if that's all right. Come myself. Sergeant Wimpey can come tonight if you like."

"Tomorrow will do."

"Let you know at once if there are any developments. I'll put out an alert. Keep the bloody clothes. The blood may come in handy for matching." With luck.

Charmian returned to Les, who seemed better. Then she saw the girl to her own front door. Two women supporting each other, was how she saw it.

She saw Lesley back to her home. Johnny opened the door. Charmian explained what had happened. "There was a bit of an incident. She'll explain. She's all right."

Johnny made sympathetic noises. "I'll look after her. Come on in, Les, you're not fit to be out on your own." He looked flushed and excited himself, which Charmian put down to the Duke of Wellington.

Back in her own house, Charmian stripped off all her clothes and took a bath in scorching hot water. Then she felt better.

Before going to bed, she packed up

the stained shirt and skirt in a plastic bag. In the pocket of the skirt was the tissue with which Lesley had cleaned her face. Tomorrow she would hand over the clothes to the CID.

She opened the window to let in the soft sweet wind, an unmurderous night, not a killing air.

But across the river, a creature was dying, a pool of its own blood staining the earth. Victim of a somebody, killed to fill a hole in that somebody's life.

2

EARLY in the morning, two days later, while Charmian was still asleep, a young girl, Joanna Gaynor, whose mother knew Miriam and Flora and who might have been at the meeting in the library, except that it was her yoga night, let herself out of the house where she lived with her parents and small brother. She wheeled her cycle round the side of the house and pedalled off to feed, water and groom her pony which she kept in a field about a mile from her home. In the winter he lived, expensively, in a stable at livery, but in the summer he preferred, or so Joanna thought, to roam free in the fields by the river. But he needed daily attention and she was the one to give it. Her mother was allergic to horses and her father was a hard-working lawyer whose home scarcely saw him. He was good at paying bills though, and Joanna's pony was his birthday present to her. The brother did not care for horses and was saving up for a model aeroplane.

Joanna liked these morning expeditions when the air was warm and still. On cold and wet days she would have preferred to hide in bed, but she was a conscientious child who carried out her commitments. It had been part of the contract: she got the pony, but she looked after it. She had a slightly guilty feeling because yesterday she had missed going. Guilt and Joanna were constant companions, it was the way she was built. She had hardly needed an excuse.

Anyway, she was fond of Traveller, her pony. He had a personality, bland but obliging, that appealed to her. He never hurried but he always got there. She knew he was not a human being, but she preferred him to some who were. Her French teacher, for instance, and her cousin Beverly who was too clever by half. And others, whose presence in her life was darker and whom she preferred not to think about.

A bus passed her and she waved to it, then got a wave herself from the milkman on his rounds. Not many people about at this hour, but these two she saw every morning. They were punctual and so was she. So, for that matter, was Traveller, who already had his head over the gate on the look out for her. The arrival of Joanna meant the arrival of some of the little snacks he liked for his breakfast. Traveller enjoyed his food.

"Hi, boy." Joanna liked it that she never had to call Traveller to her. She knew it was cupboard love but still she enjoyed it. It was a kind of love and there wasn't all that much in Joanna's life. She had cast for herself the rôle of least favoured member of the family and took a quiet pleasure in playing it. She had deliberately chosen for herself the bedroom over the garage as a way of declaring herself an outsider. It also gave a certain freedom for early morning trips such as this. People did not have to hear her go.

Joanna, prudent, careful child, padlocked her bike to the gate and went in.

The field had another occupant besides Traveller. It was home, winter and summer alike, year in, year out, to an elderly grey. The kind of horse Joanna called a Dobbin.

Dobbin was not an elegant horse, whatever had been the case in the past, and always looked down at heel. Dobbin had no visitors, and little attention. Joanna knew that the horse was left there as an intended kindness rather than being put down, but she felt more was needed.

"Better to have the poor brute shot," her father had grumbled. Joanna did not agree, she recognised an act of charity, but it was not enough, and did what extra she could. She was not exactly Dobbin's friend. It was very hard to be a friend to that old pale dejected figure, but she kept an eye out.

This morning she could not see the animal.

She held out a handful of oats for Traveller, the pockets of her jeans always had a deposit of oats in them, just as a fringe of horse hair decorated her sweater. Her mother usually started to sneeze as she served her breakfast. "Where's Dobbin, boy?"

Joanna gave Traveller an apple, took a

dandy brush from her shoulder bag and began to groom him, looking around for Dobbin the while. She always carried equipment in her bag which was why it weighed so much. Her mother joked that she could kill someone with a blow from that bag. Inside, as well as the dandy brush and a curry comb, she always had a knife, and this one had a hoof pick attached as well. She liked to have a knife.

Traveller chewed his apple. Good, it was a Cox's Orange Pippin, his favourite sort. His taste buds were not subtle, but he had them. A memory for what he liked or disliked he certainly had.

Joanna finished her grooming, a lick and spit today, but a thorough going over, hooves and all, at the weekend she promised. She considered giving him some exercise, she just about had time.

She swung herself up onto him, bareback (which was strictly against the rules, but who was there to see?), and gripped his mane. At such times (and they happened more often than she would ever admit) it was her fantasy that she was riding in a circus. Sometimes she pretended he was a magic horse who could talk and fly, and sometimes that he was a polo pony she was training. Her father played polo and her mother watched it, suitably fortified with antihistamine against her allergy. Sometimes she dreamt about her pony, how they went riding, riding, riding. Exhausting dreams from which she did not wake refreshed. Now she turned Traveller's head towards the river.

Traveller made it quite clear he had no intention of going in that direction. He went the other way, he had no objection to doing a circle, but didn't fancy the river.

Joanna dropped from his back to find out why. She had a considerable respect for Traveller's own brand of common sense and thought it worth checking.

By the river, half in, half out, lay Dobbin. The water around the animal was red.

The creature's throat was cut and it had been partly disembowelled.

Joanna stared, then stumbled away.

At such a time, there was only one place, home. Her father, who was God, one had to admit it, would know what to do.

She was unlocking her cycle, when she was stopped by the sight of her eight-year-old brother, red-faced with the exertion, riding up on his trike.

"I've come to help with Traveller. You might have waited. He's as much mine as yours."

"He's not, he's totally and absolutely mine, you don't even like horses." Her response was automatic. Even in her present state it was necessary to defend her territory.

"I'm going to see Traveller and say good morning. He'll be glad to see me." Mark advanced towards the gate.

Joanna got a firm grip on his collar. "You're not to go in the field. You mustn't see."

As she moved, Mark caught sight of her blood-stained shirt.

"Golly, you've done a murder."

It was at such moments that Joanna wished passionately she was an only child.

Joanna's father put the telephone down. "The police are going to send a car down there. Plus a vet in case the horse isn't dead."

"It's dead all right," said Joanna gloomily.

"And they'll want to talk to you."

"Me too?" asked Mark eagerly. "I was there, you know."

"I shouldn't think so."

"I'd better not go to school, anyway. Just to be on the safe side."

"If they want you, they can talk to you at school," said his mother, giving a series of sneezes. "Joanna, remove those clothes and get washed."

Her husband turned to her. "I've got to get off. An important case today." He always had important cases, they paid for the charming house, the good schools, and the occasional game of polo. "I don't think either of them should go to school today. It wasn't nice what they saw." He had a more tender heart for his children than had his wife. It might be that he was too loving a father, especially to Joanna, but then he saw less of them. Except when he so desired, of course, and in his own way. "Honestly, Annabel, keep them home. I'll ring at lunch time." He kissed her, catching her between sneezes. "That is, if the judge is reasonable." He usually entered this caveat.

"Wasn't the judge at Oxford with you?"

"Yes. Mrs Justice Anstruther. Not exactly with me. She was my law tutor for a term." She had played a good game of polo for a woman, too. Got a blue. She was the reason he had taken up the game, although he had never told his wife this. She suspected already that they had occupied themselves with things other than law.

"Well, tell her to be reasonable. We've got that party at Ascot tonight."

He shrugged. One did not tell Mrs Justice Anstruther to be reasonable. Even as an undergraduate he had known that truth. She was reasonable, terrifyingly reasonable, but it was like a divine power one did not draw down on one's head.

He got into his small BMW car and headed for the motorway and the Law Courts. He would just have time to pop into chambers and see his clerk. He was always a little pressed for time.

Joanna looked warily at her mother.

A fiat delivered by her father did not necessarily hold the force of law once he had left the scene.

But this morning her mother was tender. Anyone could see the child had had a shock. She gave her a hug, ignoring the fact that she would now probably have a patch of eczema on her arm.

"Get washed and then you can choose your own breakfast."

"Me too?" said Mark.

The veterinary surgeon called in by the police delivered his verdict to Detective Sergeant Wimpey.

"A sharp knife. Cut the throat. Not in one action but quickly enough so that the horse would collapse quickly. The other stuff," he paused delicately, "was done when the horse was down."

"Nasty."

"As you say. Not nice at all. Done by someone the horse knew I'd say. Or trusted." He shook his head. "Otherwise I doubt if the killer would have got up so close."

"And when? What's the time factor?"

"That's always tricky to sum up quickly

and, of course, you'll get your own people on it, but offhand," he paused. "Well, it's hot weather, that makes a difference. Let's say about thirty-six and more hours ago. Anyway, some time." You could smell it, too.

"Any idea about who could have done it?"

The vet shook his head. How could he have? His customers did not go in for that sort of exploit. This was police work.

"You don't think the kid did it?"

The vet looked shocked.

Sergeant Wimpey hunched his shoulders. Not a good day. One that started like this never ended well. He didn't like horses, he was strictly a petrol and combustion engine man himself, but no one wanted to see an animal end like this one.

And then there was the kid. She had a knife in her bag. And she had left bag and knife behind. He had them now, wrapped in plastic for forensic examination. Beneath the horse and on the river bank was a certain amount of debris, bits of paper, old tins, the odd bottle, all these would have to be collected and examined.

Altogether he had a nasty bundle of problems on his plate. There was this little episode. There was a housewife from Datchet, just down the road, who had not come home all night and been reported missing that very morning, and in addition, there was this flasher, who might or might not be identical with the man who had attacked Miss Daniels. He had had a meeting with the Chief Superintendent the day before to get the details. She had a fine black eye. He doubted very much if he would get far on that one, it was too intangible, but he had to try. He certainly had to try. Chief Superintendent Daniels was not one to play games with.

As they parted, the vet said, "You don't know much about horses, do you?"

"No."

"It's a mare. I don't know that it's significant. But I thought I'd just mention it."

Joanna stood very straight and answered the Sergeant's questions.

They were all in the kitchen of the

Gaynor house. Joanna, her mother and the boy. A policewoman sat in the corner of the room, a silent observer.

It was a comfortable room, large and cheerful, with evidence of good food prepared and eaten. There was a roast chicken cooling under a wire mesh cover on a side table, with the makings of a salad. On another table stood a freshly baked cake awaiting its icing. Mrs Gaynor had been busy. She looked tense, though. Maybe she was one of those who worked out their anxieties with cooking.

He looked at Joanna who answered him clearly.

Yes, of course she knew Dobbin was a mare. She knew about horses. She called Dobbin that because it suited her.

Her mother did not see the significance of this question. To be honest, neither did Sergeant Wimpey, but it had seemed necessary to ask it, somehow. Also, he was finding this questioning difficult. The thoughts he had of this child and the way she looked, fragile but battered, somehow, disturbed him. He could sense her extreme anxiety. He asked about the knife. He thought the mother looked

45

startled. She did not like this line of questioning.

Joanna made no bones about answering, but she did not look at her mother.

Yes, she always had a knife in her bag.

Sergeant Wimpey put his questions quietly, and methodically, observing her in as unobvious a fashion as possible. He did not want to worry her more than he had to.

No, she had not taken it out to use that morning.

No, she had no idea how blood could have got on to it.

Whether it was horse blood or human, or from any other animal, was not at that moment established.

Her answers were delivered in a monotone. It was like a kind of catalogue. He was puzzled and concerned about her without knowing why and he thought the woman detective, an experienced officer, felt the same.

As they left, Mrs Gaynor said, "Somehow I get the impression she's being accused of something. She only found the animal."

"I know that, Mrs Gaynor."

"As long as you do." She was alert, protective. Well, any mother would be.

"I didn't mean to imply anything else," he said mildly. "But she might know something."

"The knife means nothing. She always carries that knife."

"I'll just need to get the blood tested."

"I don't like there being blood on the knife any more than you do," said Mrs Gaynor irritably. "She may have dropped it without realising it."

"I should think that's quite likely. Don't worry, Mrs Gaynor and don't let Joanna worry."

"It's only an animal."

Whose death did not rate an inquiry? But she had not seen the horse and thus did not have the feeling he had of something badly wrong. It might have nothing to do with Joanna, yet he would like to be sure.

"She's had a bad shock." That much was certain. "Do her good to be with her friends. She has got some?" Not quite the way to put it, but it popped out before he could stop it. The woman detective looked surprised.

Mrs Gaynor, oddly enough, did not.

"Of course, a lot at school." She added in a distracted way, "And then there are the pony girls."

"The pony girls?"

"From the stable where Traveller goes in the bad weather. The girls work there. They give Joanna advice."

All comforts catered for, he thought, money no object. So what, if anything, was wrong?

He remembered that Chief Superintendent Daniels had done special work on women and violence. He could ask her for advice. Unofficially, of course, but from all he had heard of her she would give it. Not a difficult woman to approach.

He had a child himself, a boy. He would not like that boy to have the look he saw in Joanna's eyes.

Mark waved to him from the door. Nothing in that lad's eyes except cheerful self-confidence. So what was different about Joanna?

Charmian and Sergeant Wimpey had met on equal terms. He was a little nervous of her, but she liked him at once. He had promise. A good policeman and probably going to be a first-class detective. Only he wasn't there yet. He had, she thought, a face like a wary Botticelli angel, one that had seen the world a bit, and worried over it.

"We haven't got very far on the man who attacked you. A man did go into Casualty in the Feltham Hospital complaining of a broken nose. He walked out, without treatment, before anyone could get a question in. He could be your man. And when we lay hands on him we might find out if he is, or is not, also the flasher." He added carefully, "And of course, he might be a completely innocent party."

"No one got his name or address?"

"He did give a name, said he was called Roberts, but then when the receptionist tried to take a few more details, he made an excuse, went towards the toilets and never came back."

"Suggestive."

"Yes, suggests trouble," said Wimpey bluntly. "He's got something to hide."

"You think he's the man?"

"Taking it all together," said Wimpey with slow deliberation, "I do, and if we do manage to lay hands on him I think he will turn out to have a record."

Then he added, "But I think we are a long way from doing that."

"Meanwhile, he might attack some other woman."

"Almost certainly will do."

After a moment's thought, Charmian gave him Mr Pilgrim's name and address. It would be interesting to see how his nose was. He could have followed her. If that was his style.

Sergeant Wimpey said he did not believe in coincidence, but he would check on Mr Pilgrim, and it was no trouble. He liked to know of any weirdos who might be in his area.

"I've got a problem myself I would like to ask you about." Speedily and briefly he outlined the story of the slaughtered pony and his worry about Joanna.

"You seriously think the child might have done it?"

"She just might have done. And she's not quite a child. She's half on the verge of growing up." Which was always

50

a dangerous time. "And she troubles me. I think there is something seriously wrong."

"Do you think she is being abused, ill-treated in any way?"

He shrugged. "Can't say. Perhaps. It's something I am bearing in mind. It could be what lies behind the slaughter of the horse. I'm not sure about anything. But I would be grateful for any help you could give."

Charmian considered. "I can't do much unless you ask me in officially, and I don't imagine you want to do that? No. But I'll keep it in mind and see what I can come up with." She would go through her case histories and see what parallel, if any, she could find. Nothing more active. She had her own load of work in London.

Next day Sergeant Wimpey was back. He had news.

"Mr Pilgrim is known at the address he gave, but not often there. A rented room. Looks like an accommodation address."

"That's interesting."

"I think so. Glad I could help."

Then he told her that he also had news about the slain horse.

The blood on the knife was from the mare.

"And the child insists she knows nothing."

Once again he was seeking her advice. She was a specialist on women and children in crime.

"Could the child have done it?"

"Perhaps. It's not impossible. But we have to imagine she is in a very odd state of mind."

"I think she is."

"You haven't told me her name."

"Gaynor. Joanna Gaynor. Aged thirteen, looks older. Father's a barrister. Nice house out Eton way."

"Are you asking for my help?"

"Yes, ma'am." Suddenly he was very official.

"It will have to go through channels."

He nodded. "I have already had a word with the guv'nor. We are taking this seriously." They had to. Last year they had had a bad case concerning two children abused and then killed by their own father, while that same year had seen another bloody murder case where a child had been involved too. Charmian

Daniels had solved that one, as a kind of by-product of another case. Now no one was taking chances with cases about children.

Charmian too remembered that case which she had not so much solved as extricated herself from. She still occasionally saw the little boy involved, out of a kind of loyalty to his father.

"You'll hear from me," Wimpey promised.

Thus simply was Charmian Daniels brought into the case. But before she could take action, she had to prepare herself.

Within an hour of this conversation she was on the telephone to the psychiatrist who had worked with her on her thesis, which had been on the subject of violent women, criminal women.

"Ulrika?"

"Speaking." The slow, deep voice was deceptively hesitant. Ulrika Seeley knew her own mind. Usually yours as well. Charmian had found this disconcerting at fast — to be so easily seen through — then got used to it and now found it useful.

She put her problem. The horse, the slaughter, the knife, the blood and the girl.

"Could a child do this, Ulrika?"

There was silence. Ulrika never hurried herself. "This will take time," she said at last.

"I thought we could do it on the telephone."

"Oh no. We must meet. Talk. We need a good hour."

"Right." Charmian was resigned.

"You will come here." Ulrika, half German, half good Yorkshire stock, lived a solitary, but not, Charmian supposed, a completely celibate life, in a large, immaculate South Kensington flat, ornamented by black, firmly priapic African carvings, her household gods.

"When?"

"I must study the cases. Similar cases of child violence."

"Are there any?"

"I do not know of many. There was the case of Mary Bell. But that was different. I must think."

Charmian hoped that events would wait upon Ulrika's steady progress. She wondered if it would.

"And there is the case of Saul Paul."

"I don't know that one."

"It did not come to court. Anyway, a boy was involved. You are interested in females."

"I'll take anything you've got."

"My advice now is to look at the family. The real trouble may be there. Simply transferred. Taken up by the child like a parcel."

Or a kind of infection, Charmian thought.

"I will telephone," said Ulrika. "The weekend approaches."

"Not Sunday." Charmian remembered Humphrey and polo. "I have an engagement." Suddenly she knew she wanted to see Humphrey.

"Why are we tramping around like this?"

A fine Sunday afternoon in the Great park at Windsor, that ancient hunting ground of English kings, now a gentle wooded space enclosing a great lake named after the Virgin Queen, Elizabeth, where people took picnics, walked dogs, and rode horses.

And played polo.

Charmian and her escort, Humphrey Kent, an eminent public servant, so high-ranking as to be anonymous, but exuding the unmistakable air of power which Charmian found at once attractive and exasperating, were on the flat piece of grass known as Smith's Lawn. Cars were parked on the margins, horse-boxes behind them, with even the odd bicycle. And of course horses. They seemed everywhere, attracting almost as much attention, only not quite, as those of the Royals who were there in force. In sight was the pink and white marquee where a large party had lunched and drunk champagne.

Now the whole crowd of spectators had swarmed on to the pitch and were walking all over it with firm feet. Charmian was puzzled. You didn't walk on lawns. Or did you?

"Everyone always comes out on the pitch between chukkas to tread down the turf. Makes it smoother. Helps the players."

It seemed a popular spectator sport. She had already caught sight of her friend

Anny Cooper, and surely that was Flora with Emmy, her twin? No mistaking them, they were both dressed in yellow with matching hats. Now she came to think of it, she would put Flora down as a devoted, if secret, royal watcher, and it was probably to see them rather than the horses that she was here today. Emmy just went along. Anny's motives were more doubtful. It might just be that she had some new clothes to show off. Anny wore a smart trouser-suit that looked like Jasper Conran, but Anny had both money and taste. She was also tall and thin. Charmian who had started having trouble with her weight again wondered if her friend was anorexic. If so, she rather envied her, she was too greedy herself. The lunch today had been delicious. A kind of chicken dish with curry, almonds and cream, then strawberries, the first of the season, and more cream. She had eaten far too much.

"I'm getting mud on my shoes."

Humphrey laughed. "You look very nice in that blue and white thing. Well chosen. What do you make of polo?"

"Not sure yet." Charmian was looking

around. It was a smartly dressed and prosperous looking crowd. Not the sort of people she usually mixed with. They seemed friendly enough, though, and she had found plenty to talk about with both her neighbours at lunch. "Seems energetic. And I didn't understand it altogether." Not at all, really, but she was not going to say so. Surely they could not be trying to knock each other off their mounts? Occasionally it had seemed so. Humphrey said it was called 'riding-off' but it looked like something much nastier.

"I'll get you a book on the subject."

The group trudging next to them was made up of a mother with two young children, a boy and a girl. They were treading down the turf, silently but efficiently. The girl, in particular, was working with a fierce concentration. Charmian observed her with amusement. A tough, muscular figure, she was doing a good job. Those booted feet were grimly grinding away at the sods as if she really hated them. A pretty girl, though, with long blonde hair and big blue eyes.

"Don't overdo it, Joanna," her mother,

an older version of the girl, called. "Let's go across and talk to Daddy." She started to sneeze. "Damn these horses."

The trio made their way towards the players. So father was in one of the teams? And Joanna? Charmian took in the name, watching the girl, as Joanna trailed behind her still-sneezing mother.

They began to move that way themselves, because Humphrey wanted to talk to a friend who had a polo string. They got close to the area where the horses and grooms were parked. Ponies were being walked by young women. Most of the grooms seemed to be girls.

"I know that face." She did indeed, and the faces holding the next two animals. "It's Lesley. And there is Johnny. Gillian and Freda behind. So that's what they do." Not acrobats or a pop group, but work with ponies.

Humphrey looked across. "Oh, that's Tommy Bingham's string."

Next day, while Charmian was preparing to go to work in London, she had a telephone call from Sergeant Wimpey.

He said what he had to say without preamble.

"We've got a body. Young woman. Reported missing earlier. Now she's turned up. Or what's left of her. In some bushes in the Princess Louise park."

"But that's where — "

"Yes, where you were attacked. Want to come and have a look?"

It was a request with its own built-in imperative.

There was only one possible response and she made it: "Give me a minute to make a 'phone call and I'll be right there."

She had no idea then that she was going to see the Frisian beard. She had not thought of the thing for decades.

But the idea of it must have been there all the time in her mind, ready to pop out as a comment. That was an interesting thought in itself.

3

THE Princess Louise Park is small, but not as small as it looks, it narrows towards the river where there are hidden, secret places, the occasional haunt of lovers, drunks and vagrants. Beyond the tennis-courts which are bordered by the path where Charmian had been attacked, is a rough, undulating area of trees and shrubs containing a small pond where hardly anyone goes. Apparently not even the park-keepers.

The body of the woman was lying in a hollow, hidden by an overgrown clump of rhododendrons and azaleas, now in full flower.

She had been resting there for some time. Her body, so long exposed to the sun and rain, was at the moment covered with a plastic sheet. The whole area around had been taped off so that it could be searched. As Charmian arrived the photographic group was still at work. Later teams of searchers would go over the grass with intense care. Ever scrap of paper, threads of fabric, shreds of wood, pieces of plastic, dog hairs, and birds' feathers, the detritus of everyday living would be rescued and examined to see what they could add to the picture of how this woman had died and at whose hands.

"It's your sort of murder," said Sergeant Wimpey.

"Thanks." But she knew what he meant. Here was a woman violently assaulted and killed.

The scene-of-the-crime officer with his bag had already arrived. No one she knew, but a figure easy to recognise. There was a peculiar worried look that those chaps had. A civilian specialist, this one, like the photographer. The divisional surgeon whom she did know was talking to a man she knew to be Detective Chief Inspector Merry. Behind them was the specially equipped police van.

And further behind them still, in the nearest police station, the major incident room would be assembling itself, ready to take on this new investigation.

There was no doubt in anyone's

mind that this was a major criminal investigation. She could see it on Sergeant Wimpey's face, even if her own instincts had not informed her.

"She is lying so close to where you were attacked that we thought it was worth bringing you in to have a look. Just in case you saw anything or thought of anything that related to the attack on you."

It was a tribute to Sergeant Wimpey's standing that he seemed to have got a foothold in this new case, although he had started out investigating the slain horse. Of course, they might be short staffed.

"How long has she been dead?"

"Long enough." His face was thoughtful. "Don't really know yet until the scientific boys make an estimate, but I saw her and I'd say soon after she was reported missing."

"And that was?"

"Soon after the attack on you. Reported missing that next morning. Might have been killed the night before."

So that would place the death only hours after the attack on Charmian. It might even have taken place before. Only a check on the last time the victim was seen would make that clear.

I could have been lying there, Charmian thought. My kind of murder, indeed.

"And in the same space of time, roughly, when the pony was killed," said Wimpey.

"You aren't associating this killing with that?"

Wimpey paused. "Perhaps you should see the body before I say any more."

As they approached the body, Charmian was conscious of a sweet, sick smell and the lazy movement of a cloud of flies in the bushes as if not too long disturbed.

Wimpey brushed angrily at the bushes. "Makes me sick."

The young woman lay spread-eagled on her back, arms flung above her head. She had worn jeans and a cotton shirt with a pale blue cardigan. Or it had been pale once, now it was dirty and bloodstained.

Her throat had been cut and there was one great slash from the navel downwards.

Charmian, experienced officer that she

was, turned her head aside, from the swollen, discoloured face.

"Who found her?"

"A tramp who drops in here around Ascot time. Just a bit early this year. He's at present crying in the local nick and saying he's innocent."

"You don't suspect him?"

Wimpey shook his head. "He's a known figure. No violence. Used to be a groom before he took to drink."

"Identity?"

"Well, I agree you couldn't do it on her face the way it is, but there are the clothes, and she had her bag. Mrs Irene Colman, twenty-three, reported missing on the morning of 23 May by her husband."

"What about him?"

"As suspect? Well, I agree that a look close at home is a sound rule, but in this case, perhaps not. Mr Colman has multiple sclerosis and has been bedridden for some months. He can't even walk to the front door, he can just about pick up a telephone. His wife worked as a shop assistant in Baileys selling stockings during the day, and at night

65

she worked in the Buzz night-club. That way they paid their bills. Makes you sick, doesn't it?"

"So she would always have had a late walk home."

"No, not always. Usually she drove. She had an old car, because she was nervous of the walk, but that night it broke down. Or she was out of petrol or some such. The car is still outside the Buzz." He spoke as if he knew the night-club, as indeed he did, although not as a patron. The Buzz had known fights with knives, had had a death on the premises, and found itself under suspicion of selling drugs. The Buzz had survived unclosed and unchanged, but it was always of interest to the police.

"Remind you of anything?"

Charmian looked down again at the body. There certainly was something familiar about those wounds.

"Are you relating this to the mare's killing?"

"The knife work looks the same."

"You think the other was a practice run?"

He shrugged. "Who knows?"

66

"The pathologist may be able to tell if the same knife, or the same hand used the knife. Be a bit speculative. But it would be worth advising a look at the mare."

Tentatively, he said, "If both killings are by the same hand, this would rule out the child, wouldn't it?"

"One would certainly hope so. I may have seen her yesterday, by the way. Blonde girl, pretty fair hair, tall. Out in the park watching polo with her mother and brother."

"Sounds like her."

"Let's be content to call this killer a man, shall we?" said Charmian. "For the time being."

As she turned away, she thought, If the two killings prove to be connected, it may not be that the first was a rehearsal, it might be that the killer wanted to kill but drew back at first from a human victim.

Now something had driven him over the edge. It was a chilling thought.

"We might be at the beginning of a Ripper-style murder series."

"My thought exactly."

Chief Inspector Merry had started to move in their direction. He had kept an eye on Charmian ever since she arrived. Knew the woman, of course. Wasn't sure if he approved of her, but he had colleagues that did. Also she had influential backing. One had to watch one's step. He was not a man for watching his step, preferring to step heavily on whatever was in his way, but life had taught him that this was not always the way to go on.

He greeted Charmian cheerfully and politely. He liked women and she was attractive enough. "Good of you to come."

"I'm interested."

"So what do you make of it?"

"So far?" asked Charmian cautiously. "Alarming. Whoever did this killing is almost out of control."

"I hate these 'met-by-chance' killings, if that is what it was. You know where you are if it's a straightforward domestic crime. In the family."

"She may have known her killer."

"Doesn't look like it. Not how I see it. He was just hanging around in this

68

area and she walked into him." He did not say, "Just like you did," but it was in his mind. He turned to Charmian. "Anything you see here that ties in with the attack on you?" His eye strayed briefly to the bruise still staining her cheek-bone.

"Nothing except the place."

"We'll be moving the body soon. Stay around and watch. You may see something."

The removal got under way with the usual slow care. The body, still covered, was lifted onto a metal stretcher and carried to a waiting mortuary ambulance which moved off across the grass.

As the body had been raised, a piece of paper which had been caught underneath fluttered in the breeze.

Wimpey bent down quickly to pick it up.

A cheap sheet of plain white writing-paper. On it, drawn in thick, hasty pencil, was a rough shape.

A kind of squared circle, not quite a square, not quite a circle, somewhat oblong towards one end and the other end not completely joined, although it might have been meant to.

Charmian took a look. "A Frisian beard," she said spontaneously.

Years ago, while an undergraduate, she had had a boyfriend who was studying early Anglo-Saxon society. He took her to museums and archaeological digs to see their remains. He had taught her to recognise a Frisian beard. A line of sturdy stone warriors on an ancient church porch, busily laying about them with axes and staves, and each wearing a short spade-like beard had been his teaching ground. "That's a Frisian beard," he said.

It was all she recalled about the episode, she hardly remembered him now except that he had had red hair, but the image of the beards seemed to have stayed.

The two men looked at her in surprise.

"Sorry," she said. "I don't know why I said that."

After a day of routine work in London, plus two committees, one of which she chaired, Charmian returned to her home in Windsor. It already felt like home.

There was a card on the doormat from Kate, she was no longer in Venice but had moved on to Florence. More than that could not be read since Muff had chewed and clawed at the card, apparently giving it the rôle of supermouse.

There was also a parcel, delivered by hand, which felt like a book. She put that aside to look at after she had fed Muff, who was making angry but hopeful noises of welcome and hunger.

She opened the packet while she ate an omelette. A book on polo by Marco.

"Oh good, a joke."

It was a battered old green volume, obviously much studied and much loved. A note from Humphrey came with it.

"I'm getting a chum to drop this in." (Humphrey always had a chum to do useful chores.) "Look after the book. It belonged to my father. Hope you enjoy it, should tell you a lot about polo."

She looked at the pictures while she drank some coffee. There was something called a 'wooden horse' that was useful to have, which you kept in a polo pit which was not a pit but looked more like a hen-run.

71

Noises of music and happy shouts from next door suggested that her neighbours were having a party. At least she now knew where they worked and that they were grooms to a rich man's string of polo ponies.

As she finished her coffee, she watched the television news. The Windsor murder was briefly reported, with pictures of the Princess Louise Park, together with a flash of the castle in the background for no known reason except local colour. There were no fresh details. She got up, dislodging Muff from her lap, to turn off the set.

The Frisian Beard episode had opened a kind of hole inside her, stirring up memories, not oddly enough of the archaeologist or the young girl she had been, but of an affair she had worked on in Windsor.

She had lost touch with most of the characters in that story. Life itself had drawn them apart. Death, imprisonment, in some cases promotion and ambition had separated them. She still kept up with a clever, young policewoman, Dolly Barstow, whom she had met then, because she saw in her a mirror image of herself when young.

But not the group of women criminals she had been studying. (With the exception of the one called Baby. Baby was always an exception and might pop up in her life any day.)

Her friend Anny Cooper had taken her to task.

"Do you still keep up with those women?"

"No," she had answered slowly. "No, life does not work like that." She had had other tasks, other responsibilities. They represented a job done. But in a sense, they had never left her, walked with her still, far from silent ghosts, reminding her that she was a woman. "I know what became of them. But I don't see them." Except for Baby, Beryl Andrea Barker, who seemed a permanent element in her life.

"So that was all they were to you? Another job?"

"Opened my eyes to a lot in myself that, perhaps, I had not been aware of."

"A certain ruthlessness?" Anny was dry.

Charmian shook her head. No, that she'd known about. A kind of softness in her, rather. An unwillingness to cause pain. To Anny, she said, "A lot in the way I see women and women police officers."

All day, while engaged in her routine of work, thoughts of the murdered woman, the slain horse and the girl Joanna, had kept breaking through. Now, as she thought of Anny too, she had a picture of Anny walking on the polo field.

Had she not spoken to Joanna as if she knew her?

Without waiting, she telephoned Anny.

"Mmm, yes. Sure. I know the Gaynors. Well, not him, but Annabel and Joanna. I did a portrait of Joanna." She added thoughtfully, "Not one of my best. She's hard to bring out, that girl."

"Can you arrange a meeting for me?"

"I don't know what excuse I could make."

"Oh come on, Anny, you can think of something."

"What are you up to?"

Charmian did not answer. She pretended not to hear and put the telephone down.

74

Anyway, it was the sort of question to which Anny did not expect an answer.

But Anny had been prompted to action. In a short while, she was back on the telephone.

"There's going to be a display of books and a talk in the library in aid of a charity for disabled riders. There are also going to be stalls with produce and flowers, that sort of thing. The Sesame Club is sponsoring it. Annabel is helping, Joanna will be there. Runs till Wednesday, but get yourself there tomorrow and you will see both of them helping to set it up." Her turn now to ring off quickly without waiting for an answer. Charmian knew what that meant: Anny wanted no more responsibility for anything that might happen.

"I'm aiming to help the child, Anny," she said to herself, hoping that Anny would somehow get the word.

Muff, who had escaped to freedom in the Houdini way which she had perfected, mouthed at her from the window, demanding entrance.

Charmian opened the door. "You shouldn't be out on the street. Dangerous for cats." Dangerous for girls, too, she thought as she saw Les pedalling down the street. No lamp on her machine, either, and the pale summer night had arrived.

"Hello, Les. Not at the party?"

"I'm going in now. Not my scene, really."

"How are you? I mean after what happened the other night?"

"Fine. I don't know what came over me then, I'm usually tough as old boots. How are you? Your eye looks better."

"I'm all right. Making good use of cream and powder." Charmian thought the girl looked tired. "Johnny said you go out every night to see your father and feed your horse."

Les laughed. "I do go to see Dad, he's not up to much. No horse though, that's just their joke."

"Did you hear about the horse that was killed?"

Les nodded. "Knew the poor old thing. I know the kid who keeps her pony there."

"Joanna Gaynor?"

"She's pony mad. Hangs around us a

lot. Her father occasionally rides one of our boss's string. Saw you on Sunday."

"It was the first time I knew what you lot did."

Lesley laughed. "It's no secret."

"What do you make of Joanna?"

"She's a nice kid," said Lesley, bending down to fasten her bike to the railings. "Seems to prefer horses to humans. We must see more of her than her family do."

"Is that so?"

"Oh well, you know what I mean. I suppose she gets a lot of freedom. She's a bit of a loner."

"Talking of being alone, the streets round here may not be the safest place in the world just now."

"You mean because of the murder? Are you thinking of what happened to you?"

Charmian shrugged. "Be unwise not to." And the flasher who had been seen in Maid of Honour Row. "Have you noticed anyone? Hanging around?"

"There's been a man exposing himself on and off all the summer. We don't take any notice. He's not dangerous."

You should, and he might be, thought Charmian. "You should have reported it."

Lesley laughed. "You ought to know how they look at women who report that sort of thing."

Damn you, Charmian thought. And she did know. Even in her case, there had been that something in the air.

"You think the police will catch the killer? I don't."

"Oh yes. Because the murderer was stupid?"

"Stupid?"

"Yes. It was a chancy killing. Opportunist and therefore fundamentally stupid."

"Oh well, if you say so. You ought to know. We were talking," went on Les. "Johnny thinks we know the girl that was killed. We go to the Buzz occasionally."

"What even you?"

"Even me. Bit pricey though. Johnny says she was a waitress there."

"She was." And it was to be hoped she had earned danger money. Lesley picked up the note in her voice, and responded to it.

"Don't worry about the girls, we can look after ourselves. Johnny is the tender one."

I must tell Kate, thought Charmian. But I thought I'd heard otherwise.

"Keep a eye on the girl Joanna, will you?" Lesley looked at her in surprise. "For me," Charmian added ironically.

"OK. For you. I do anyway. She's always around."

"Thanks."

"My pleasure. "'Bye, see you later. Come to the party. It's going on all night."

"Celebrating something?"

"Do we have to be? Oh well, yes. Our boss's team did well in the Champagne Cup. He gave us all a rise, and we love him. That's it for now."

And with a wave, Les supremely confident, bounced into the house next door with that slight lift to her walk that all good riders seem to have.

Charmian picked up Muff and returned to her own house, where she slowly got herself and Muff to bed. The party went on for hours, so that she lay in bed listening to it. She didn't want to join

79

it, but it sounded good fun. Was that Johnny's laugh?

And exactly how tender was Johnny?

She found herself thinking about the piece of paper and the drawing on it. It presumably meant something to the killer, and apparently it did to her too.

Why had the phrase the 'Frisian beard' sprung so readily from her memory? It puzzled her, but it was something she would take care not to mention to Ulrika who would worry away at it until she dug up something that Charmian might not want to hear.

At last the noise of the party died down and she went to sleep.

4

NEXT day, when the local paper was full of the murder in Princess Louise Park, but it had not yet hit the national headlines, there began a period which Charmian knew occurred in every case and which experienced police officers sensed without naming.

It was a time, she said, when a lot of things were happening in a case that you never got to know about but ought to know.

Sometimes, later, you found out. A few things always stayed underground, you made a guess that was all.

She was in such a time and knew it, but she was not idle. Next day, as well as the normal workload entered in her diary, Charmian had an engagement to see Ulrika in the morning ('Come to breakfast,' that early riser had said) to talk over what her cases on violent children had turned up and then the evening was booked for a visit to the library in Crescent Street where she would see Joanna herself and Annabel her mother. No one had mentioned whether the father would be there or not, his permanent non presence seemed taken for granted.

Ulrika, when seen, handed out strong coffee and a piece of slightly burnt toast, but not much information. She had found no cases which were helpful. A child could certainly kill a horse, a child might be strong enough to kill an adult and some had, but she personally had not had such a case. She could point to several American cases, but drugs or fantasy games had been involved. Charmian could check these points.

Just watch the whole family, she had said again. If there is a hole, it may be theirs. She was cheerful, as ever, and cynical. Also, as ever, "One cannot always help people," was her attitude. Only when they admit they want help can one move forward, and when they have had enough of you and say so, then you know you have succeeded. Do not look for joy.

"As if I did," thought Charmian sourly, as she drove away, heading for her normal day and the viewing of Joanna in the evening. She had withheld by a hair's breadth her remembrance of the Frisian beard which placed her in the company of those not admitting they wanted help. One day, she too might say goodbye to Ulrika and then Ulrika would know she had done her job, whatever it might be.

One of the episodes which Charmian should have known about happened that very day in the time space between her breakfast with Ulrika and arriving at the library in Crescent Street.

Windsor has a small but elegant branch of Madame Tussaud's Waxworks. It is housed in one of the two railway stations, both of which were used by Queen Victoria. She is the principal character of the display there, although you may also see her eldest child, the Empress of Germany, and one of her prime ministers, the Marquess of Salisbury, beside other relations and courtiers whose features you may recognise after a little work.

You can see the Royal Train arriving with its burden of illustrious guests, peer in through the window to observe the cosy interior of the carriages, and then stand to watch and listen as the National Anthem is played and the guard of welcome present arms.

A visit there by the elder girls in the private school attended by Joanna Gaynor had been both popular and educational. Even the sleepiest and least interested girls (which Joanna was not, although everyone who taught her felt an occasional loss of contact with her) had responded. For a while, a keen interest in Victorian social history had swept through the upper forms.

Miss March, who taught history and was also Deputy Headmistress of The Brockington School, had been so encouraged by her success that she arranged, by popular request, a visit to the main Madame Tussaud's in London.

"I am so grateful," she said earnestly to the Headmistress, who was an elegant administrator but not much of a scholar, "for anything that arouses a spark of academic interest." Most of her pupils, charming, well-bred girls, were heading for a finishing school and then a husband for whom they would gracefully entertain. Joanna, elusive as she could be, was an exception. But then both her parents, elusive as they were too, were intellectuals.

So a booking was made, a coach hired, a guide engaged, and the party, carefully selected to weed out those who might slope off and go shopping in Harrods. Or worse. There had once been a child who took off for New York and Bergdorf Goodman's, but she was an heiress, with thrice divorced parents. One forgave her.

While not wanting or expecting it to happen again, nevertheless Miss March kept her eyes open. A small group of girls made a spirited rush to view the model of Madonna, recently introduced, but Miss March soon foiled this and led them on a carefully planned tour of historical interest. The guide did the talking, she did the watching.

She did not miss Joanna until nearly the end. They were going to regale themselves with a session of tea and cakes in a nearby restaurant, so she was counting heads.

"Where is Joanna?" she demanded. The usual silence followed by a small mutter of ill-informed speculation reached her. "Who saw her last?"

"I did, Miss March." A hand went up. If Joanna had a close friend in the school, and this was not to be taken for granted, it was Maria Andrews. Maria had travelled, knew her way around the world, and had been heard telling everyone on the coach that she had visited a tiny waxworks museum in Rome where there was not a single woman depicted, what a disgrace! Maria was a spellbinder. "We were together in the Chamber of Horrors. I think she may have gone back."

Maria was well informed as usual. Miss March found Joanna staring silently at the figure of Jack the Ripper. She must have been there some time.

"What are you doing, Joanna?" Miss March said sharply.

"It's really interesting."

"You're a bit on the young side to be

interested in all that." Not the cleverest remark in the world, Miss March realised as she spoke. You could be interested in 'that sort of thing' at almost any age. She was herself. All the same . . .

On the way home Miss March thought, I wonder if I ought to tell her mother? But she decided not.

That evening, Joanna made a more than usually hurried visit to the stables where Lesley and the others worked. "Can't stay. Got to help mamma with an Exhibition."

"We can manage," said Lesley tersely. Joanna got on her nerves sometimes.

Joanna helped with fetching buckets of water, assisted in rubbing the ponies' coats down with a wisp of straw to massage the skin, checked the feet and carried food. Ponies like small meals often.

She did it all silently, expecting no thanks and getting none. They were so used to her that they hardly saw her. Sometimes she was there, sometimes she wasn't. When she was, they made use of her, and at other times forgot her.

Completing a small errand connected

with disinfectant for Lesley, she said softly, "We went to Madame Tussaud's today."

Lesley did not answer.

"I saw Jack the Ripper. Face to face."

"What did you do that for?"

Joanna shrugged. "Just wanted to."

"Why are you telling me?"

"Thought it might interest you. It was interesting. He looked so ordinary. Of course, it's just imagination. No one really knows. He was never caught."

"Forget it," said Lesley. Basically her reaction was the same as Miss March's. "I suppose it's because of the horse?"

"'Suppose so."

"Tell your mother. Not me." Kids picked things up sometimes like an infection. Especially this one.

"No," said Joanna, roughly.

No, thought Lesley. It's not the sort of thing you do tell your mother. Like your first brush with sex.

"You're an imbecile sometimes for an intelligent girl. Get off home."

"I'm just going."

Lesley proceeded with her work. There was still plenty to do and, in spite of what she had said to Charmian, with her deliberate lightness, there would be much to do looking after her father. He was sicker than she liked to admit. And he was not the only one. The boss was not too good. He had looked bad today, a colour no one liked the look of. Which after their party of yesterday when all had seemed well, made them sad.

But as she worked she thought, Wonder if I ought to tell the kid's mother what she said about the Ripper? Or possibly the policewoman.

But you did not always do what you were supposed to do. She would think about it.

Charmian inserted herself quietly into what the architect had called 'the reception area' where the display of books and photographs, together with the stalls, were being set out by the Sesame Club. Charmian saw at once that these were what attracted the crowd already surging through the door to pay their entrance fee. A few people were looking at the books, most had their purses out ready to buy. Home-made cakes and jam, old books and second-hand clothes made a brave display. Joanna and her mother had a flower and pot plants stall, with trays of seedlings.

Miriam Miller together with Flora Trust and her twin sister had no stall, shifting around as required, and were now bustling around behind the tea and coffee stall. Flora was buttering scones. "How much are we charging for biscuits?" Charmian heard her ask.

But the price was already written up: "Tea and biscuit 15p.", and Miriam was already pointing this out to her.

No sign of Mr Pilgrim, which ought to make Miriam and Flora feel better and perhaps Emmy feel worse. Charmian had already observed that in a quiet way Emmy encouraged him. Perhaps it was an old-fashioned courtship going on after all. Not everyone wanted a talkative wife. On the other hand, not everyone wanted two for the price of one which is what he might be getting here.

No Mr Pilgrim then, but to her surprise she saw Sergeant Wimpey walking towards her.

"Didn't expect to see you here."

"The wife's got a stall," he said with slight embarrassment. "That's her over there with the home-made jam."

"Mr Pilgrim is not here."

"He is, though. He's over there." He nodded towards one corner. Sitting quietly on a chair was Mr Pilgrim, wearing a dark suit and a small smile.

"No sign of a bruise or a broken nose," said Wimpey.

"So I noticed," said Charmian. "He's in the clear then for the attack on me. He's a puzzle, though."

"Oh well, I'll find out," said Wimpey confidently. "I mean to. He's up to something. I smell it. Maybe he's a con man. He's got the cut for it."

He did have the smooth, cheerful air of a man who knew how to get away with what he wanted.

"I've got a nice line-up of chummies ready for you to have a look at," went on Wimpey. "Quite a few broken noses and bruised faces have turned up among some of my friends. You'd be surprised. Worth your taking a look. I'll set it up, give you a bell. Right?" He looked across the room, "I'd better get over there and help the wife with the jam." He added, "And on the way I might just have a word with Mr P. He's just bought a pound of my wife's marmalade. That shows initiative on his part."

"And I thought you came to get a look at Joanna Gaynor."

"And I thought you did."

"I came to see if she was on drugs or into fantasy games."

Wimpey grimaced. "You do have nice ideas."

"My expert says to look."

"First, let's both talk to Mr Pilgrim."

"You do the talking, I'll do the watching," said Charmian. "That way it's less official. I take it you won't be introducing yourself?"

"No fear. This will be strictly man-to-man talk."

She watched as he moved smoothly across the room, and Mr Pilgrim as smoothly got up, holding his jar of marmalade, and walked towards the door.

"Rapid exit," she murmured. Well done, too, an expert job. He was certainly a pro of some sort. But probably not a murderer. In fact, almost certainly not.

A quick look in the direction of the twin sisters convinced her that Emmy looked disappointed.

Wimpey came back, looking disappointed also. "Slippery bugger." Charmian made a sympathetic noise, trying not to sound as amused as she felt. "Wait a minute." Wimpey went across to speak to his wife, returning briskly. "My wife says he's a nice man."

"So he may be."

"She said he told her he was buying the marmalade for his old mother."

"Perhaps he was."

"Knows how to handle women."

"And his exits."

"Yes, damn him. That was too bloody professional for words. And you see what it means?"

"Oh yes, he knows what you are. He's recognised you for a copper."

"I'll get him, you know," said Wimpey with conviction. Across the room, Anny had arrived at the Gaynor's stall. She caught Charmian's eye and smiled. It was a smile that said, Come over here and let's get this over and done with.

Charmian obliged, holding out a hand as Anny introduced her. Mrs Gaynor gave a cool nod. She seemed well informed on who Charmian was, and what she did in life. "Sorry I missed your talk. Looking back I ought to have come, seeing what has happened to my child! And what she seems to need protection from is the police. Just because she had the bad luck to find an animal that had been killed in a particularly nasty way she has been pursued by you people. You act as if she had killed the animal rather than just finding it."

"Sometimes routine investigations do seem like that," said Charmian. "Don't let it worry you."

Now she was close to Joanna she had a chance to observe her. A pretty girl, nicely dressed in clean jeans and a pastel shirt. Her long fair hair was caught back with a tortoiseshell band. She was tall, as tall as her mother, with the promise in her strong straight back of growing even taller. She was handling the heavy pots of geraniums with ease, shifting a big tray of tomato seedlings without obvious effort. She gave Charmian a small smile.

"Hello, Joanna. Think I saw you at the polo on Sunday."

Now the smile became broader. "Yes, Daddy was playing."

Mrs Gaynor put in defensively, "My husband occasionally plays in a friend's team. Of course, he can't afford his own ponies."

He must be pretty good, thought Charmian, to get a ride in a champagne match.

"Daddy's marvellous," said Joanna. "Super." She gave her mother a hostile look. "I'm going to play myself when I'm older."

"Over my dead body," said Annabel.

A little trickle of cold ran down Charmian's spine. She had heard people say such things before, and it was never a good way to talk.

Anny reacted briskly. "Oh come on, Annabel. Why shouldn't the kid have that ambition?"

"Because it's such rubbish. Women never make first-class polo players, and what's the point if you aren't good?" Joanna's pretty face had a set, mutinous look. "Wait and see," she said.

'No love lost there,' thought Charmian. But she had to say the girl looked healthy and well groomed, with no sign that drugs of any sort formed part of her life. No running nose, no red eyes, no spots. Nor did she smell of them. She looked fresh and robust. Normal, in short.

Perhaps we are wrong about this girl, she thought. But even as she thought so, she saw what worried Wimpey. There was something hard to penetrate about Joanna. You got so far and then no further. She presented a barrier.

And there had been blood from the mare on her knife.

Charmian stayed at the plant stall as long as she could, making conversation and observing the girl.

But somehow we are reading her wrong, she decided. And no blame to us. If she was a sentence you'd have to say she was indecipherable.

Quite an achievement for a thirteen-year-old.

She began to stroll round the room, now crowded, predominantly with women. Most of them would have heard of the murder in the Princess Louise Park.

Some of them might be talking of it. None of them were frightened by it as yet. They were a prosperous protected crowd for whom the death of a woman in a park seemed far away.

But Charmian knew how fragile a bubble was this confidence. Her work with criminal and violent women had made her realise how thin was the dividing line between these two worlds. There was no great wall, no barbed-wire barricade, but a fence over which anyone might fall. And once you were over, it was very hard to get back.

She bought some embroidered napkins at one stall and some books at another. Then two pots of marmalade from Mrs Wimpey who gave her an alert amused look and passed her on to the cake and biscuit lady in the next booth.

Charmian stood hugging her purchases to her. Good bargains all of them, they served you well, these ladies of the Sesame Club — an average group, about whom statistics told her that in a year or so or more, two of them would have contracted cancer and one of those would die. Another of the wives would have a husband who suffered a coronary arrest; she might lose him. Another two would be divorced, and the same number take lovers.

And one might die violently. By accident, or suicide, or murder. Domestic or otherwise.

Perhaps it would be her turn.

Statistically she was in a profession where death came close. And she had certainly run her luck hard once or twice in the last few years. But at least she had learnt not to say over her dead body.

Flora and Emmy emerged from the racks of clothes over which they seemed to have a temporary proprietary interest. Emmy was holding a tin box into which the sales money was to be put while her sister hung up a dress of printed silk in maize gold and dark blue.

None of the clothes were unattractive. In fact, as Charmian soon saw, all were of excellent quality and more than one had labels of distinguished designers. Perhaps they were no longer top fashion, but they were still more than wearable. They confirmed her impression that the women of the Sesame Club had money to spend.

She fingered the printed silk. Dare she?

"Want to try it on, darling?" Flora had adopted her sales manner. "We've rigged up a trying-on room at the back." She nodded towards some curtains.

"I think my bones are too big." It was an honest admission and one that cost her something. She had always been tall, and although she was slender her frame was bold. There was a mute and unexpressed rivalry between Anny and Charmian which had been going on since they were both students. Charmian had been first the plump one, then more recently the thin one, but she had to admit that marital unhappiness suited Anny who was now looking good.

"Squeeze in," said Flora. "Cram yourself in. See how you like it. You could let it out."

Needlework and letting out was not quite her style, but the urge to try it on was not to be gainsaid. Ever so often, just when she thought she was over all that, Charmian surprised herself with feminine desires. She did love good clothes, always had and always would.

"Yes, I will." Besides, she had just seen the label in the dress.

"Beautiful silk," said Emmy. These were the first words Charmian had heard her speak. True as well. The silk was lovely, thick and heavy. Emmy took the dress and held it up against herself admiringly.

Flora whisked it away. "No good," she said. "Forget it." She handed the dress to Charmian. "Wouldn't fit her. Wouldn't fit me. Have a go."

A minute or two later, Charmian had added another purchase to her marmalade and paid over a sum surprisingly much larger than she had anticipated. But the dress was worth it.

Sergeant Wimpey came towards her. "Guess what I've just picked up."

"You're going to tell me."

"I've just been talking to my wife. She has a friend who lives next door to the Gaynors. Not such a big house, but a nice little bungalow. She has a girl at the same school as Joanna. They both go to a private school out towards Ascot.

It seems there have been ructions today because Joanna disappeared on a school trip to Madame Tussaud's."

"She's back now all right." Charmian looked across the room to where she could see the girl and her mother.

"Oh they found her: staring at the waxwork of Jack the Ripper. Been there all the time."

Charmian pulled a face.

"Yes," went on Wimpey. "Not nice, is it? Not what we wanted to hear. But interesting. Adds to the picture."

"Did she talk about it afterwards?" It was the sort of question Ulrika would expect her to ask.

"Not a dickybird. Just got on the coach home with the rest of them and sat quiet. Didn't say a word. So what do you make of that?"

"Not quite normal, no. On the other hand, it's what a lot of children must have done." A taste for horror was not unusual.

"That's not all. The neighbour says the kid has a room over the garage that belonged to the chauffeur in the days when they had chauffeurs, and this place has its own door and staircase. She can come and go as she pleases. The neighbour says she does. Out all hours."

"Might be just talk."

"No. She boasted of it at school. They all knew."

"Do the parents know?" asked Charmian, looking across the room at Annabel Gaynor, so pretty, neat and normal.

"Do they hell!" said Wimpey. "What do you think?"

Joanna and her mother packed up the flower and plants stall together. Their goods had sold well, Annabel would be able to report a good profit to the Sesame Club. She was famous for her seedlings and cuttings, she had green fingers and usually turned in a good sum. Not much was said between them until they were in the car.

As she fastened her seat-belt, Annabel said, "I heard about what happened this afternoon at the waxworks."

"How did you find out?"

"Maria told her mother."

Joanna muttered something that sounded like 'sneak'.

"Why did you do it?"

"I was just interested."

"It was a silly thing to do. Drawing attention to yourself like that."

"I wanted to look. After all, it's a murder case Daddy is trying. The woman that's killed her husband."

"Your father is not trying the case, as you put it, the Judge does that, and the jury decides whether she did kill her husband or not. Your father is just the prosecuting counsel."

"I think he's made up his mind, though. I heard him say it was a nice little domestic murder."

Annabel started the car in silence. As they reached their gates, she said, "I think you have entirely too much freedom. I shall have to do something about it. For a start, you can bring your things in from the garage room. As from tonight, you sleep in the house."

She parked the car in the drive, where it would effectively block her husband's car when he got home, and walked into the house. This is all your fault, is what she was saying. Your work, your habits, your life touches all of us, all of us.

"I'll kill her," said Joanna under her breath. "I'll kill her, I'll kill her."

If Charmian had heard this conversation, she might have advised Annabel to watch her step. On the other hand, she might not. Plenty of girls threaten to kill their mother without planning to do anything much about it.

5

BRIAN GAYNOR worked late at his papers in the room he and Annabel had created as a study for him. It was a charming, book-lined attic with solid plain furniture, which gave it a comfortable feel, nothing fancy. The whole house was the same, quiet but good. The taste was Annabel's, but she had designed it for him and he matched it. Brian Gaynor was a tall, fair-haired man with big solid bones like his daughter. Finally, he went to his bed. Annabel was sound asleep in the antique French bed upholstered in a William Morris chintz. He touched her gently, but she did not stir. He knew that he and Annabel had created a pleasant way of life in this house, now he had the uneasy feeling it was threatened.

He looked in on both children; he tried to be a good father, do all the things expected of him, when he had time. The boy, small-boned like his

105

mother, was lying on his back with his arms sprawled above his head, the duvet on the floor. Brian replaced the duvet and tucked him in. Joanna was curled up like a ball with her head buried in her arms. He left her alone. Untouched. She looked peaceful enough. So did Annabel for that matter, although he well knew this could be deceptive. He had heard about the murder in the Princess Louise Park, of course, but he was more interested in the murder he was engaged with professionally. More interested in that than in his family, Annabel would have said.

As soon as he was in bed, and the house dark, Joanna got up and conducted a quiet investigation of possible exits and entrances. She knew most of them, naturally, like the pantry window, and the broken lock on the kitchen window, and the exit from the attic widow over a roof and down a drainpipe, but it was wise to check.

Oliver Colman, the husband of the murdered woman was asleep too, well sedated by his doctors who could do nothing about his dreams. The couple had lived in a small flat on the ground floor of a council estate. Twenty other flats constituted their block, but theirs had been the only one with window-boxes full of flowers. Irene would not be around to water them any more. Asleep too, in his set of rooms above the club was the murdered woman's employer at Buzz. By the time he got to bed he was usually exhausted. His living quarters were in their usual state of chaos.

Before he slept, Oliver Colman had given as complete a statement as he could manage of his life and Irene's. Where she worked, the people she knew, the contacts she might have made, he had named all the people he could think of. He had once worked as a special policeman so he knew that his statement would be read by the whole investigating team, and it was up to him to do his best.

Repose too, in Maid of Honour Row. Johnny, Freda, Gillian and Lesley had such a sparsely furnished house that it was easy to keep tidy. Their employer, who owned the house, provided a cleaner once a week. She used to say that you wouldn't know from looking whose room you were in, they were so alike. Their real life was in the stables. Or just possibly in the Duke of Wellington or at Buzz. Charmian had seen inside the house once, handing in some misdirected letters and come to the same conclusion. Immaculate, but empty.

Miriam in her large Victorian, mother-dominated house; Flora and Emmy in their neat, semi-detached house with a bird-table in the front garden; Sergeant Wimpey in his heavily mortgaged two-garage bungalow: they were all asleep. Flora and Emmy were both dreaming of Mr Pilgrim, a fact which, had she known of it, would have surprised Charmian, but which Ulrika Seeley would have said was only to be expected. Miriam was not dreaming, she was far too tired and her mother too restless. Mr Pilgrim was not dreaming because he was awake and travelling.

All around them the police machine was still working. Information was settling itself into several police computers, bits of the machines gently talking to themselves.

In the Home Office Forensic Laboratory tests were in process on the clothes of the murdered woman. The scraps of rubbish found under her body had been preserved for a thorough study. Nor was the matter of the slaughtered mare forgotten, a little bundle of evidence awaited investigation too. In another laboratory, the clothes in which Charmian had been attacked were spread out.

There was a kind of nightmare about this going on in Charmian's mind, one in which every piece of evidence got lost or muddled and it was all her fault. A piece of paper kept fluttering into her face, then floating off before she could read it. Read it? Was there anything to read? An anxiety dream, a responsibility nightmare. She woke up and took a drink of water, dislodging Muff who had settled on her chest, weighing her down. Eventually, she slept heavily, Muff on her feet, failing to hear the telephone ring.

Ulrika Seeley finally managed to wake Charmian.

Charmian stretched out a hand with her eyes still closed. "It's so early." She knew it was Ulrika. Telepathy?

"You are never home."

"Not a lot, no."

"So I ring early. I have had a few thoughts. About the girl's father and his profession."

"But I didn't tell you," began Charmian.

"No, you did not tell me the child's name. But I have my own ways of finding things out." Ulrika sounded amused. In fact, it had been a combination of luck and good guessing. A patient who worked in Lincoln's Inn and had a mother who lived in Eton, together with the intuition that Ulrika used all the time.

Charmian sighed. They could do with Ulrika in the police. "Go on."

"He is a very successful man. Rather tough, they say, but with all this charm. He specialises in criminal cases. And for the last few weeks he has been much absorbed in prosecuting in the Debarton murder trial. Not his first murder case, by any means, he has done several in the last two years. Have I got the right man?"

"You've got the right man."

She hated to give Ulrika best, especially when she knew there must be a lot of guesswork involved.

"You can't guess in my work," she said somewhat sourly.

"Oh go on. You do it all the time."

Charmian abandoned the contest. "So? What are you telling me?"

"That the father's work and life-style must be considered in relation to the girl. They may constitute her problem. Making a kind of hole in her life."

Holes, thought Charmian. Why all this talk about holes?

"Why don't you go and watch Gaynor in court and see how he operates? He may open your mind for you."

"I've really not got time."

"Then read the account in *The Times*. He is masterly."

"That's easier to do."

Only half awake, Charmian heard herself say, "Ulrika, I've been wanting to ask you . . . " Wanting, but not willing to admit to it. "I saw a bit of scribble, really looked nothing more, on a piece of paper under the murder victim. It was collected as part of the forensic residue. But it reminded me of something I had forgotten and I found myself saying so, as if it mattered. Just popped out, yet I hadn't thought about it for years. Why should I have remembered? It worries me. And I don't know why. So that worries me, too. What do you make of it?"

"I'm not a magician, dear," said Ulrika, sounding amused. "It'll have to be do-it-yourself therapy. Work on it. Think about it. Round and round, till something pops out once again. It may be important to the case. I should say it was."

"That worries me too."

"Of course it does, because then you must say: and was it important, that scribble to the killer? That's the other question."

"I think it may have been important," said Charmian.

"And what was it?" asked Ulrika.

"On the paper it looked like a squared-off circle, or a rough oblong, the outline not quite complete. Rough, very rough."

"And what did you call it?"

"A Frisian beard. If you know what that is. It's the name of a style of beard the early English went in for. And I'm not saying that's what it really was, just what it reminded me of." She appealed to Ulrika. "What do you think it represents?"

"Not having seen it, I can't say, but offhand I'd say it sounded like a hole."

"Thanks," said Charmian. "A hole. That is really helpful."

Ulrika did not laugh. "Holes as symbols are very important. Think about it. From a hole something is gone, something must be replaced. And perhaps that was what the murder was: a replacement."

Charmian got up, fed the cat, made herself some coffee. With the bitter coffee, she read *The Times*, turning to the Law Court reports. And yes, Brian Gaynor was brilliant, with a nasty cutting edge to his tongue in prosecution, a formidable mind.

Then she dressed herself in the sort of clothes, neat but on the dowdy side, which might be suitable for watching a line-up of sexual offenders, one of whom might be an exhibitionist who had later tried to rape her, and then gone on to kill Irene Colman.

It was not clear if they were looking for three men or one. But she would turn up to survey the suspects dragged in by Sergeant Wimpey.

He met her himself, polite as ever. "Thanks for being so punctual."

"Least I could do. But all I've got to go on is his smell!"

She let herself be led along the row of men he had got lined up for her. All of them men with a record of sexual offences.

In the daylight of the bleak room at the back of the Alexandria Road Police Station, they looked, and smelt, so ordinary. She shook her head and came back to Wimpey.

"No, I'm sorry."

He was philosophical. "Well, it would have been so easy if you could have said yes. And the we might have moved on to see if chummy fitted the Park killing. But I didn't expect it. One or two bruised faces, as you saw, but nothing you took a fancy to? No."

He walked her to her car. "Got one thing to tell you, though. Our bright young police surgeon, at my suggestion, photographed and measured the slashes on the horse, as far as he could, mind you, decomposition having set in, and compared them with cuts on the girl. He detected a remarkable resemblance. Same knife, same hand. Or so he thinks." He gave her a straight stare. "Makes the position of Joanna Gaynor interesting."

"We really have to talk to her again. About her knife, if nothing else." The incredible, the incomprehensible, might be true. "Have you said anything to your boss?"

"I told the Chief the way our thoughts were wandering, and he said he could not accept that nice child as a killer."

Chief Inspector Merry doesn't like me, Charmian thought, and would never see things my way. And then she had to admit that all policemen hate children to be criminals of violence, it cuts into something basic about the way they regard their work.

Moving on to another point, she added, "So the horse could have been a trial run?"

"Could be," said Wimpey, with the air of one who kept his options open.

Or something more complex and terrible, thought Charmian. The first work of a killer who was needing to kill, but struggling not to kill a human being.

Yet it had happened.

"If such a killer could kill once, then it could happen again," she said, following her thoughts to their logical conclusion.

Starting from a different point, Wimpey had got there before her. "I reckon," he said, "if we don't get lucky, we will have a series."

"We should use the media to get a message out to the women in Berkshire and this part of Buckinghamshire to tell them a killer is around, and to be careful."

And some more than others, Charmian considered.

Later that day, she parked her car in the garage at the back of her house and strolled back down the small side road to Maid of Honour Row. The garages had once been a kind of mews, she supposed, although the houses themselves did not look grand enough to have supported coachmen and horses.

It was a warm, quiet evening and she strolled on, enjoying the soft scented air after a day in London. Before she realised it she was in a road of large houses, lying back behind hedges and gardens. From what she could see of them, they had a comfortably shabby air as if families had lived in them for generations.

Ahead of her a familiar figure was strolling. She caught him up. "Johnny, out for a walk?" Not her business, but the police are constitutionally curious, and just now everyone's movements were of interest.

He turned. "Hello. Yes, I'm just dropping in to see Lesley's old man. He likes a bit of company."

"I thought she went every evening."

"Oh she does, gives him his supper, checks his freezer to see he's got enough food for the week in it and takes away the laundry. He can't do a lot himself, got terrible arthritis, poor old boy. But she's a bit austere, is our Lesley, and the old chap likes a bit of male company. So I pop in now and then before she arrives. I don't think he's too keen on women."

"No?"

"Had a bit too much, probably. Or not

enough of the right sort. Lesley's mum walked out on them when Lesley was a kid, so I'm told, and I don't think life was too jolly when she was there."

They had reached the entrance to a detached brick house, surrounded by a large, dejected looking garden. The front door stood wide open, a tall thin figure leaning on a walking frame was looking out.

Johnny waved. "I've brought him today's paper. One of the more entertaining kind. Lesley only allows him *The Times* and the man likes a bit of gossip occasionally. I suppose you could say I pander to his lower taste." Johnny gave Charmian a cheeky grin.

"Does Lesley know you call?"

"I think so, but we don't talk about it." He turned into the garden and left her with a wave. "Right, I'm off. Don't stay out too late, Miss Daniels, not too safe out for ladies these days."

Cheeky devil, thought Charmian. Thinks he can get away with murder. All the same, she turned back homewards. After all, the evening was closing in.

6

THE Sesame Club had a committee meeting the next day. Miriam Miller telephoned first Flora Trust to remind her, and then Annabel Gaynor who had only just been elected to serve as treasurer. Annabel was known to be good about managing money, and if she wasn't, then her husband was. People quite often got elected because of their husbands although this was never openly admitted. There were five other ladies on the committee, all close friends and enemies (in the Sesame Club it often came to the same thing), but she had already been in touch with them and knew that four would come and the other was in America with her husband, who was a banker.

"Flora?"

From the moment of silence at the other end, she deduced with long experience of the Trust household, that the telephone had been picked up by

Emmy and was now being handed over to Flora. Why did Emmy lift the receiver if she didn't mean to answer it? No answer to that one, but it was irritating.

"Oh there you are, Flora. About tonight, I think you ought not to come on foot." The sisters usually walked the short, wooded street that led from their house to the library building.

The district between Eton High Street and Windsor was almost a village with its own atmosphere. It even had its own name. It was called Merrywick. Merry had been the name of the farmer who had once owned all the land upon which most of it was built. He had been gone for about thirty years, but a son was an officer in the local police and the name Merrywick was a perpetual memorial. There had been quite a nice large sum of money too, but he had left all this to a lady friend that no one knew he had.

In Merrywick a group of leafy roads with houses set well back behind hedges surrounded an open green where cricket was played in summer down to the river bank. On the other side of the green was a church, the post office and the small infants' school. There were very few street lamps which meant that it could be dark at night, if there was no moon.

"It's not safe," she went on. "We've been warned. Did you see the evening paper? Take a taxi." Flora did not drive at night if she could avoid it.

"Don't go on, Miriam. We aren't coming alone. We are coming with Nancy Waters and she's bringing her dog, Bruce."

"I don't like that dog."

"No one does. That's the point of him."

Bruce, a cross between an Old English Sheepdog and a Dobermann pinscher, combined the fiercest traits of both, and was indeed an alarming creature, rightly feared by friends and enemies alike. Nancy said he had a sweet soul, but no one else saw the evidence for this.

"I grant you ought to be safe enough with Bruce," admitted Miriam. "But if he's coming to the meeting, mind you see he has a muzzle on."

"Won't be much good to us if he can't bite," said Flora briskly.

"Muzzled!" Miriam put the receiver down and then dialled the Gaynors' house. "Annabel? You're coming tonight. Don't bring the dog."

"I wasn't going to," said Annabel in surprise. The Gaynor dog was a Pekinese with the aggression of a Jack Russell. He was rarely allowed out. Certainly not when Bruce was to appear.

"Drive. Or come in a group. Don't walk on your own. Not safe. I'm telling all the committee."

"I'll drive, of course. Or my husband will bring me." Annabel knew he would not, of course. Too busy, but she liked to pretend.

The usual arrangement was for the teenage daughter of a neighbour to stay with the Gaynor children when their parents were out in the evening. She was a reliable girl who took her duties seriously. Another thing Millicent took seriously was food.

"I've left you tomato soup with Brie and chutney sandwiches." This was what

122

Millicent liked best at the moment. Her tastes varied, you had to keep up with her. Annabel took pains to do so. "Ice-cream in the refrigerator, strawberries in the glass bowl."

"Oh thank you, Mrs Gaynor, you always leave me lovely things to eat. I'm looking forward to raspberries coming in."

"Right." Annabel registered that next time it had better be raspberries. "I've left Joanna chicken sandwiches."

Joanna tolerated Millicent without liking her; Millicent was baffled by Joanna, but tried to make good blood.

"Oh, she's eating meat again? I thought she'd gone vegetarian."

"Yes," said Annabel briefly. "White meat."

"And Mark?"

Mark would eat anything. "He's having the same as you. But no strawberries. They make him sick."

He would try to get some, of course. He never seemed to learn, but she could count on Millicent.

"Mr Gaynor will probably be back before I am, then he will see you home."

"If it's not dark I can see myself home, Mrs Gaynor."

"No, get him to do it." Partly because the girl ought to be escorted back, but even more so that Brian should not get away with doing nothing. She saw it as a kind of score.

Her last birthday present had been a small red Fiat car. Whatever other criticism you made of Brian, and Annabel made many, she had to admit he was not mean. Although life between them was often a battle, she did admire him very much. He was so clever.

She hurried to the garage to get the car out. There against the wall rested the children's cycles and the lawn-mower, but no car.

"Damn."

"Car been stolen?" said Joanna's amused voice behind her.

"No, of course not." Now she remembered that she had taken the car to the local garage for a service and had forgotten to collect it. She looked at her watch. Too late now, the garage would have closed an hour ago. "I'll have to walk, that's all." Run really, she was late already and Miriam was a stickler for starting the meeting on time. "Where is Millicent?"

"Eating her sandwiches and counting the strawberries."

"Now, now, don't be unkind. Go and eat yourself, love." She gave her daughter a peck on the cheek, her standard non kiss, meant to convey abstracted affection, and which Joanna deeply resented as being meaningless. "I've left you a slice of chocolate cheesecake. Made today. I must rush."

Joanna nodded. Whatever you thought about Annabel, and Joanna thought many different things, you could not fault her cooking. She stood watching her mother hurry down the drive and disappear into the dusk.

"She needs wings." She had a quick, satisfying picture of her mother flying away through a hole in the clouds, like a black hole. That might be the way, a good idea. Not painful in any way, of course, just gone. Thoroughly, completely gone. For a moment she contemplated life without her mother.

The committee meeting started on time without Annabel.

At eight o'clock on the dot, Miriam checked her watch, and looked around the table where the committee was seated. "She's late, we won't wait. Let's have the minutes read and get going. We have a long agenda." There was a quiet pleasure in her voice. She liked a full agenda, it showed that the Sesame Club was important and that she, Miriam, counted for something in it.

Two vital topics were to be discussed. First, they had before them a report by a committee member on a home for battered wives recently opened, and which they were asked to support financially. Such an enterprise was bound to provoke strong discussion. In theory, the committee was all for protecting battered wives, but in practice, as Miriam well knew, it would call into play any number of prejudices, dislike and inhibitions, not all of which the members would admit to owning although powerfully moved by them.

In addition, they were going to discuss

the idea of joining with other groups to fund a day hospice for the terminally ill. For this there was a great deal of enthusiasm, but it was a heavy responsibility and one which, once taken up, could not lightly be put down again. It was for the financial burden of this that they secretly desired Brian Gaynor's expertise. Also that of the banker at present in New York.

"Everyone has a copy of Mrs Baxter's report on the shelter in Listow Road, I think," she began. "She reports very favourably on the place. Seems to be working well. The police and the Salvation Army say it fills a need in the district."

"She ought to know. I'd call her an expert on battering. If there was one for husbands . . . "

"Now, now, Nancy."

"That poor husband of hers."

"I don't know that she actually beats him," said Miriam uneasily.

"He's completely under her thumb, that's why."

"Well, we must agree that Joy has written a very good report and we have to thank her for that. I think we should circularise the whole society and ask for responses. Shall we vote on that?"

This done, the membership secretary reported a rise in numbers. "Very satisfactory. And one of our speakers, Chief Superintendent Daniels, has asked to join."

"I'm not sure we ought to have her," said someone. "She's only going to study us. Make a report, write a book." The speaker knew something of Charmian's history.

"Still, it's flattering," said someone else.

"We can't refuse her," said a third. "We don't have a blackball."

"Perhaps we should have," said the first speaker. She was a lady of explosive temperament in whose hand a blackball would have been like a grenade.

The committee drew in a sharp corporate breath, preparatory to bursting into speech. A nice little argument over Charmian was about to explode.

In the distance the big front door banged.

"That must be Annabel now," said

Miriam with relief. "Shall we wait for her?"

They sat for a minute, then another.

"Must have been the caretaker leaving," said Flora.

"She'll be here soon," said Miriam.

Charmian got home late that evening, parking her car just about the time the committee meeting was getting under way. The small terrace of houses in Maid of Honour Row had been built well before the days of motor cars, so she used the old mews behind.

It was a calm, quiet evening, but overcast. She noticed the sweet scent from the lime trees that lined the road. This was one of her favourite summer smells for the pleasure of which she easily forgave the sticky fruits that later in the season would splash on the pavements. Tonight she could smell the scent of roses from her own front garden. She must remember to do something about them later in the year. Wasn't there something about pruning? Either you did it in the spring, or you mustn't do it in the spring but in the autumn. Either way it was a skill she must learn. It occurred to her that someone like Annabel Gaynor could set her right.

It had been a good day: lunch with Humphrey at his club, surrounded by actors and lawyers, a mixture of which Humphrey was himself, now she came to think of it. She both liked him and did not trust him. But she had paid him the compliment of wearing a dress in printed indigo silk, which had been made by a famous *couturière* who owed her something and who had 'made a special price'.

She walked up the short path, fumbling in her bag for the key to the door. She paused, staring.

There was something dark on the step. No real shape. A dark furry splodge. And blood.

Oh god, Muff.

Eyes blurred, not really seeing, she knelt down by the heap of tawny brown fur and blood. The cat must have been struck by a car and crawled home to die. She must have been hit by something very heavy. The wreck of her body was total.

The head didn't look right.

Charmian sat back on her heels and took a deep breath. Not only the head was all wrong. The tail was wrong. There was no tail.

She looked up at her sitting-room window to see Muff's face peering out at her, with her mouth opening and shutting in silent protest.

Not Muff, never Muff, not even a cat at all. A dead rabbit.

A tremor of mixed relief and disgust ran through her.

"No, not you, Muff dear, thank goodness. Not you, so horribly dead. Someone has deposited a very dead rabbit on my doorstep."

A flash of white underneath the animal's head caught her attention. She touched it, drew it out, stared at it: a sheet of paper with a message on it in large, staggering letters as if the writer's hand had trembled.

SUPPOSING IT WAS YOU
NEXT TIME.

No question mark. It was more of a statement than a question.

Holding the piece of paper with care, she stepped over the rabbit to let herself into the house. Muff descended the stairs, calling loudly. Food, food, me, me, she shouted.

"No, Muff, wait. I must make a telephone call first. Can I speak to John Wimpey? At home? May I have his number? This is Charmian Daniels."

Her name had the desired result so that the number was produced at once.

"John? I've had a little present delivered to my doorstep. And a message." Briefly, she told him about the rabbit. "Yes, I've left it there. I thought one of your lot ought to inspect it. And the message." She read it aloud to him. "Yes, I'd call it a threat." She turned the sheet of paper over, still handling it carefully because there might be fingerprints. With any luck the forensics would be able to get something from it. "Yes. I'll be in, I'll wait for you." She wanted to say, And be quick about it, but she restrained herself and turned to examining her clothes and the paper. There was a lot of blood about.

Blood on the paper, blood on her

hand, a smear of blood on her dress.

On the other side of the page, as well as blood, there was a scrawl. That shape again. A square that was not a square, a jagged empty shape.

It felt wicked, evil. Evil was washing over her.

Annabel slid quietly into her seat at the committee table, hoping no one would notice her.

"Annabel, you're late. The meeting started some time ago."

"Yes, Miriam. I am sorry. I took the long way round because of the street lights. I didn't want to go the dark way."

"I thought you were going to drive."

"No car."

Flora said, "What's that on your face?"

Flustered, Annabel extracted a glass from her make-up bag and looked at herself. A long streak of mud was dashed across one cheek.

"I fell over." She took a deep breath. "Oh, I might as well say. I thought I was being followed. I don't suppose I was. But I panicked."

"And quite right too." Miriam reached out to pat her friend's arm.

Annabel's head drooped, her small figure in the soft cotton dress seemed vulnerable and fragile.

Flora and Emmy looked at each other in sympathy and alarm, almost, but not quite holding hands for self-protection. Women had to look after themselves, they knew it in double strength. Mr Pilgrim had not been around lately, and Flora would have to admit that, although he had been a worry to her and she would like to know what he was about, she missed him now he was not there. He had held a kind of promise for the future in him.

Voices of alarm, sympathy and support rose from around the table. Annabel was a popular person. There was a general feeling that although her husband was distinguished and generous, he neglected her. The Gaynor children were looked upon with alarm as being out of control, although no one could say exactly what, if anything, they had ever done wrong. It was just a feeling of unease they engendered.

"You're not walking home alone," said Miriam in a decided voice.

"We will see you back," promised Flora.

The meeting proceeded, ending by common agreement, a little earlier than usual. No one wanted to stay for coffee and cake, they preferred to get home. In little groups, they departed. Miriam with a neighbour, Flora and Emmy walking with Nancy Waters and Bruce. Annabel, refusing offers from other people with cars, chose to go with them. Bruce looked fierce enough to protect four women, nor did his looks belie him as she well knew.

The three women and the dog walked Annabel to her own gate. Brian's car was in the drive. So he was home. Annabel felt the usual mixture of pleasure and anxiety. What mood would he be in? It counted for so much with the whole family. The happiness of the family swung with his moods. Moods he always denied having, but which were instantly perceptible to his wife and children.

"We'll wait till we see you go through the door," said Nancy, who had constituted herself as head of the party by virtue of Bruce and his powers.

"No, don't worry. I'll be all right." You couldn't see the front door from the gate anyway, because of the curve of the path, overshadowed by flowering bushes. She got the key to the front door out of her pocket and into her hand, ready for a quick entrance.

"Sure?" Nancy wanted to get home herself, while Bruce himself was straining on his lead in a way which, she knew, foreboded badly at his temper. He had been known to prevent her and her husband going to bed by getting on the bed and growling at them all night. She did not want a repeat. "We'll push off then."

Flora and Emmy waved goodbye and let themselves be led away.

Annabel closed the gate and started up the path towards the lights of the house. Brian's car loomed darkly before her, blocking some of the light. Bushes and flowering shrubs hung over the path. 'We ought to have all this cut back,' she thought. 'It's a jungle.'

She was a few yards up the path

when she stopped. Beyond the bushes she sensed a presence. The feeling of being looked at, of being watched, was strong.

She felt the evil. A cloud of evil was floating over her, filling her nostrils. She could smell it.

A branch moved in the bush on her right. Annabel gave a small scream and ran towards the house.

The key turned easily, she was inside.

All seemed quiet and at peace. Thank God, no sense of evil here. The hall was softly lit, she could see through the open door into the kitchen. Down the hall she could just catch a glimpse of Brian working in an armchair, books and papers all around him. He turned a page.

Her mouth and throat felt dry and sore. She went to the kitchen sink to get a drink of water. The bowl of strawberries was still on the table, untouched. Millicent really must be giving up eating strawberries in favour of some other fruit.

She rinsed out the glass to replace it on the shelf. Brian hated a mess so that over the years, and under his influence, she had come to dislike it herself. A natural muddler, she had become tidy. What had she done to him? The bowl of strawberries went into the refrigerator to join Brian's supper which he had obviously not eaten.

At once jealousy flooded into her soul: he had eaten in London with someone.

At the sitting-room door she stopped. "Brian? I'm back. Why are you working down here and not in your study?"

"Just felt like it. Doesn't matter, does it?"

"Of course not. Children all right?"

"Asleep when I looked in on them."

"You didn't eat the meal I left for you."

"Had something in town."

"With anyone special?"

"I was working, if you want to know. I worked as I ate. Papers I had to study." He was very tired, wearier inside than Annabel would accept. She didn't know much about mental fatigue, didn't even accept that it existed. He loved his wife, but she could never understand that after a tough day in court, all he wanted was silence, solitude, and to get ready for the next day. He saw her sceptical little smile and tried again. "I just ate and worked."

She didn't believe a word of it. All the same, it might be true. She strained to believe him. "Want some coffee?"

"Don't think so, thank you. I haven't been sleeping well lately."

"It's because you work till all hours."

He ignored this remark, eyes turning to what he was reading. Sometimes she wished he'd go blind.

"You saw Millicent back home?" Her eyes were fixed on something across the room.

He jerked to attention. "No, I didn't. She'd gone before I got here, leaving the kids on their own. I don't think it's good enough. Don't have her again."

Annabel said, "Are you sure she has gone home? That's her bag on the floor by the window."

"She's just left it behind. She's not in the house."

"How do you know? Have you looked?"

"Of course not, but she'd have

appeared. Or we'd have heard her."

Annabel moved towards the door. "I'm going to look."

The boy was sound asleep with the dog on his bed. The dog raised his head when they came in, yawned and went back to sleep again. The boy did not stir.

"That dog shouldn't be here," said Brian.

"Leave him." Annabel was crisp.

Joanna opened her eyes as her parents stood at the door. "Hello," she said, sleepily. The sleepiness was false, her body was tense. Wait for it, she seemed to be saying.

Annabel sat on the end of her bed and kept her voice calm. "Joanna, what time did Millicent go?"

"I don't know. I left her downstairs and went to bed to read. She's such a bore. I must have dropped off. Does it matter? What's happened?"

"Nothing. Go back to sleep again."

Annabel pushed her husband back down the stairs before her. "Go and 'phone Millicent's parents. See if she's there."

Reluctantly he went to the telephone.

"I don't want to alarm them."

"They've got to be alarmed."

His hand on the telephone, he said, "Where are you going?"

"I'm going to look in the garden."

Brian put the receiver down, he had caught her fear. "I'll come too."

But Annabel was ahead, running down the garden path. She stopped at the place where she had felt movement, sensed evil. She pushed through the bushes to the little grass patch beyond. A dim light from the house illuminated it.

Millicent lay on the ground, spread-eagled, arms and legs flung wide apart, tossed there like a doll thrown by a child. A tumble of clothes lay beside her.

On a branch of the scented azalea bush hung her jeans. Their legs waving in the breeze.

Here was the evil she had sensed.

Annabel turned round to see Joanna behind her, staring, eyes wide. The girl's face looked swollen and flushed, her mouth was wide open, so wide that it looked like a black hole with a scream waiting to burst out.

Annabel's hand came up and she

slapped Joanna's face, with a hard stinging blow.

"Take her away," Annabel screamed at her husband. "Take her away. This is evil, evil."

Confused, Brian found he did not know if she meant Joanna or the murdered girl.

7

JOHN WIMPEY looked down at the dead rabbit. "I have to say we are not being smart about this. Someone is running rings around us." He stood up, wiping his hands on a paper towel provided by Charmian from the kitchen. "For what it's worth, I would say this was a bunny from the butcher's."

"My impression too. Doesn't make me like it any more." The sense of evil was still there.

"Yes, I don't blame you. Not carved up on your doorstep, but brought in ready to serve up. I suppose it's a slightly better picture. All the same, I don't think you'd better feed it to your cat."

Muff, hungry spirit, was prowling around the house, looking for her supper.

"Because in a little while you are going to have the whole CID outfit down here pretending to be SOCO's and getting in each other's way."

"Because of the paper?"

"Because of the paper," said Wimpey seriously. "It does tie in with the death of that girl in the Princess Louise Park. As you had already decided for yourself." He turned to her. "Let's leave this dead animal where it is for the moment, and go inside."

They went back into the house, where Charmian put down some food for the cat. "Seems to make a definite threat to me."

"It does."

"And what I want to know is why? Why me?" The classic question that victims probably always asked themselves if they had time to speculate, and here she was asking it. "Do you think it has anything to do with the flasher? Or the man who attacked me?"

"I have news for you. We've picked him up. You did a better job on him than you knew. He went back to Oxford where he lives and was put into the John Radcliffe Infirmary with pneumonia."

"That wasn't my fault."

"You helped. Anyway, when they got him out of the oxygen tent and he'd had time to think about why he'd given a false name, he'd decided to confess all. Apparently his brush with death had given him a desire to purge his soul. Plenty there to purge as it happens. A lot more assaults on his conscience than the attack on you. More than he could remember, he claimed, but he remembers you because you were the last and the most painful. For him, at least." Quite a number of attacks on women in a wide area south-west of London were going to be cleared up by the man's statement.

"So he's out of all this?" She waved her hand indicating everything from the murder in the Princess Louise Park to the mess on her own doorstep.

"Yes, he was under constant inspection during that period. He could not have got out and done a murder, even if he'd had the puff to do it. I'm not saying he might not have had a try, not a nice man, and dislikes you. Said so. But he couldn't have done it." Wimpey gave a tight, mirthless smile. "Says he's trying to struggle against it now he is so holy, but I wouldn't count on too much. Still he couldn't have done this tonight, or killed the girl."

So one man, a possible suspect, had been removed from the scene, but another, faceless personality had taken his place.

"Perhaps he's got a friend," said Charmian.

"What horrible ideas you have. But whether he has a friend or not, you have an enemy. I don't think you ought to stay in this house. Not now it is marked as where you live. I don't like that. Can you go somewhere else? Friends? London?"

"I shall certainly stay. I'm not going to be frightened out. Besides, there's Muff." She looked down at the cat who was clearing her plate with the efficiency of a vacuum cleaner. "You can't move a cat around like a parcel. I have good neighbours." She had waved to them as she had set off for work that morning. All four of them had been piling into the old car that took them back and forth to the stables. A postcard from Kate in that day's post (she was in Padua now, looking at the Giotto frescos) had spoken of that 'bonny boy next door'.

He was bonny, they all were, healthy bright young creatures like the animals they tended.

"Do you think they saw anything? After all, it must have taken a few minutes to put the dead rabbit on your doorstep. They'll have to be questioned."

"Doubt if they were around. But I'll ask." Lesley might have noticed something.

"It's the Bingham house, isn't it? Where Tommy Bingham keeps his stable team. Those that don't live with the ponies."

"How do you know that?" She was surprised.

"It's the sort of thing I'm paid to know. Bingham's had that house for years. This is the latest team, that's all. Might be his last, I hear he could be giving up. Three girls and a lad, he's got there, hasn't he?"

"That's right."

"I don't think they're locals."

"One of them must be. Her father lives here. Lesley something." She had never heard Lesley's surname.

"Oh yes, old Barraclough's girl. I heard

she'd got a job at Bingham's. He was Headmaster of the local Grammar before he retired early. She'd be a cut above stable work, but I suppose she wanted to stay at home to look after Dad. The mother left them."

Johnny certainly didn't think the work above or below him. No class worries there. A natural bouncy born egalitarian Lesley could be the same "I think she just likes the ponies."

"That too."

Behind their conversation another dialogue was going on. He thought she was more shocked by the bloody threat on her doorstep than she would admit, and he wanted to get her out of the house. He felt protective, which was amazing, really, because she was such a strong woman. But against some people, some evil, what was your defence?

Charmian was silently resisting the pressure she sensed. But she too knew that there was a killer loose who seemed to have her number. Man, woman or child? Charmian was the one who put the unspoken query into speech.

"The question we have to ask now is:

what about the child, Joanna?"

"I knew we'd be coming to that. And the answer has to be that it is the sort of trick an adolescent might play."

"True enough."

"She might have guessed you've been observing her, and that could turn you into someone to attack."

"She's hard to read, that child. I think it would take weeks, months possibly, really to assess her, and then it ought to be done by a professional. But what I did see was that the mother is anxious. It all adds up to a troubled family." She shook her head. "But where the trouble comes from I can't say, whether it's the girl, or the parents or all of them rubbing against each other. It's been suggested to me," (she was careful to keep Ulrika's name out of it), "that the father's professional preoccupation with murder may come into it."

Wimpey said, "If we get any closer to the girl, then we're going to have to take on the father." His tone suggested this was not something to be undertaken lightly.

Charmian bent down, removed Muff's

empty dish and replaced it with a bowl of milk. Not wanting milk, Muff stalked away with the angry gait of a cat engaged in keeping its owner in her place.

"Shouldn't your outfit be here by now?" she asked Wimpey.

"Yes, they are slow. About the Gaynors, ever met the father?" Charmian shook her head. "I have once. Came to a community meeting we had, police and the neighbourhood, that sort of thing."

"So?"

"Lot of charm. But something cold and hard inside."

How could he really know from one meeting, Charmian thought. Ulrika had taught her that people were harder to know than that.

"Let's have a cup of tea while we wait," said Wimpey. "I'll put the kettle on." He was a domesticated animal, well able to find his way around other people's kitchens. A strong relationship was growing up between them, not entirely professional. He admired her, and she liked him. They worked well together, they could be a team. Age didn't come into it, but intellectual sympathy did.

The teapot was next to the book on polo. He moved it carefully aside.

"Hello, you interested in polo?"

"Don't say you play it?"

"Never. You have to be a millionaire to do that. But I watch it. I love to see them shoving away at each other. Mind you, it's the ponies you really admire." All the time he was putting in the tea, pouring water, with quiet expertise. The kettle seemed to have boiled faster for him than it ever did for Charmian. "Tea's made."

The telephone rang loudly in the quiet room.

Charmian bent to answer it. With a sudden flash of precognition, she said to Wimpey, "Did you leave the number here with anyone?"

He nodded. "My wife. Always do."

It wasn't his wife. She recognised the voice of an assistant to Chief Inspector Merry without being able to put a name to him. "It's for you," and she handed the receiver over.

She knew from the way his face changed as he listened that something had happened. Something over and beyond

151

her little episode on the doorstep, nasty as it was.

He listened carefully, saying little beyond 'Yes' at intervals, and finally, "OK. I've got the message." He put the receiver down with a gentle hand as if it was both hot and explosive.

"A car is on its way over. DC Oliver and a photographer will be in it. You can talk to him. But the stuff on your doorstep wasn't chummy's only activity tonight. Or it may have been just a curtain-raiser. There's been another murder. Copy of the first."

"Where?"

With real pain in his voice, he said, "In the garden of the Gaynor house."

"And the victim? Is it Mrs Gaynor?"

"Funny we should both think that first? No, it's a girl who was baby-sitting for them. The daughter of a neighbour, Millicent Ward."

He was getting himself out of the house and away with the same skill he had shown at the tea-making. He looked regretfully at the steaming pot. "Won't have time for that. Still, it's all yours. And you'd better have it." To his eyes, she looked as though she needed it. Sweet hot tea, that was what you gave women in shock. Always had and always would.

"I'll be following," said Charmian. "Don't think I won't."

He was gone and the second police car had arrived before the tea was cold.

DC Oliver eyed the teapot with appreciation. "Milk and two sugars, please." He looked round hoping for a biscuit as well, and not seeing any, drank his tea with a wide mouth. "We'll get your bunny measured and photographed. It's being done now, if you want to look." Charmian shook her head. "Then you can fill me in on the details. Is that the bit of paper?" He took it carefully between tweezers, inserting it into a plastic bag which he labelled. All between big gulps of tea. "Got your prints on it, I suppose?" He pushed his cup forward again. Unlike Wimpey he was one who naturally thought tea was a woman's job. You were a man and thirsty, they poured out the tea. It was the way things worked.

"Yes." Charmian filled his cup and,

weakening, opened the tin of biscuits and offered him one. "Shortbread?" He couldn't help being young, hungry and brash.

"They won't be long with the photographs." He helped himself from the tin. "Then we'll get your doorstep tidied up and be out of your way, ma'am," he added, as if remembering for the first time who and what she was. No doubt he was marvellous with lost dogs and old ladies. "I'll just get out there to check."

While he was gone, Charmian tidied the kitchen. In a short while DC Oliver was back, Muff hanging from his arm like a fur boa.

"Found her out there trying to get at the rabbit, ma'am. Better shut her up."

Muff looked sour, but dangled there limply, determined to co-operate in no way.

"Something out there you missed, ma'am," Oliver said, as he handed Muff over. "Well, when I say missed, you couldn't have seen it without moving Brer Rabbit because it was underneath." He held out a small brown label. "Tied round one leg. Got the butcher's name on it. Came from a local shop."

Charmian read the name. "Fisher and Brown, Windlesham Street." She knew the name, occasionally shopped there herself. "About the best butcher in Windsor."

"Right, ma'am." He was still looking pleased with himself. "And there's a bit more. Underneath, a bit blood-stained and mucky, you can read where it was meant to be delivered."

Handling it carefully, although any fingerprints were unlikely to have survived, Charmian made out the letters:

The Housekeeper,
WINDSOR CASTLE

She stared at Oliver in surprise. "The Castle?"

Oliver laughed. "Never got there, of course. I reckon the Queen's had her lunch nicked."

Still laughing, he took a brief statement from Charmian and then departed. Charmian shut Muff in her bedroom, collected her handbag and keys, preparatory to departing for the Gaynor house.

No one had invited her to this murder, but she meant to be there.

The police party had left her garden, it was dark outside, but she had put lights on inside the house.

Slowly she walked down the path, she paused at her own gate for a moment. Finding a label on the rabbit was a valuable pointer. Possibly, just possibly, it might be a way to identify the thief.

The thief might not be the person who had left the rabbit and the threatening note on her doorstep, and that person might not be the murderer. Nothing could be taken for granted. You were balancing one probability against another. But the finding of the piece of paper with the open circle on it, made it very likely. It was a kind of signature. She had had anonymous messages before in her time, but nothing like this.

Why me, she thought again, why me?

Because you are Chief Superintendent Charmian Daniels and somehow or other you are a threat to the killer.

The moon had come up, but there were clouds scudding across the sky, so that the scene was sometimes brightly lit, then at other times clothed in darkness.

As she closed the gate behind her, the moon came out from behind a cloud, shone brightly for a second, then disappeared again. Just for that second, she thought she saw a figure standing in the shadows of the garden across the road.

She believed she had made out a shape. Tall, slender and still.

She stood looking, wondering what to do. Then the moon came out again, and she saw nothing remarkable, just bushes and a lime tree.

With resolution, she turned down the road towards her garage, and stepped out.

A dark figure detached itself from the shadows, crossed the road, and padded behind her.

Further down the street Marigold Marshall, a middle-aged widow, was walking her dog, a tall Irish wolfhound which she had inherited from a dead aunt together with a large sum of money and a house in Maid of Honour Row, a valuable freehold. There was not much love lost between Fergus and Marigold, but she did her duty on account of the inheritance. Also, she had loved her aunt.

She saw the figure creep out of the shadows like a dark stain and start to walk behind Charmian. For a moment she stood still and watched.

"Fergus," she said. "That man is following that woman." She quickened her pace. Fergus gave a yelp of joy. He saw the chance of action. It was a long time since he had bitten anyone. He lifted up his head and made a delicious moan.

The figure in front heard, looked round and saw the dog. He seemed to hesitate, and then ran back across the road and down a side street.

Charmian walking fast, turned the corner towards her garage.

Marigold moved more slowly. Should she tell the woman? She knew where she lived, having watched Charmian move in. Tomorrow perhaps.

She turned round and plodded off home. Not a very nice night to be out, felt like rain. She did not listen to the television news that night, she never did, it was always so full of unpleasant things better avoided. For the same reason she did not take a newspaper. She relied on the milkman and her neighbours for news of importance. They would certainly tell her if the Queen was dead. Or if the Princess of Wales had another baby: But they had not bothered her with the murder in the Princess Louise Park.

She went to bed and read the diary of Noel Coward. Much more her style.

8

SINCE Merrywick, although crowded by Windsor, Eton and Slough, regarded itself as a village and behaved like one, soon many people knew that there was trouble in the Gaynor house.

Flora Trust and her sister Emmy were among the first to know. They had gone back with Nancy Waters and her dog to drink the coffee they had so badly missed at the Sesame Club meeting. As they were now in mufti, as it were, not representing the club or anything else, all three ladies, Emmy silently assenting, decided to take a little whisky with it. It was the sort of night, Flora said, when you needed a nip, and then they would be off home.

From the sitting-room of Nancy's house you could see the lights of the Gaynor house. Nancy, who was a keen neighbour watcher, knew how to read the signs.

160

"Something's up there," she said, sipping her whisky. It was a double enjoyment to have something to drink and something to watch. She was a woman who knew how to appreciate her pleasures.

Flora got up to take a look. Emmy followed. It was she who saw the flashing blue lights, just discernible over the hedge. She looked at her sister, then pointed at them.

"A police car." Flora's eyes went wide. "Or an ambulance."

"Or both," said Nancy, being taller she could see the lights better than Flora could. Besides, it was her garden, she knew what to look for. "I think there is more than one light." Anxiously, but happily too because it was so interesting, she said, "Do you think we ought to go round to see if we can help?"

Flora rightly interpreted this as meaning to see what was going on. "I'd like to." It was an honest answer and got an honest response from her hostess.

"I won't sleep a wink if we don't."

No one asked Emmy, but she was moving before they were.

"What about Bruce?"

Nancy considered. "I think we'd better leave him behind."

Flora thought she would like to leave Emmy but of that, of course, there was no hope. She had nourished a vision of Mr Pilgrim somehow being her saviour but this golden dream was fading fast with his prolonged absence from their scene. Had he ever really been interested in them at all? Perhaps, as Miriam had been ready to hint, it was no more than a female fantasy. Did women have such fantasies? More pertinently, did this woman? It was something you wanted to know about yourself.

By crossing the road to stand on the opposite pavement, the trio of women could see the Gaynors' house. Not only were there three police cars lining the kerb, but an ambulance was drawn up behind them. A uniformed police constable stood on guard. The significance of this was not lost on the three women.

"Oh, my goodness," said Flora. "It's bad all right. What can have happened?"

"Let's go a bit closer." For a better

look, Nancy meant.

As they moved down the road, they were joined by two other people and then by a man who had been watching from behind his hedge. There were muttered greetings as the group formed.

"See that ambulance?" said the man who had emerged from the hedge. "Look at the black windows. That's the police mortuary ambulance." He added lugubriously, "If there's more than one body they will bring up another ambulance."

In silence, they stood watching. They were all there in time to see Charmian drive up, park her car, and walk in through the gate.

"Do you think that means it is Annabel?" whispered Flora. She didn't expect an answer, nor did she get one. But the hedge-watcher said, "There's another police car round the corner. I could see it from my bedroom window. The third house round the bend, the one with the tulip tree."

"Who lives there?" said Nancy Waters.

He didn't know, said the hedge-watcher. Hadn't lived there long himself, he said. Hardly knew anybody.

Emmy nudged her sister. She knew that tree. Say so, she was urging her sister.

Flora spoke, "The tulip tree? The Wards have a tulip tree. Milly Ward sits in for the Gaynors when they go out."

"Oh well, there you are then," said the hedge-watcher. "Looks as if something happened to her."

In a village you always get to know things about your neighbours. You have valuable source material from which you work it all out.

Charmian Daniels made her way straight to where her friend Sergeant Wimpey stood in the garden of the Gaynor house. A canvas blanket like a black pall had been thrown across Millicent's body. An assembled cast of police and lay technicians were performing their customary tasks. All the lights were on in the house, but none of the family was visible. Through the sitting-room window she thought she caught sight of Annabel. There was no sign of Chief Inspector Merry.

"Where's your boss?"

"In there talking to the family. I'm in temporary charge out here."

"What about the girl's family? Who's talking to them?"

"Jack Fraser." Jack Fraser was Inspector CID, based on the Alexandria Road Station. "As you can guess, we are a bit stretched."

Charmian looked across to the black shrouded figure. Then her eyes went to the jeans hanging from the tree. "Same MO as before?"

"Exactly the same. Same sort of knife wounds as we have see before."

Twice, if you counted the mare.

"Before you do anything else," said Charmian, "I have something to tell you. I was followed to my car. I was just about to confront the follower when a dog made a racket behind and the fellow ran off. I lost him."

"It was a man?"

"Of that I can't be sure. It's possible. I thought so at the time, but I only caught a flash. A figure wearing jeans and dark shirt and woolly hat pulled down low."

So she'd seen that much, Wimpey

thought. "Right." Without another word, Wimpey was off, and she heard him talking on the telephone in the front police car.

While she waited, she considered the scene before her. She walked towards the tree where she could see the jeans. They were hanging, legs apart, suspended from two branches at eye level. Her eye level, she was a tall woman. Draped across the top were a tiny pair of white bikini-style knickers. It was a macabre sight, as if the murderer had a sense of humour but did not know how to express it.

She removed herself a few yards, leaning against a tree and thinking. Now would be the time to smoke a cigarette, except that she had give up smoking several years ago. She was still here, thinking, when Wimpey returned.

"That's fixed. A search of the area is under way. Probably too late, but if he surfaces, we'll get him."

"Fine. Thank you." Then she said, "Has anyone spoke to Joanna?"

"I presume that Merry has done. He's in there with one of the WPCs. But I don't think anyone is going to be able to speak to her easily."

"Not even me?"

"Especially you. If he knew you were in the garden, he'd have you out. Your name has been mentioned."

"By whom?"

"By the mother. The father is busy erecting a stockade around the whole family. When he gets them all inside, he might come out himself and say a few words."

"You're joking, of course."

"Not altogether. We're dealing with a chap who knows the ropes."

He took her arm and turned her towards the gate. "I'd go, if I were you. You won't do any good."

And might do some harm, he meant.

Charmian moved her arm, gently but decisively. She wasn't going. Or not yet. The male establishment was firming up against her.

"There's one thing I can tell you. No note. No scrawl on a bit of paper. That way this case is different."

"You think so?"

"What do you mean? I assure you no paper has been found."

"May I take a look?"

The covering on Millicent's body had just been drawn back to allow a final photograph as they approached. Charmian knelt down beside the body to make, without touching, a concentrated survey.

She had been looking at dead bodies for over twenty years now, and specialising in violent attacks on women and by women for the last eight years, but this death and the other that had gone before it had a special quality.

She leaned back on her heels. "It's one in a series," she said. "It may have its differences, but it's one of a kind. We've got a serial murderer here. Not private, personalised hate, but anyone will do."

"What about the threat to you?"

"In spite of that. I am the exception that proves the rule." She stood up, brushing earth and grass from her skirt. "And you are wrong about there being no message. There is one."

"Where?"

Charmian pointed to the tree where the jeans were strung up. "There, there is the message, a hole spelled out in clothes not written paper." A hole which signified something to the killer, a hole which the killings were, in some way, filling.

Wimpey looked sceptical. She could see he did not believe her. He had never really believed in the hole. He had not seen the scribble as a hole, just as scribble.

A scribble was a scribble was a scribble.

She was irritated. He didn't believe her, and she felt it was because she was a woman. Wimpey too! She'd thought better of him.

"Well, we'll see. When this killer is caught, you'll see I'm right."

It's a lock and key, don't you see, she wanted to shout. The hole is the lock and the killing is the key. The image of the Frisian beard had faded from her mind for the moment, but she had not forgotten that it had once seemed important to her.

Wimpey was silent, thinking he would settle for just catching this one. Theories and justifications could come later.

"I think we've got a psychotic; I'm with you there." He added. "Also, I think you ought to take care yourself."

"Oh yes, about the bunny." And she told him about the label attached to the rabbit. "Looks as though we owe the Queen."

Again, she detected a sceptical look cross his face. What did that look mean?

All he said, however, was, "Drive home a different way, and park the car outside your house."

It was what he might have said to his wife, or his daughter, but he should not, Charmian felt, have said it to her. Professionally she was more than his equal. She was also older, but she understood he meant to be protective rather than patronising.

They stood aside as preparations were made to move the body. Still no movement from within the house, but an unseen hand had drawn the curtains in the living-room.

"I wonder what's going on in there?" Charmian wondered aloud. "I'd like to know."

She followed Sergeant Wimpey's advice on taking a different route home because he stood at the gate to watch, thus making it difficult for her to do anything else. Turning, as she did, up the road, enabled Flora, Nancy and Emmy to see her while Charmian flashed past pretending she did not know they were there. A little of her bile was thus relieved. A bundle of crossness, put together because of a man, and deposited, she was ashamed to admit, on her fellow women.

The group looked at her sadly. "She might have told us what was going on," complained Flora.

Inside the house Annabel Gaynor was glad to let her husband take charge. Sometimes she resented his managing ways, now she was glad to be protected.

She avoided looking at Joanna, on whose cheek a soft bruise was spreading. "I did that," Annabel told herself. "I hit my child. But I had to hit her. I had to wipe that look off her face. Brian didn't see it, I did. Joanna liked what she was looking at."

At the memory of what they had both seen, she felt sick. Millicent was so young, so innocent in her own way, and they had destroyed her. If she hadn't been in their house, surely she would not have been killed? "I left her strawberries when she really wanted to eat raspberries. I thought of her in terms of food, brie and pickle sandwiches, fruit and cream. She was a lot more than that, even if I couldn't see it. And now she's dead." It was somehow the Gaynors' fault. Or more her fault than anyone else's. Guilt sat heavily on Annabel's shoulders.

She tried not to think about Millicent's parents. It was not parents' day. Especially not mother's day. Could you fear someone to whom you had given birth?

She shook herself. What was she saying? Joanna was just a child who had had a bad shock, a very bad shock indeed. Anything else was her own imagination, after all, she too had been shocked, and she had slapped Joanna to ward off the attack of hysteria she had read in her child's eyes. A slap was the recognised therapy. She'd been more than a bit hysterical herself. Brian had been calm enough, but then murder was a money-earner to him. But thank God for that calm which was erecting now a protective stockade around his family. He knew exactly how far the police could go in their questioning.

Suddenly she wondered if that very protectiveness was not an admission that something was terribly wrong in this family. Brian was so very very clever, you always had to remember that. She looked across the room at him, and saw that he had his clever face on. She hated that face.

The policeman, Chief Inspector Merry, was asking them all questions about where they had been that evening, and the times when each had returned. He had asked Annabel when Millicent had arrived, then asked her if she could think of any reason that had taken the girl out into the garden where she had been killed.

None of them could or did help him. There had been no noise, no alarm, Millicent had not screamed or called out. Just gone quietly into the garden to be killed.

"I was asleep," said Joanna, shrinking against the protective figure of the father. In her nightdress with her hair in plaits, she looked vulnerable and childish.

Mark sat squarely on the sofa next to his mother and said very little at all, even when asked questions. Just yes or no. He didn't appear frightened, just dazed and uncomprehending. Annabel confirmed that he was a very heavy sleeper.

"I'm one myself," said Chief Inspector Merry, with apparent sympathy. "And you just sat there working when you came in, Mr Gaynor?"

"Yes. I was tired. I had had a heavy day. I made myself a drink and sat there reading my papers and waiting for my wife to come in."

"But you were alarmed that the children had apparently been left on their own?"

"I was cross," said Brian shortly.

Nothing was said about the affair of the slaughtered pony, which for Annabel, and perhaps for Joanna too, was the beginning of this terrible affair, but there was no doubt it was in the mind of Chief Inspector Merry. Annabel could feel him collating the facts.

The policewoman, a clever girl called

Dolly Barstow, leaned forward. "Joanna, how did you get that bruise on your face?"

Annabel sat very still. Joanna raised her hand and touched her cheek tenderly; she looked at her mother.

"I did it," said Annabel, in a loud clear voice. "I slapped her because I thought she was going to be hysterical."

"Joanna," asked the policewoman. "What about those scratches on your hands? Where did they come from?"

Joanna held out suntanned hands, muscular and thin, on the backs of which were several parallel scratches. She stared at them in apparent surprise. "I think I must have got them this evening grooming my horse."

She might have done, thought her questioner, or she might not. Dolly Barstow felt she would like a closer look. They could have been scratches from someone's fingers.

"No, I remember," said Joanna, with an air of believing what she said. "I was playing with the stable cat."

Annabel could see Brian gathering himself together to put an end to this questioning. It would only be a delaying action. In the end they would have to go through this process over and over again with the police. You couldn't stop it.

"Would you like some tea or coffee?" she asked Chief Inspector Merry wearily. "I think I would." It would keep her awake, but she wasn't going to sleep anyway.

"I'll help you," said the policewoman, rising with her, either to watch her or protect, Annabel was not sure which, but she knew she would rather have been alone.

As she filled the kettle, she wondered about that other policewoman, Charmian Daniels. She was all for women protecting women. The water began to boil while Annabel pondered if Miss Daniels could be of any help.

Charmian was thinking about the Gaynors as she drove home. If I can get the mother on my side, then I may be able to have a session with Joanna. She knew Ulrika would say she must see them all together, as a family unit. But that was the way Ulrika worked, she herself would have to do the best she could. She guessed that the father, in whom all the trouble might lie, would raise difficulties.

Obeying Sergeant Wimpey's advice, which she admitted to be wise, she parked her car under a street lamp, checked the front of her house, then let herself inside.

The doorstep where the rabbit had rested had been cleaned up by the police. A stain remained, not everything could be washed away at one attempt. In the morning she would scrub it herself. She stood for a moment letting the events of the day run over her, the good bits and the bad. Then she went to her bedroom, stripped off all her clothes, threw them into the laundry basket and stood under a hot shower, letting the water rush over her. That dealt with the day.

Drying her hair, she saw the minute hand on the clock by the bed tick up to the hour. Although so much had happened, it was not so very late. She could still hear sounds of life from next door.

Ulrika never went to bed early.

Night was a time for working, she said. Charmian belted her dressing-gown round herself, drank some cold milk, checked that Muff had food and drink (she was dozing on the bed, in fact) and picked up the telephone.

"Ulrika?" It might be that the current lover was in residence, in which case Ulrika would not have answered the telephone so readily. Six rings and no answer and you knew to put the receiver down. She did not know the name of the present incumbent, nor had Ulrika ever mentioned him, but she retained a strong belief in his existence. Not here tonight, however. "Can I talk, or is it too late? Or perhaps you are working?"

"Thinking, just thinking."

"I can give you something to think about. There has been another murder." Quickly she gave Ulrika the details about the murder, and not only the murder: telling her about the rabbit and the threat to herself first because that was how it had happened to her in time, but presenting the facts as dispassionately as she could. "In the Gaynors' garden. Their child-sitter." One really could not call either Joanna or Mark babies, they were not infantile. "Do you think that significant?"

"Yes."

"But of what?"

"What do you think?"

"Does that matter?"

"Certainly it does. What you think becomes part of it."

"I don't know what to think. I find it hard to accept that a girl like Joanna could do two murders."

Ulrika did not commit herself to what a girl like Joanna could or could not do. "We shall have to see."

"And then there is the man." She told Ulrika about the figure that had followed her. "What does that mean?"

"Perhaps the girl and a man," said Ulrika lightly.

"And what about the rabbit on my doorstep? What does that mean?"

"You will have to decide that for yourself."

Ulrika gave one of her attractive, baffling laughs. Charmian recognised it for a kind of finial. There was no more to be said for the moment.

Charmian put the receiver down, half amused, half frustrated, this was always the way with Ulrika. She offered you questions where you asked for answers. But when you thought about it afterwards, you realised she had shown you the way to the answers.

She sorted out one of her favourite books, Keats' letters, to read in bed to soothe her to sleep, but she had no sooner placed it on the table with the lamp turned on when the front-door bell rang.

Keeping the door on the chain, she said, "Who is it?"

"Johnny and Lesley. We've come to see how you are. We know there's been trouble, we saw the police car."

"Come in then, and I'll tell you." A strictly edited version, she said to herself.

"We know a bit," said Johnny, following Lesley and Charmian into the living-room. "We saw a policeman doing something to your doorstep. I thought it might be your cat, then I saw her at a window. So I knew she was still alive."

"It was a dead rabbit. I suppose you

could call it a kind of billet-doux." She had decided to tell it with a light touch, she didn't want to alarm them. Lesley looked tense as it was. She said nothing about the threat to herself. Leave that out.

Johnny looked grave. "There's a nutter around."

"Yes, I think you all ought to be careful. Especially the girls."

"We usually go around as a group."

"Lesley doesn't."

"True." He turned towards Lesley. "Watch it, Lesley."

"I will. Believe me, I will."

"No more coming or going late at night on your own. One of us will come with you."

"I don't think it's that bad," protested Lesley.

Charmian said gently, "It may be. Better take care. There has been another murder. Another girl."

"Where?"

"At the Gaynors'. In their garden. A girl who was with the children for the evening. You'll read all about it in the papers tomorrow, I expect."

"So that's why you went out again," said Johnny. "I saw you go. We would have come round before, but you were on the telephone."

"How do you know I was on the telephone?"

"Oh, our telephone always gives a little chirrup when you start a call. Something wrong with the line, I expect."

"Can you hear my calls?" She was alarmed.

"Never tried. I don't suppose so."

I watch them and they watch me, thought Charmian. We all ought to be the best of friends.

"If you are all right and there's nothing we can do, then we'd better be off," said Johnny. His eyes fell on a large framed photograph of Kate, looking her most radiant. "What a beautiful girl."

"My god-daughter. She's in Italy at the moment, but you will probably meet her when she comes back." In fact, if Kate has anything to do with it, you certainly will. "Thanks for calling, you two. I appreciate it."

She closed the door behind them, grateful to have such good neighbours, but glad to be on her own. She collapsed into bed, and was asleep before she had read a page. Muff was there before her, eyes closed, nose buried in her paws, snoring gently.

Charmian awoke to a sudden, strong sense of a presence in the house.

She sat up, muscles tense. She remembered that she had not put the chain on the front door. Daylight filled the room. Muff had disappeared.

Then she realised she could smell coffee. Tying herself into her dressing-gown, she sped down the stairs.

Kate appeared at the kitchen door. She was wearing white jeans, a soft blue shirt and a sweater. "Let myself in quietly. Good job you hadn't got the chain on the door." She came over and kissed her godmother. "Sorry I disturbed you."

Charmian got her breath back. "How did you get here?"

"My flight was delayed, got in after midnight. I hitchhiked from Heathrow."

"Kate! The risks you run."

"I'm here, godmother, aren't I?" She went over to the kitchen stove from which came the smell of coffee. A bag of croissants from goodness knows where was on the side. "I know how to look after myself. I'm the condom generation, remember? Coffee?"

"I hope you are." She accepted the coffee, and the two women sat facing each other at the kitchen table. Muff was on the floor eating an early breakfast.

"I didn't expect you."

"I sent a card. Probably get it next week. The Italian post office had a little strike. They have them all the time."

"It's lovely to have you back. You look good, Kate."

"How's that gorgeous lad next door?"

"Is that what brought you back? He thinks you are beautiful."

"I must work on that."

The telephone rang in the hall. Charmian went to answer it. Kate watched her thinking that a call so early must mean trouble. She was very protective, without admitting to it, of both Charmian and her mother. On the table she saw a book on polo. A new subject for her godmother; she was interested in polo herself. Aesthetically, of course, not with any intention of playing.

Men and horses in motion looked so beautiful.

Charmian heard Wimpey's voice, it sounded gruff and tired — early morning and no sleep tired.

"Sorry to wake you."

"I was up." He had probably not been to bed. "So what is there?"

He took an audible breath. "First, we never caught up with the chap who might or might not have been following you."

"I never expected you would."

"But on that road leading out to Merrywick we found hoof-prints on the grass verge. And droppings. Could be, just could be, that was the way he went. Or how. Had a horse tied up somewhere, ready for escape. Couldn't follow the prints very far, though." He sounded disappointed. "And it's been raining since, damn it. Got some casts of the prints, fortunately before they were washed away."

This road, a mere unmade-up track really, was a short cut to Merrywick running from the bridge and behind Eton High Street. There were meadows on either side behind low hedges.

"Thanks for telling me. It'll bear thinking about."

"Not quite all."

"No?" Somehow she had known that much. He had more to tell her. "Anything to do with the hoof-prints?"

"No, not directly." He paused, "Another body has been found. I don't know many of the details yet, but there is one. Out on the Slough road, beyond Merrywick. A girl as before, same sort of killing as before."

"Ah," she was trying to take it in. Two in one night was going it.

"Only difference, she's been there some time. Perhaps a week."

She felt defenceless, at a loss, with nothing to say.

"You there still?"

"Yes. I'm just thinking. Trying to take it in."

"I'll leave you with it." Then he said, "Oh one more thing: that rabbit of yours. It wasn't on the way to the Castle. Well, yes it was, but not the Queen in her Castle. The Windsor Castle, the pub down by the railway."

A pub and not the Queen, you could

laugh at that. She thought that Wimpey had guessed from the first. But another murder? So already they had a series of three.

Your turn next, had been the menacing suggestion. For the first time, Charmian felt a sense of danger.

9

KATE exploded into Charmian's life. Suddenly the house was full of light and movement. Not noise, Kate was not noisy, but the house seemed to vibrate to her passage. She was not untidy, her room was neat, she left the kitchen in order, the bathroom immaculate; but the very air registered she had been there. Perhaps it was her scent, a peculiarly sharp, sophisticated scent brought back from Italy, full of verbena and rose. Little snatches of it met you as you came in the door, or on the landing, or breathed at you from the chair she had been sitting in. Even Muff smelt of it after she had been stroked. Kate was out a good deal, but her presence was always there. Charmian did not know if she loved it or found it maddening. Muff, after a period of jealousy, decided for Kate, and slept on her bed, nose to nose on the pillow if she could get there, or at the foot of the bed if not.

By breakfast time Kate, together with Merrywick, Windsor, Eton and Slough — not to mention the rest of southern England — knew what had happened in the way of murders. For the next few days it was the main subject of conversation at many breakfast tables.

The killer now had three deaths to his credit. It had to be a man, Kate said. Mass murderers were always men. The newspapers agreed with her, the killer was definitely 'he'. Charmian hoped this was the case. The evidence seemed to point in that direction. She herself swung this way and that, sometimes influenced by Ulrika's neutral, open-eyed belief that anything could be possible, sometimes influenced by her own deep-seated feeling that only a male could do such things.

If she had put this feeling into speech she would have been ashamed of it, but she never obliged herself to do so. Instead she took refuge in a kind of fatigue. It would be nice, she thought, to take things easy, not to work today, to stay in bed, if possible to sleep. Instead, each day she got herself into her clothes, put on a suitable amount of lipstick for a high-ranking police officer about whom there was a certain amount of gossip, and drove to London. She had more than one life to live.

She knew that she had left behind her a police machine clicking itself into position to deal with an investigation that might cover several counties and more than one police force. There was a lot to be set up when this happened, and she knew it all. First a major incident room, code named Miriam with its linked computers. In theory all the forces now had compatible machines. But she knew that, in practice, there were going to be hiccups here. Not all the computers had the same language yet and could read each other. Nevertheless, the police had to act as if they could. So there would be indexers, putting statements into the computers and numbering them, then statement readers underlining all significant points. Action allocators sending out inquiry officers who would come back with statements to feed into the machine, thus to start the whole cycle off again. She wondered where her friend Wimpey would find his stake in all this. By rank and temperament she would call him a natural 'Action allocator'. It was to be hoped that the local force had enough officers, but they would be calling on lay personnel.

In her capacity as an acknowledged expert on women and violent crime she would be talking to Joanna and Annabel Gaynor later today. At present they were said to be 'under sedation', but she suspected this was part of Brian Gaynor's protective apparatus for them. In addition, she would have to speak to Millicent's parents to find out what her relationships were inside and outside her family, and what sort of curiosity could have prompted her to go into the garden where she met her death. That would come later. There were the other two victims also to be considered.

Charmian knew that her position would not be easy. No one loves an expert, least of all another expert, and she suspected that Brian Gaynor would have his own specialist opinion on hand.

Being punctilious and careful, he would no doubt name this person in advance.

She knew enough about the subject by now to realise that it would have to be one of a limited number of people.

She knew the names of most of them.

E. J. Halliday, of the St Freda's Hospital, West London. Brian might call him in and would not regret it: a good gentle man with great insight.

Dr Francesca Risehanger, Department of Psychology, University of Middlesex: but she was said to be mainly interested in ethnic problems.

Bill Sanders, formerly of Edinburgh, but now in New York: not likely to be called in, therefore.

And the most likely of all, because she was so eminent in the field and yet so approachable, her own friend and mentor, Ulrika Seeley.

Should I consult Ulrika? she wondered. She could alert me to any prejudices and scruples I ought to guard against in myself and in anyone I may work with. But Charmian knew from experience that she could not be too careful, and if Ulrika herself were to be called into consultation, it might be better not to talk to her.

With the permission of the police, Brian Gaynor had moved his family that morning into a cottage in the Great Park owned by his friend Tommy Bingham. Buried in the depths of the woods, near a bridle-path leading to Ascot, it was intended to isolate them from sightseers and the press. The press would soon find out where they were, of course, but protected by the privilege of the Park, the gates, the foresters, the nearness of several royal houses, it was harder for the journalists to get at them.

As she settled herself in her car one morning to drive in the sunlight down Maid of Honour Row, Charmian knew that she would be, as usual, acting two parts, and that as well as trying to find out what made Joanna tick, she would also be seeking to discover discreetly how much freedom to wander Joanna had and, in particular, what freedom on the nights of the murders.

It was going to have to be a very indirect form of questioning. She didn't look forward to it, she hated being two-faced, but it happened to her all the time. It was part of the job.

About the third victim she still knew very little. Her name was Margery Fairlie; she was about thirty-five, unmarried and lived alone in a small flat above a shop in Merrywick. She had been dead some time, but exactly how long was not established. It was even possible she had been the first to be killed.

At the corner of the road, she saw an old friend waiting by the bus stop. Beryl Andrea Barker, sometimes called Baby, although in these days of respectable hairdressing, she preferred to be called Andrea. She and Charmian had had a long and varied relationship, in the course of which Charmian had once been instrumental in putting Miss Barker in prison. But they had got over that hurdle and were now friends who gave each other cautious trust.

Charmian drew up. "Want a lift?"

Miss Barker looked around cautiously. "Well, I don't know," she began. "I'm not sure if I ought. Are you on business or not?"

"Oh come on, get in." Charmian opened the door and Andrea, she was certainly all Andrea today, hopped in.

"What was all that about? You don't usually talk to me like that. To the shop as usual? I'm going past."

"Placed as I am," said Andrea, "as someone who has transgressed once or twice — "

Charmian laughed. Once or twice was a euphemism for what had looked at one time like a life dedicated to crime.

"And paid her debt to society," continued Andrea, "I have to be careful. People might wonder if you were picking me up. You weren't, were you?"

"Not unless you've done something."

"Innocence is not always a protection," said Andrea. "We both know that."

For the last five years she had been working at her old trade of hairdresser. She had now bought her own business. The money for the purchase coming from somewhere, begged, borrowed or stolen, Charmian chose not to ask. Andrea was prosperous, successful, and as Charmian detected, as restless as a cat. It was in such moods that Baby stood a strong chance of reappearing and pushing aside Andrea. Of the two persona Charmian preferred Baby as being the more straightforward. You were always catching your foot on something the Andrea person had prepared for you and falling over, whereas Baby didn't prepare traps.

"I heard that a friend of mine had got herself done in."

Charmian slowed the car, turned into a parking slot and stopped.

"Were you waiting for me?" It no longer looked like a chance meeting by the bus stop.

"She'd dropped out a few days ago, we all wondered where she'd got to. Now we know."

So it was the last found body, thought Charmian. The one she so far knew least about. It looked as though she was about to learn.

"You were waiting for me," she said answering her own question.

"She was gay, poor cow," said Baby, making a sudden appearance.

Charmian said nothing, but she was thinking hard.

"I know you believe I am too," said Baby.

"I've never said so."

"Don't have to. Let's say you've wondered. Anyway, I'm not. It's just that when I've been inside that sort of person has always been very nice to me."

"I see."

"And not for favours received, either," said Baby hotly. "They just took to me."

You could, Charmian admitted to herself. You just could. Beryl Andrea Barker could be very likeable.

"And was she one of them, this woman who has been murdered? Did you meet her in prison?"

Baby nodded.

"What was she in for?"

"Fraud. She was a clever girl."

Not clever enough, Charmian thought. She looked at her friend, who had that sharp, cat-is-watching-the-mouse look on her face. Charmian hated being the mouse.

"Are you telling me something? That because she was gay she was killed?"

"Could be." Baby started to move, putting her Andrea face back on again. "I've got to get to work."

"No. You're not leaving this car without talking a bit more. Tell me everything you know about this woman, beginning with what you called her and how she came to figure in your life again."

"She was Maggie to me, but I think her real name was Margery. In prison we called her Tops, just a nickname, I don't know why. I never used it. I've always thought that may have been why she liked me. I think there was some dirty joke there that I never caught on to." Miss Barker sounded disappointed, as if she had searched her mind to work out this joke, but had been unable to do so.

"And after prison?"

"I didn't see her for a long while. Then she turned up one day looking for a job."

"Was she a hairdresser?"

"No, a bookkeeper, she did the accounts. That's how she got into trouble."

"But she still wanted that type of work. Did you give her a job?"

"No, I hadn't got one. Do my own

books." Baby had a sort of native self-protection. No one would ever swindle her. "But I found her one. With the restaurant next door."

She stared out of the car window at the Chinese takeaway.

"I don't think they paid her much there, but it was a start."

"How did she get on to you again?"

"I keep up with some of the girls," said Baby defensively. "You know that."

"You were sorry for her."

"Never." Baby hated to be thought soft. "But she had a quick tongue had Maggie, and quite a reputation. I mean she was always good to me, but I've known her beat someone up when it suited her. If anyone had got violent death labelled on them, then she'd be the one."

It altered the picture somewhat, made the victims not a random, any-woman-would-do choice, but selective. If Baby was right.

"Thanks for telling me."

Miss Barker, all Andrea again, this face neatly fixed on for the day, got out of the car.

"I hope you get him, and the sooner the better." She and Kate saw eye to eye on the sex of the killer. "I bet when you do you find some poor cow has been sheltering him all this time and thinks he's the most lovely man living."

"Think so?"

"But underneath she'll know," said Baby, and on this matter, Charmian took her to be an expert.

She drove off smartly; she had other work, other engagements. When she got to her London office there was a message for her.

A telephone call, a recorded message which told her that while she 'could not give all her time to the murders in the neighbourhood of Windsor, you are requested to assist the local force.'

It was the formalisation of what she had already been doing and, no doubt, in accordance with the accepted practices of the machine for which she worked, it would be repeated in writing.

What she thought at once was that it would strengthen her hand with Brian Gaynor. Her second thought was that someone had fixed it, and she wondered who?

A telephone call soon brought enlightenment. It came through on the grey telephone on her desk, used only by certain channels. But this was, in its oblique way a personal call. She knew the voice even before he announced himself: Humphrey Kent.

The relationship between them, although happy, was not unclouded. He had been married, Charmian had been married. Her husband was dead. About his wife there was a breath of mystery. Certainly there had been a divorce, so quiet and unobtrusive that some people still did not know it had taken place. Charmian suspected he still loved her. The story had reached her that he had discovered his wife to be a CIA agent (or it might have been a Russian spy, that was the other version) and that the divorce had taken place on this account and not due to any loss of feeling on his part or unfaithfulness on hers. Who knew? Charmian didn't, but it added a spice of uncertainty. Spouses, she thought, should be comfortably disposed of before you embarked on anything else.

One day she would ask him herself, but she had the uneasy feeling it was not the sort of question you put to Humphrey. Or if you did, it didn't get answered directly. But then he never asked questions himself. Still, it was a question that ought to be asked.

Of course, they both had means at their disposal to get the answers to any number of questions, but Charmian had never used this for her own ends. She wondered if he had to find out things about her? There were one or two episodes she kept quiet about. If he had investigated her in any but the most professional way (police officers expect to get scrutiny but there are limits) and she should discover it, then it would be over between them, and she would withdraw gently from the relationship. Or would it be so gently? Unluckily, she knew herself well enough to guess she might explode.

"How's the study of polo going?"

"Not badly," said Charmian cautiously.

"It seems to play a big part in your life."

"It will in yours once you meet Tommy Bingham."

"Am I going to?"

"He wants me to bring you to lunch."

I am to be taught a lesson, she thought. But in what?

"I won't be nasty to the Gaynors," she murmured. Not unless Brian Gaynor is excessively obstructive.

"He didn't mean that."

"Well, he might have done. When is the lunch?"

"Sunday. Will you come?"

"Of course. Work permitting." For both of them there was always that proviso.

Their conversation then ceased to be personal and turned to the professional matters in which they were both involved. After this, she telephoned Wimpey to let him know what Beryl Andrea Barker had told her about Margery Fairlie, receiving back the message that he knew, it was common knowledge and that he would be giving her the up-to-the-minute info' some time today. Something to look forward to, she thought sardonically.

When it was over, she sat back to drink

some coffee. She had her own machine on a table by the window, her badge of office she called it, since lesser ranks had to share a coffee-maker in the corridor. To her mind the coffee thus produced was never quite hot enough, but the flavour was tolerable. Her office had been furnished by an unknown hand and was workmanlike without being beautiful. Serviceable was the word for it, she thought. Brown chairs and a shiny brown desk with a leather top. At least it looked like leather, but it didn't smell like leather.

A few touches of her own had arrived with her on the day she settled in. A small clock in a glass case that had belonged to her grandfather and still maintained good time, a green morocco blotter from Italy — a present from her mother on her first promotion years ago, and which she kept as a good-luck token — and a matching desk diary. The diary she replaced every year. She had gone to a lot of trouble to find the expensive shop in Bond Street that sold them. Her mother thought it was the old one going on and on, restoring itself as if by magic.

Now she drew it towards her and wrote in the luncheon engagement. She would ask if she could bring Kate on Sunday. It would be a treat for Kate and interesting for her to see how Humphrey coped with her god-daughter.

The thought was cheering, it rested at the back of her mind, making the day pass quickly. But all the time she had the interview with Joanna Gaynor ahead of her, which for some reason disturbed her. In the end she told herself this worry was because she feared she would not perform well.

She decided to go that evening unannounced. Just turn up on the doorstep and see what happened.

She had been given the address, and a map of the Park: Fletcher's Cottage, Rider's Gate, The Great Park.

She approached her home that evening with circumspection. After all, she was under a threat of some sort, even if she was convinced she could defend herself. Perhaps all the victims had had that simple faith.

She found the house empty, no sign

of Kate. Was she off to Italy or foreign parts again, or just out for the evening?

There was no note, but Kate had left cold chicken and salad ready for her in the refrigerator, the manner of its presentation suggesting she might be back soon. It occurred to Charmian that she had not told Kate about the rabbit and the threat to herself, and that perhaps she should. Kate might not feel invulnerable. On the other hand, at her age, she probably did not believe that she and death were running on converging lines. Yes, Kate would feel safe and therefore be all the more at risk. So she must be told.

On the kitchen table was a thick envelope which had been delivered by hand. Kate had added a note:

'Handed in by a smashing bloke. Hope it's a love letter.'

The smashing bloke was certainly Wimpey, who was personable; she had registered this fact for herself.

But it was not a love letter. Instead she drew out a file of papers on the three murders. They were drawn from various sources, starting with a survey of work so far from the Chief Investigating Officer (in this case, Chief Inspector Merry), through to reports from the pathologists on the knife wounds, and another from the laboratories on the so-called 'forensic debris'. These documents were photocopies of reports, and attached to them was an assessment of the current position as seen by the CIO. In addition, there were maps, diagrams and folders.

In fact, she had a skeleton of the case before her on the table. She read while she ate, abstracted, but enjoying her food. Kate had anointed the chicken with something like honey and brandy before she cooked it and the taste came through the crisp skin. Everything that the girl did she did well. Down on the floor Muff too was tasting a chicken supper. She was less appreciative, honey and brandy were not quite to her taste. Moreover, the mixture made her whiskers sticky, something no cat could endure. She patted them with an angry paw.

Charmian spread out the photographs of the three bodies, pictured as discovered. There were close-ups of the faces. Not pretty. Then long shots of the whole scene. The killer seemed to choose grassy, wooded spots, as if these milieux offered what he or she wanted. They also offered shelter and protection.

There was no sign of struggle. The killer had not alarmed the intended victim, but had had an easy ride.

Mouth full of salad, she studied the pathologist's reports. Photographs here of the wounds, all remarkably similar. On the arms, legs and trunk there were slash wounds which were longer than they were deep. But it was the stab wounds, smaller but deeper, that had probably caused death. More detailed reports would be following further examinations later. There had been no sexual assault.

The third victim, as suspected by Sergeant Wimpey, had been killed before Millicent. But the exact time difference, certainly over twenty-four hours, possibly much longer, had not yet been clearly defined.

Reading between the lines, she thought that the local pathology department was at full stretch and feeling desperate. As she recalled it was a small one, struggling hard at the best of times.

The wounds on the bodies reminded her of the very first victim of all, the mare.

In addition to all this, there was a list of some fifteen men who were investigated because of their past history, or because they had known the victim or been seen near the place of the crime. Men in the wrong place at the wrong time, in other words. Among them might be found the killer. Their names and addresses were attached.

But her business was not with them. She was to occupy herself with Joanna Gaynor.

She drew all the papers towards her again to study once more. They provided a marvellously complete outline of the case as of today. Wimpey had been very clever in his selection of them, but then he was clever. The investigation had not got very far yet; that was clear for everyone to see.

There was a note in his own hand. The horse-droppings of which he had told her were going to be analysed to see if the horse could be thus identified. Small chance, she thought, but perhaps worth trying. Casts had been made of the hoof-prints, which had been sent for expert examination. That too, she thought, could be non-productive. Turning up the type of evidence that would be helpful once you had caught the criminal and were putting together a case, but not much help in actually finding him. But it had to be done, and she would be delighted to be proved wrong. Sometimes you were lucky. In any case, every small detail had to be checked; that was good police work.

She went to the window to get a breath of air before setting off to see the Gaynors. Better change into something innocuous and casual like a linen skirt and cotton sweater. She mustn't look official. They might not let her in, of course, but she thought they would. Brian Gaynor would never put himself in the wrong. Only her, if he could.

Muff jumped past her and sped out into the garden where a garden chair and the scattered remains of a newspaper showed that Kate had been out there in the sun. It was amazing how the house felt full of Kate even though she was out somewhere. Kate would enjoy the lunch and the polo on Sunday. You've been a trouble to me and your mother in your time, Kate, she thought, but you've come through and turned into a good person. There's hope for the human race yet. For a moment the thought satisfied her, and she felt rested and happy.

Then another idea struck her about the third body discovered. No hole. Nothing that reminded her of a so-called Frisian beard.

She gave a mental shrug. Oh well, so there wasn't. I'm not always right.

Since it was wise to be careful and take precautions, she had requested that a woman police officer from the Alexandria Road Station accompany her to the Gaynors, and had arranged to meet her outside the Park at one of the gates equidistant for them both.

To her pleasure she saw Dolly Barstow already sitting waiting in her car. She had come across Dolly about a year ago; they had worked together for a short while.

Dolly had her head down and was reading. Not a newspaper or a novel but a small, heavy book that looked like some technical tome. Dolly had an alert and scholarly mind which she was always training to be of use to her in her career.

She got out of her car as she saw Charmian, putting aside the book which was a manual on police work from the University of Chicago.

Charmian smiled. "Glad it's you." Dolly was an easy person to work with, quick and clever. Charmian realised that she both admired and was fond of this young woman. 'I must be getting old,' she thought. 'I'm not competing here, I just like her.'

"I fixed it."

That was Dolly for you, she did fix what she wanted.

"Get in," Charmian opened the car door. "I'll drive." It was sometimes necessary to let Dolly know who was in charge.

As they drove through the Park, down a winding avenue through trees heavy in leaf, they talked of old acquaintances from the last case.

"How's Tom Bossey?" Chief Inspector

Tom Bossey had been a quietly helpful figure in the last case.

"Promoted and transferred to another division."

"And Harold English?" A different sort of man altogether. She had never known what to make of him.

"Still master-minding things in the back room."

They both smiled.

"A devious character," said Charmian.

"You can say that again." But then Dolly added, with that honesty and perception that one had to give her credit for, "And yet one trusts him."

"And how's Len?"

Len had been the young doctor with whom Dolly had been in love. If she admitted to anything so soft. At any rate, it had been a strong and unceremonious attraction, visible to all their friends.

"Sadly we agreed to call it a day. His ambition and mine didn't match up." Dolly shook her head with obvious regret, Len had meant something to her. "His idea, not mine."

"I'm sorry."

"He'll marry a pretty little nurse and

get his two-and-a-half children and a BMW."

After all, she had loved him more than he had loved her.

"Maybe I'll get him second time round."

Charmian supposed she was joking.

"But by then I may not want him. He will be fat and bald and on the way to his mid-life coronary."

This time she wasn't joking.

In silence, trying to read the route through the park, Charmian drove on. A signpost told her she was on the way.

"About your rabbit," began Dolly.

"Oh, you know about that?"

"Sure." Dolly was reproachful; naturally she had prepared herself. "In case you are wondering, the delivery van had an accident on the way to the Windsor Castle." There were two Windsor Castle pubs (as well as the real castle with the sovereign's standard fluttering above it): one on each side of the town, this one was the other one. "Some of the goods got lost, and someone must have picked up the rabbit. And in case you are wondering why it was not skinned, the cook there liked to do his own."

They had come to a stop outside a square brick house with white gables. A plate on the door read, Fletcher's Cottage, while on the gate a box said, Bingham. Through an archway to the right of the house, they saw a cobbled yard with low buildings ranged round it. The smell and sound of horses seemed to float out of it and over to them. Everything in sight looked newly painted and freshly polished from the brass letters which spelt out the name to the knocker on the white front door. It was bandbox trim. Charmian realised that this was where her young friends Johnny, Lesley and Co. worked. Pololand.

Charmian looked at the house again. She could see a face at the window, a man, Brian Gaynor probably, manning the barricades.

"Let's go in," she said to Dolly.

Brian Gaynor opened the door to them himself. He stood there for a moment as if blocking the way. He was a square, sturdy figure with a brush of short fair hair and bright blue eyes. He waited, without a word, letting them stand on the doorstep. In an inner room to the left of the small entrance hall Charmian could see Annabel sitting stiffly upright on a sofa, her eyes focused on nothing much, but turned towards a window. Three suitcases by the stairs suggested that not much effort to settle in had yet been made. The house looked comfortably furnished with chintz and old oak, but unused as if Tommy Bingham only put in an odd appearance. But when he did, he smoked, or someone did, the smell of old tobacco still hung around, strong and thick. Either a rich pipe or strong cigars.

Charmian did not fail to notice that Brian Gaynor seemed totally unsurprised to see her.

Charmian introduced herself, he nodded silently, and motioned them to go through. He still had not spoken. Words were obviously going to be handled seriously, like a currency in short supply.

Annabel looked at them as they came in, her eyes flicking over Charmian and then Dolly, then she shook her head and went back to staring out of the window.

"We have talked before, Mrs Gaynor," Charmian reminded her. "But this is WPC Barstow."

"Hello," said Dolly cheerfully, she was busy assessing the atmosphere. Heavy, she thought, no help for us here. "You met me before, remember?"

Annabel did not turn her stare from the window.

Brian Gaynor moved so that he was standing behind his wife. "I think you will understand that we are all in a shocked state, Chief Superintendent." His voice was carefully neutral.

"I see that, naturally. It was a terrible thing that happened. But it would be helpful if I could talk to your wife and daughter. In your presence, of course."

"I understand your position, Chief Superintendent, I know you specialise in dealing with violent crimes concerning women and children."

"It's one of the things I do, yes."

Someone had been talking to him, he had been expecting her. If not now, then some time soon. It had probably been Humphrey Kent. Oh, nothing overt, nothing direct, but he had got the message across. One protected one's friends.

"You have, as you would doubtless say, your job to do. I am the last person to impede that. Since I am a lawyer, I am not asking you to wait before questioning my wife and daughter until I have a solicitor present. I waive that right. For the time being."

Dolly Barstow coughed. Charmian eyed her repressively.

"But I must ask you to wait until I have my own expert present." He moved round to the front of the sofa, partially blocking out the sight of his wife. "I have asked Dr Ulrika Seeley to assist me."

Charmian took a deep breath. So she and Ulrika would now be on opposite sides, be a challenge to each other.

But she seemed to hear Ulrika's shocked voice. No, no, she was saying, we shall be working as one, forming a picture between us. No rivalry, no competition, that is not how I work.

It might be so, nothing to do but wait and see.

"May I at least see your daughter?"

"She has been questioned, you know.

By Detective Chief Inspector Merry." There was a perceptible hostility in the way the full title was rolled out. Merry clearly had not scored a success.

"This is something quite different," said Charmian, she was prepared to show infinite patience.

With difficulty, as if his lips could hardly get round the words, Brian Gaynor said, "My wife got the distinct impression that you suspected my daughter of involvement in the killing of the pony."

Charmian remained silent, but Dolly made a soft noise.

"If you can suspect a child of anything so dreadful," said Brian, his bright blue eyes full of pain, "then I have to face the fact that you may suspect her of something even worse."

"I would just like to see her," said Charmian. Just to satisfy myself of the state she is in, whatever that may be. Or to find out what chances she might have had of getting out of her parents' house to do what she might, just possibly, have done. Anything could happen here in this family, she thought; the parents did not seem to communicate at all.

"I love my child."

"I know, sir."

She waited for Annabel to say something similar, but she did not. Brian Gaynor seemed to feel the omission, for he gave his wife a quick, anxious look, then suddenly yielded.

"Very well. I'll take you upstairs. The children are there."

If Joanna is a child, thought Charmian, which I seriously doubt.

"Thank you." She nodded to Dolly to come with them. Dolly dutifully trotted after.

"Stay here, Annabel," Brian Gaynor said to his wife. He lightly touched her shoulder as he passed. Annabel remained silent.

"She's had a tranquilliser," he said, half apologetically, half defensively to Charmian.

A narrow stairway of polished oak led to an upper landing from which four doors opened off.

"This used to be the head stableman's house," said Brian. "Tommy uses it as his base now when he's down here. Decent of him to let us have it. He's there now with the children. Couldn't leave them on their own."

He took them up one more flight to an attic room, flooded with light, which had been turned into a kind of games room with a bar at one end. A camp bed in one corner was made up with a pale blue duvet on which lay a girl's blue cotton dressing-gown.

A tall thin man looked up from a low table on which a chess set was arranged between him and the boy, Mark. The boy had a broad grin on his face, no shock and tension there.

"Just taken my Queen, this lad of yours," the man said. "He's a better player than I am."

"He's always been good. Just the way he is. Born good at chess." Gaynor introduced the two women.

Tommy Bingham stood up and shook hands politely. "Know your name, of course," he said to Charmian. "Humphrey's spoken of you." He did not mention the luncheon engagement, and Charmian saluted his tact.

He had a charming smile, in a lined, tanned face with a hint of pallor under the tan. Charmian remembered that Lesley had mentioned an illness.

"Want to see these two, do you?"

Charmian looked round the room for Joanna. She was seated on the window-seat with her back to the window. Her face was empty of all expression, but there was a bruise across one cheek where her mother had struck her. Possibly other bruises elsewhere. There were certainly hidden bruises. Her mother had been staring out of a window. Joanna appeared to be reading a book.

Her eyes looked dull and quiet.

No one at home, thought Charmian, but she would have a try.

"Joanna?" Behind her, Charmian heard Brian make a noise of protest; she ignored him. "I'd like to talk to you sometime. Do you agree to it?"

"What about?"

"About Millicent."

"Oh." Joanna absorbed this idea, without reaction. It wasn't what interested her. "Not about the knife?"

"The knife?"

"The knife in my bag. The one you took away and kept when Dobbin was killed. Only we did all that. I think it would be beastly to ask about it again."

"That's enough for now," said Brian Gaynor.

Charmian walked to the window and looked out, giving herself time to think.

From the windows of this room, which were barred, and in which, judging by the bed, Joanna slept, she could see down into the stable-yard in the centre of which stood a large box-like structure. The bars made the room like a prison and in this prison Joanna was placed. By this action Charmian was convinced that in her own home Joanna had her exits, and that her parents thought she might have used them.

"What is that object in the stable?" she asked.

"A polo pit, for practising polo on a wooden horse." Tommy Bingham gave her the answer.

"Oh yes." Charmian turned away from the window. "The child doesn't seem well," she said.

"She's had a bad time. The doctor prescribed some stuff."

"You don't think it's too powerful?"

"No. She'll sleep it off. I wouldn't mind some myself." Brian's eyes looked bruised and sore behind their brightness.

"I'll come back," she said to Brian Gaynor. For the moment, she felt she had seen enough.

Joanna returned to her book but her thoughts were elsewhere. She had read that the mind was a powerful weapon, able to wound and even kill. She concentrated her mind on her mother.

As they drove away, Dolly said, "You didn't get much out of that."

"No? 'Rather beastly'. I got that at least. The father stopped me at that point. Did you notice?"

"He would have stopped you before if the girl hadn't started answering. I reckon he thought that would look worse."

"True."

"The kid looked blind in both eyes."

"Vividly put, Dolly."

"Perhaps that's how you look after killing."

"Don't pass judgement too soon."

"Sorry. She scared me that kid."

"If there has been any violence from her, I'd say it was over, wouldn't you?

From the look of her?" Joanna had looked drained.

She drove Dolly to her own car, left her then with a promise to telephone, and drove back to Maid of Honour Row.

Remembering the threat to herself she considered parking outside her house, but decided to put her car to bed for the night in the garage. She was proud of her car, and inclined to cherish it.

As she walked back down the street which was quiet and empty, she looked across the road to where a side road snaked away into the darkness.

She stopped short, staring. Surely that was Lesley? She could see the bike resting in the road. But what was Lesley doing? Was she kneeling on the grass verge? Or was she hurt?

Charmian began to walk across. "Lesley, are you all right?"

The girl was on her knees on the grass, because there was no pavement here. Behind Lesley was the broken fence of an empty old house with its neglected garden. It was soon to be knocked down and a block of flats put up in its place.

Then the road would be paved and its charm gone.

Lesley waved at her. "Come over here." Her voice sounded thick and distressed. "It's an animal."

Charmian reached her side and stared down at a dark, furry patch that was no longer even animal in shape, except for the head and glazed eyes.

"It's another rabbit. But very dead." Another from the load dropped in the accident, one that hadn't got to her doorstep, perhaps dropped here as an unwanted extra.

"It's horrible." Lesley was distressed. "Is that blood through there under the trees?" She pointed at a gap in the fence through which you could see the dishevelled garden. "I'm going to look. Will you come with me?" She held out a hand.

"This animal has been dead some time," said Charmian, undecided.

Suddenly they were caught in the glare from the headlights of a passing car. The pair of them were picked out in silhouette. The car slowed for a second as if the driver was looking at them.

What must they look like? Decided, Charmian said, "Forget it, Lesley. This creature is well dead." She put her arm round the girl's shoulders, they were shaking. "We're all upset by the things that are happening, but we mustn't let it get out of hand. Come back with me and I'll give you a drink."

And have one myself, she thought, more distressed herself than she wanted to admit. Was there no end to nastiness?

"But there might be something else there."

"I don't think so. But I'll look myself in daylight."

Whatever was there was going to be very very dead.

10

FAITHFUL to her word, Charmian was out of the house early and across the road, studying the scene that had so distressed Lesley. Kate went with her, having been an interested observer of the steadying down of Lesley last night. Or, as she put it herself, 'stiffening her sinews with strong drink'.

Kate had been in the kitchen, drinking coffee and talking on the telephone. Kate did a good deal of telephoning. Now she was back home, she explained, she had a good deal of gossip to catch up with.

When she saw Lesley and Charmian come in, she had put down the telephone and hastened to their assistance.

"Don't tell me, another murder."

"Not quite. Look after Lesley for me while I get us a drink. Then I'll tell you."

But Lesley was already pouring out the details in an excited way, explaining and apologising in the same breath. "I am sorry for being such a nuisance, but it was so horrible."

Then Kate had offered coffee and sympathy to Lesley as Charmian poured out some whisky, and the colour came back into Lesley's cheeks. Kate saw the girl back home, and was gone so long that she caused Charmian to remember her expressed interest in Johnny.

"Nice bunch," Kate said, when she returned. "She'll be all right with them, they'll look after her." She studied her godmother. "You look done in yourself."

"It's been quite a day."

"I'll come with you in the morning." Then she tactfully took herself off to her room, from which she very shortly returned with Muff hanging over her arm like a furry lappet with bright eyes. "Here, you can have her. She's just knocked over my bottle of scent."

A fragrant Muff sat down on the floor to wash her face. She smelt strange to herself, not nice at all. Where was that lovely fishy smell she had started out with?

Charmian went to bed, to sleep lightly

and to dream of knives, and blood and Frisian beards that were really holes, and holes that were beards, red ones, at that, all mixed up with death and Joanna.

She was surprised but not particularly grateful to have Kate appear at her side as she left the house in the early morning.

"You needn't have come. I didn't really expect it."

"I said I would, so I am. Besides, I'm interested."

The milkman delivering the early morning bottles gave them a surprised look, and a newspaper delivery boy shooting down the road on his cycle had to swerve to avoid them as they crossed.

"Where were you last night?" asked Kate, looking around her.

"About here. Yes, there. I can see the animal."

Calmly Kate bent over the remains. "Not much to see really. Hardly more than a dead rabbit skin. I don't know why Lesley got so worked up."

"I don't, either."

In daylight there was nothing frightening, although the garden beyond was lonely and desolate enough.

Charmian took a quick walk through it, but there was no sign that anyone had been there recently. The house itself was locked and barred.

"Come on, Kate, there's nothing here. I'll give them a ring at Alexandria Road, and someone can come down and have a look, but I don't think they will find anything. The rabbit, I suppose, might be one of the consignment that went missing on the way to the pub. Might have been meant for my doorstep."

"I suppose the joker who did it (not that I think it was a joke, godmother, far from it), might have thought one was enough."

Kate walked briskly back to the house muttering about orange juice and coffee, with perhaps bacon. Getting up early made her feel so hungry. Charmian stood alone for a moment, staring through to the deserted garden. Evil, wickedness could not hang around, and yet she felt a sense of malignancy, as if the blood that had been spilt was bad blood. Perhaps something terrible had been planned for her here.

Charmian duly telephoned a message to the Receiver in the Major Incident room who took it without much enthusiasm.

"Our computer's gone down," he said. Like most other forces, they used the HOMES (Home Office Major Enquiry System) in which the computer network was a vital part. "We won't have it back till mid-morning, so they say. But I'll tell the Office Manager. If you say it is important, ma'am." His tone implied that he most certainly did not. But his not to reason why before a Chief Superintendent.

"I didn't say so, I just said it might be."

Later, from her London office, she telephoned Ulrika who agreed, Yes, she had consented to advise Brian Gaynor. It was an interesting case as she already knew. She had had perhaps a slight reservation whether it was entirely ethical of her to undertake the case when she had already heard details from Charmian, but she had decided it was permissible.

Ulrika could be maddening sometimes,

thought Charmian. Of course she always meant to accept Brian Gaynor's request, but she would have to have this great debate inside herself first. It was the German side of her coming out.

"So you and I are to be on opposite sides of the fence." Possibly Charmian came out with it more sharply than she might have done.

"But of course it is not like that," said Ulrika, in a predictably reasonable manner, calculated to irritate. Charmian recognised she was getting the professional treatment. "And why should you mind? But I sense you do."

"It's a very emotional and tricky situation with the Gaynors as you may imagine. I can see it getting into drama. And I do not want there to be a scene, I don't like scenes, especially between you and me."

"Doesn't have to be a scene. Unless you want one."

"What makes you think I do?"

"I think you are looking for a way to cut loose from me. To assert yourself."

There was so much truth in this, so much acute observation, that Charmian found it painful. Perhaps this was true of her in general, that as soon as she settled into a relationship, she wanted to be free of it. In retrospect, it certainly could have been true of her marriage, which had lasted and yet not lasted until her husband's death. She had always blamed the alienation on her career, her ambitions, but perhaps it had been her own character. Ulrika caused her to ask if she had nurtured the ambition itself as a route out; if her career had been an excuse and not a reason.

A sudden rush of thoughts like this is not easy to handle. At this point Charmian would have liked to withdraw from the Gaynor case, but she knew her job and suggested, with more docility than the alert Ulrika (who knew exactly what she was about, and rather enjoyed prodding her friend) had expected, that Ulrika telephone Brian Gaynor and set up a meeting.

Soon; she had a sense of urgency.

"This evening?" It was not an easy day, she had two committees and a report to write but she would push to get away. "I'll try to finish early and come out to

Fletcher's Cottage between six and seven if that suits. What do you think?"

"See what I can do," promised Ulrika. "I have a full case load today, also a lecture to medical students in the late afternoon. They will all be asleep after playing rugger. Maybe I will let them sleep on. I will ring you back."

Charmian found herself waiting for the call. She was glad when she was drawn out from a committee to hear Ulrika say that Brian Gaynor had agreed to the evening appointment. Mother and daughter would be ready to see them both.

"Thank goodness."

"Are you uneasy about them?"

"There is a bad feeling in that house. I don't like what they might do to each other." What they were doing, what they had done.

"Do you suspect the parents of ill-treating the child?"

"If I was sure of my ground, I would have acted at once. No, it's not as simple as that. Both mother and child bear bruises."

"The father?"

"I don't know. He doesn't seem the type."

"Who does?"

"He's not a killer," said Charmian, who had not liked Brian Gaynor, but thought she had got his measure. An intellectual tough, who must be an aggressive and alarming counsel, but who loved his family and provided for them well. Of course, love could be violent and terrible, one always had to remember that fact.

"In a family you cannot always be sure who will kill whom," said Ulrika.

It was a warm day in Windsor, one of the hottest in that hot summer. Brian Gaynor had taken his son to school, then proceeded to his London chambers to consult with his clerk. Some cases might have to be postponed, others handed over to other counsel. It was a mark of his state of mind that he even considered doing this; he was not a man who gave up work lightly. Annabel had been left in charge of Joanna, and Annabel herself was under the gentle supervision of Tommy Bingham. It was Annabel's belief that she was looking after Tommy, who had been ill, but the truth was the reverse.

"It's very decent of you to have us here, Tommy," Brian had said before he left that morning.

"Glad to do it."

"Don't let Joanna make a nuisance of herself."

"She never does. I like her. A bright child."

"Oh, there's nothing wrong with her intelligence."

"Anyway, she'll be mostly out with the stable lads, if I know her, and what could be healthier than that?" They were both men who thought that the open-air life and the noble animal, the horse, promoted a healthy mind.

"I'm thankful they put up with her."

"Yes, I've got some decent lads." Tommy referred to them all as lads, regardless of sex. The term indicated status rather than gender. "And they seem fond of me. Couldn't have been better when I was ill."

"You're a good employer. You deserve it."

"Doesn't always follow. Don't always

237

get what you deserve."

"True enough." Brian was getting himself out of the house by degrees. Coat on, brief-case checked and ready, car keys out. "Don't let Annabel fuss over you. I know she's longing to. She doesn't get enough to do now the children are grown up."

"A girl who looks like Annabel can fuss me as much as she likes," said Tommy Bingham stoutly. He had always had an eye for the ladies, and although he couldn't do much about it these days, he still enjoyed a pretty face.

The morning passed quietly. Annabel received from her husband the message about the evening's appointment with Ulrika Seeley and Charmian Daniels. She pulled a face, but undertook to have Joanna there as arranged. And yes, they had both recovered from the effects of the sedation. Joanna looked quite bright.

She herself had a headache, which she did not mention, but cooked a light lunch for them all, finding her way around the strange kitchen with quiet skill. Tommy read *The Times*, then worked on accounts at his desk. He had given up smoking on his doctor's orders, so he sucked peppermint humbugs and groaned at intervals at the price of feed and farriers. He was a rich man, but he had a frugal nature.

Joanna read one of the books she had brought with her. After lunch, she politely asked her host's permission to go out into the stables.

"By all means. But they'll be pretty busy out there."

"I can help them."

"Right you are." He watched her depart, neat in clean jeans with a white shirt. "Very knowledgeable about horses for her age," he observed to Annabel.

"Oh yes, she's fine with horses." Too fine, thought Annabel, who did not have the same feeling for horses that her husband and daughter shared. But she had to admit that Joanna worked hard at school and did not fail there. She kept her end up, whatever she had in mind for her life, and Annabel wondered sometimes what this was. There was an enigma locked up inside Joanna that she could not get at. It was fair to say that it maddened her.

Tommy eyed her. He was sensitive about women, especially good-looking ones. But any woman, like any horse, would get good treatment from Tommy.

"You're not too keen on this woman coming this evening, are you?" He took Annabel's silence for assent. "Can't say I am myself. Although the one we saw the other day seemed a nice enough woman."

After his illness he had become alive to changes in the atmosphere around him. Smells, the taste of food, sounds, all struck him harder. Emotions also. Now he felt as if something strange had come into his house with the Gaynors. They were his old friends, he had known Brian from a boy, Annabel since her marriage and the children since they were born. They were nice children, the boy clever, with his father's logical mind, and the girl a taking little creature. Perhaps too much in the stables at present, but she would get over that; girls always did. And as for being mixed up with murder, nonsense! So why did he have now the very strong feeling that he was in what he called 'a situation'?

In the first place, little as he liked to admit it, murder had come sailing close to the Gaynor family. You couldn't forget the girl killed in their garden. It was why they were here, in his house. He had invited them.

So if there was 'a situation' then it was his own fault.

More troubled than he would have admitted to either Brian or Annabel, he went to the window of his sitting-room to stare out at the stable-yard. The sky was darkening with a belt of clouds coming in from the west while a yellow haze suffused the sun.

He might have a word with Joanna herself. Or with Lesley, she was a sensible girl, a nice girl with a practical nature and marvellous with the ponies. Originally he had given her the job because he knew her father. The old boy had taken his Latin in hand when he had to cram a bit to get into Oxford. No one learnt Latin today. He could see Lesley now going into the tack-room, walking with her long, graceful stride. He had a soft spot for Lesley, another thing he would never be ready to admit, liking her almost as though she were the daughter he had never had.

Lesley turned round, saw him at the window and gave a smile. Then she disappeared inside the tack-room.

No sign of Joanna, but she'd be there somewhere.

He turned back into the room. "Look at that sky," he said. "There's going to be a storm."

Darkness visible began to crowd into the room where he sat with Annabel. After a while, she saw he was dropping off to sleep. She sat quietly with him for a time, then climbed the stairs to Joanna's room.

Finishing her day surprisingly early, because of a cancelled committee meeting, Charmian decided she would go to see Millicent Ward's family. It might be wise to have spoken to them, to see what information they had to hand on, before she saw the Gaynors. She needed all the ammunition she could get. And then she was ashamed of herself for thinking of her interview as a battle.

She went to her car, parked in a neat underground bay, so handy for her office, as befitted an officer of her seniority. To have a parking slot at all in this city was a privilege.

To her fury, the car failed to start.

Several frustrated minutes later, she decided to get a taxi and go to Windsor by train. She had told herself when she bought her house how useful it was to have a good train service. Well, now was her time to try it.

Waterloo was hot and crowded but she threaded her way through to the Windsor and Eton train, grabbing an evening newspaper on the way. She could hide her face behind it if she didn't like the look of her fellow passengers. She knew from past experience that she had the sort of face that encouraged people to speak to her in public places. As a rising young policewoman it had been an advantage, but it had its contrary side too. She didn't always want to talk.

The carriages were crowded with ladies

carrying bags from Harrods and Fortnum and Mason, with a touch of purple contributed by a Liberty carrier bag here and there. Did she also get a glimpse of the soft mauve of a bag from Asprey's? She remembered that the summer sales had just started.

She got the last empty seat in a carriage near the engine, sitting down gratefully, aware that the first drops of summer rain were falling.

She had read a few words of her evening paper, another scandal in the city, no news to someone who had already been fed the richest details by Humphrey Kent, when she began to feel she was being stared at. She raised her head, to see two pairs of interested eyes gazing upon her.

Sitting opposite, identically dressed in trim town suits of dark brown linen, with a pale violet shirt for Flora and a yellow one for Emmy, were the Trust twins. On each lap was a carrier bag from Harrods, and in each hand was an ice-cream. Emmy was eating with easy enjoyment, but Flora was a little abashed at having been caught out.

"Had no lunch, you see, couldn't spare the time. And we were so hungry and thirsty."

"Don't blame you." Charmian's hands felt hot and sticky. "I could do with a cup of tea."

"One could not totally recommend a cup of station tea," said Flora. "In fact, it's not a cup but a plastic beaker which spoils the taste. Such taste as there is. But the ice-cream is excellent. Do you hear the thunder?"

Charmian nodded. A flash of lightning had seared her eyes, the roll of thunder was long and loud. They were travelling into the storm.

"Had some good shopping?"

Flora looked pleased with herself and Emmy finished her ice-cream and gave a small nod. It was the most positive response from her that Charmian had ever witnessed.

"Yes," Flora nodded. "We decided we needed some new clothes. Emmy particularly."

Charmian felt surprise; she had never heard Emmy's interests receive mention before.

"You see Mr Pilgrim has come back into our lives."

"Ah," said Charmian alertly. The reclusive Mr Pilgrim with an accommodation address.

"Yes, he came to a public lecture on Florentine art at which Emmy and I were present and spoke to us." She gave Emmy a look. "It seems Emmy and he have been in correspondence." Flora did not sound angry. "He declared his intentions. It seems we shall soon have a wedding in the family."

Emmy smiled. She spoke with a self-assurance new to her. "Flora thought blue for the wedding, but I chose white."

"A white linen suit. Very proper," said Flora, once again without rancour. "We shall all live together, of course."

I wonder if she will go on the honeymoon with them, thought Charmian and decided she probably would. She had a sudden picture of them all three together with Emmy by degrees taking over the speaking role and Flora subsiding into silence, until, with a complete reversal of their part, Emmy was the talking twin and Flora the mute one.

Charmian retired behind her paper with her thoughts. She knew that both the Trusts had small but comfortable private incomes, and since it was her belief that Mr Pilgrim was a con man of no mean skill, it behoved her to do something about it. But what?

At Windsor station, she looked around for a taxi to take her to the Ward's house in Merrywick.

"I've got the car here," said Flora. "Can we give you a lift?" She liked driving her friends to wherever they wanted to go; it gave her an insight into their lives. She got more than she bargained for this time when Charmian revealed she was bound for the Wards, and her eyes widened.

"Right you are. It's on our way." Flora drove the car neatly and fast, with Emmy in the back surrounded by her parcels and Charmian by her side. "Mr Pilgrim has heard about you," she said, as she drove, "and would like to meet you. You agree? Oh good, I will see what can be arranged." The car drew up before a large, opulent-looking bungalow. "Here you are, this is the house. Do they

247

know you are coming? I shouldn't worry, someone is bound to be at home." As the car drew away, she pointed out of the car window. "There's a bus stop. One bus every half hour. Save you trudging home. Or give me a ring," she ended generously.

Charmian walked up the garden path between standard rose bushes carefully trained over wire cages. The curtains were drawn, the house looked shuttered and blind. The bell did not seem to work so she tried the knocker. She was not so confident as Flora that someone was at home.

But no, Flora was right. Footsteps could be heard coming in response to her knock.

When the door opened she saw a short middle-aged man with a tired face. He was dressed with scrupulous neatness in a dark suit with a pale shirt. The skin around his eyes was red and puffy, as if he had cried, and not slept.

"Mr Ward?" She introduced herself. "May I talk to you? And your wife?"

"My wife isn't here. I sent her and my other girl away." He lowered his eyes and spoke hesitantly. "We have another daughter, three years younger than Millicent. They're with their grandmother. I don't want to tell you the address unless you press me. I'm here on my own. I'll talk to you if I have to, and if it will help find who killed Millicent."

He led her into a long sitting-room. Furnished comfortably but without fuss, it was an easy family room. Even now it was dusted and neatly arranged. Only the dead flowers in the vase on the table hinted at something amiss.

He offered her a chair and sat down himself facing her on a pink velvet sofa. "I know who you are."

"You do?"

"You're quite a well-known lady. My wife went to a talk you gave. Told me all about it. She admires you."

"Thank you."

"Difficult job you've got, teaching women how to look after themselves. Their own worst enemies. Look at Millicent. They think she went out into the garden because something caught her attention. Lured out there."

"Someone she knew?"

He remained silent. Then, "I'd say so, wouldn't you? Or someone she trusted."

"Any idea whom?"

"If I had, do you think I'd be sitting here, talking to you? I'd have shot him."

"Have you got a gun, Mr Ward?"

"I should get one." Charmian found she believed him. "Or I'd let my hands do the talking for me." He looked down at his hands, they were strong and square.

She knew she had to try to get him to talk about Millicent's feeling about the Gaynor household, because she was seeking for an insight into a family situation she knew must be there, but found hard to pin down.

"Did she like the Gaynors?" It seemed an easy question, a beginning, anyway.

"Didn't like Joanna much, or she thought the girl didn't like her. They didn't have anything in common. Millicent was older, they had different interests. They did get a bit closer when Millicent was working on a school project about horses. Joanna helped her there, introduced her to people. Even took her to some stables where she seemed to have friends."

"They were at the same school?"

"That's right, but Millicent was in one of the top forms. I believe Joanna was going to be sent away to school anyway."

"Was she now?"

"Millicent thought she'd be glad to go, but I think a girl needs her home."

"Did she think Joanna wasn't happy at home?"

"She didn't put it like that. I think Milly just felt it wouldn't be the sort of home she'd be happy in herself. But she liked Mrs Gaynor."

"Oh she did?"

"And of course the pay was good."

"The pay?"

"Yes, Mrs Gaynor paid well for what Millicent did, and provided a lovely meal. I never gave my girls much pocket money. Didn't think it right. Get out and be independent, I used to say; earn for yourself. I blame myself now, of course."

"You mustn't blame yourself, Mr Ward." She guessed that the younger

251

daughter would profit from what had happened to Millicent, and have an easier ride. Poor Millicent, the loser all round.

"But I do. And always will."

He got up. "Can I give you a cup of tea? I had just made some."

"Thank you." Charmian followed him into the kitchen, a light bright affair with polished pine surfaces and yellow paint, all orderly and neat in spite of everything. Mr Ward obviously ran a very tight ship. She could not help reflecting that in similar circumstances her own kitchen would have been in a state of considerable disorder. But everyone showed misery differently and his way was to keep externals tidy. It probably supported him.

The tea however was horrid, cold and weak, a whole pot made with one tea-bag and some time ago at that. It was served in thin Worcester cups which she doubted if his wife used in the kitchen.

Mr Ward sipped his tea with a puzzled look as if he sensed that something was wrong with his brew but could not work out what.

Charmian stirred her tea. "Would you say the Gaynors' was a happy household?"

"Didn't really know them that well. Brian Gaynor's a bit high powered for me. Now, for me, buying this house and sending the girls to good schools was success, but for Brian this is just a passing phase, he'll go on and up."

"Success like that often bears hard on the family," probed Charmian.

"Yes," agreed Mr Ward absently. "Millicent did say she heard quarrels. The kids got shouted at a bit sometimes."

"Anything else?"

"Millicent did say she saw bruises sometimes," he said, still absently, as if unaware of what he had said.

"On both children?"

"Only the girl."

Only the girl, Charmian echoed the words silently. She put the cup of tea away from her. "Thank you for the tea." She hadn't finished it.

They talked for a few more minutes, then he saw her to the door. As he stood there he said, still absently, as if it meant nothing to him, but was a part of his

253

dead daughter that he wanted to pass on, "Millicent said to me once when she came back from an evening there, 'They're keeping something quiet in that house, there's something they don't talk about.'"

"A lot of families must do that."

"Not my family, we talked everything out. It wouldn't be what Millicent was used to."

He ought to see some of the families I know, thought Charmian as she prepared to walk home to Kate, looking forward to telling her about the invitation for lunch and polo on Sunday. The bus she might have caught had she been quicker was just disappearing round the corner. But the rain had ceased and the storm was over. She would enjoy the walk.

When the rain had stopped, Annabel went out into the stable-yard to look for Joanna. The sky was still lowering and murky with more than a hint that the storm would come back. She wanted Joanna in the house.

The yard was empty, it seemed to her that the lads had gone home. She was well acquainted with Lesley, Johnny, Freda and Gillian and knew that they kept a sharp eye on the clock. They came in early, they liked to leave on time.

She called Joanna's name, but without much hope of a reply. Her experience was that if Joanna did not want to answer, Joanna would not. Her usual anger at Joanna's evasiveness surfaced.

"Joanna?" she called loudly and angrily. "Where the hell are you?" The girl had entirely too much freedom.

She advanced to the construction in the middle of the yard where Tommy Bingham had once practised his polo shots. He hadn't used it since the onset of his illness and it had the slightly neglected air of a piece of apparatus that was out of favour.

The door moved as if in a wind. But there was no wind.

Annabel went over and gave the door a strong push.

"Joanna," she said. "I could kill you."

Not all mothers who threaten to kill their daughters actually plan to do anything about it.

11

KATE was in the kitchen of the house in Maid of Honour Row mixing up an omelette. Charmian had not put a lot of money or effort into the kitchen, and to Kate's way of thinking it needed bringing up to date. It was easy to see where Charmian really lived, she thought, and it was not in the kitchen. In her living-room with her books, cat and music, that was Charmian's world. About the bedroom she was not so sure, she did not know too much about that side of Charmian's life. For the first time it struck her that it might really be a nuisance to her godmother to have her living there.

She smiled at Charmian and gave a small wave. "Supper is on the way. Mushroom and bacon omelette with salad." On the table was a long baton of French bread. "I thought of garlic bread but guessed you'd say no."

"I'd love it, but as you say, not tonight.

I've got an appointment." Couldn't breathe garlic over the Gaynors. Although it was said to keep the devil away, she had no desire to beat the evil out of Joanna in that particular way. "And I mustn't take long," said Charmian, putting her bag on the table, and sorting through her post. "There's not a lot of time."

"I know. I took a message from Dr Seeley that she'd meet you at Fletcher's Cottage at eight o'clock. She can't trust your timekeeping."

"No doubt with reason."

"That's why I'm whipping up an omelette."

"I didn't know you were into cooking."

"I've just taken it up. It's life giving, isn't it? And of course as an architect, which I will be one day, I ought to know a bit about how kitchens work. I've never done much, I always used to leave it to my mother who is marvellous, but doesn't really welcome help in the kitchen. But she cooks like an angel." Kate was busy chopping mushrooms.

"So she does." Charmian was remembering the many good meals she had eaten at Amy's hospitable table. "And an angel who has read Elizabeth David and Elizabeth Craig. Your father wasn't bad, either." There was nothing in the post except a short note from Wimpey to say there had been no progress of any importance on the triple murders, but it was early days, and he personally thought it would be a long hunt. The horse-prints and the droppings had produced nothing helpful, as yet, but the prints of the shoes had interested their expert who would be coming back to them with his conclusions. The animal had been small and limber, shoes size three and fed on the usual feed of several thousand local nags. And yet the horse matters, Charmian said to herself. The appearance of those prints, the very use of the horse is telling us something. Murderers like this don't do anything by accident. This is a proclamation of sorts if we can read it aright. What is it saying to us?

Kate broke into her thoughts.

"You know they are divorcing?"

"No, she hasn't told me."

"Ashamed, I expect. Never think it of her, would you? But she is beating the breast a bit. She thinks it is her fault."

"Half of it probably is."

"Yes," said Kate, pausing in her cooking to consider. "I suppose it is. Yes, you are right. But I think they will miss the quarrelling. It's the way they are." She turned to the stove. "You need an omelette pan, but I'll make do with this."

"There's one in the bottom of the cupboard," said Charmian. "I think my mother gave it to me. By the way, I have an invitation to lunch and to watch polo from the Bingham box on Sunday."

"What, that rusty old object?" Kate pointed a contemptuous finger at the waste-bin. "It's in there and should have been dumped ages ago. When did your mother give it to you? Nonstick is the name of the game now and heavy metal at that. About the lunch, good. I'd fixed up to see Johnny anyway."

"You'd better watch out with him."

"Oh he's an angel."

"Angelic but ruthless."

"Like me," said Kate smugly. "You get back to your case load and leave me to myself."

"I will, you ungrateful child." Charmian

picked up a crust of bread, buttered it and started to eat. Muff gave her a reproachful and hungry stare from the floor. I too am peckish, the look said. "Do hurry up with that meal," Charmian said, "I have to get on with the said work."

"I know how your mind must be working on this case. I know because you are working with Ulrika Seeley and I read a little book by her in the London Library."

"I didn't know you belonged to the London Library."

"I don't, but Anny does." It was Kate's belief that they thought she was Anny, in which she was wrong. The librarians knew exactly who she was and meant to stop her next time she came in. "I use it all the time. As a kind of club. It's very handy."

"What was the article?"

"It was called 'From Saint to Sinner: the Myth of Woman'. So I know the sort of thing she does. It was about the view of women as criminal through the ages," Kate said appreciatively. "It was jolly good. I was supposed to be researching the arch in Florentine pictures and this was much more interesting. Didn't understand all of it, but I enjoyed it."

"Good for you."

"She seemed to think the female of the species can do anything."

"I didn't need telling that. And I shouldn't think you did either."

"No." Kate was thoughtful. She had had in her a streak of violence, now dying down as she grew older, and knew that women could kill.

"Seeley seems to extend this judgement to children. She cites the case of a female child who killed at least three people and possibly more. So I suppose I knew what you are both thinking."

"Thank you. It's nice to be understood."

"Oh come on, Charmian, don't be sarcastic. I'm only talking. And I suppose that dishy policeman thinks the same."

"I'm not answering that."

"Well, you just have," said Kate, showing she had learnt something in questioning technique from her god-mother. She was adding the last touches to her confection in the pan.

"That's an enormous omelette for two people."

"Look at the table," suggested Kate.

Charmian did so, fending off an anxious cat. "Three places? Who else is coming?"

"Dr Seeley. She seemed so anxious, I invited her round." As if to underline her invitation, the doorbell rang. "And that must be her now. You feed Muff and I'll answer the door."

She came back with Ulrika looking cool and elegant in a natural silk suit with a transparent raincoat over it. "The storm is over, thank goodness. I don't like thunder. Irrational but true." She smiled at Charmian, but included Kate in the smile.

"I'm not sure if we ought to arrive at this interview like a team," said Charmian, flustered.

"Not at all. The way to do it, a good thing. Exactly as I want it." She smiled at Charmian and now the smile did not include Kate.

Kate, gazing with interest from one to the other, thought, That woman loves this woman. And how was it that her godmother, with all her training and expertise did not seem aware of it? My godmother doesn't know she's born, thought Kate. And what about Humphrey Kent, that enigmatic figure waiting in the wings, in whom Kate took a sharp interest? Kate had her own method of rating a man's attractiveness, and she rated Humphrey at several megawatts.

Charmian bent down to give Muff her bowl of food, offering to Kate, as she did so, a sharp look that said, Watch your thoughts and cover them up better. Aloud, all she said was, "Is supper ready, Kate?"

Kate divided the omelette into three equal portions, placed the salad bowl in the middle of the table and produced a bottle of white wine from the refrigerator.

"Is this child discreet?" asked Ulrika, between mouthfuls of omelette. "Can we talk in front of her?"

"No," replied Charmian, "probably not. Nevertheless we will talk."

"We have two women and a girl who have been killed, in the same manner and certainly by the same killer."

"Or it's a copycat crime."

"But I think not."

"I understand the investigating team here agree with that," said Charmian.

"And at the very beginning we have the slaying of the pony."

"I wonder if that is the beginning?"

"It is where you and I have to start. Then we go forward from there." Ulrika sounded sure of herself. Charmian wished she felt the same. "You know I think that the female is as capable of Ripper-style killings as men. What I have always wondered is whether such a person would kill women or men. And my answer is coming to be that it depends what kind of hole inside themselves they are filling."

"Oh, those bloody holes," said Charmian.

For a few minutes, while Kate made some coffee they talked over the problems that faced them tonight and how they would approach the Gaynor family, whom they both believed to be at the heart of it.

Kate poured coffee, acting out the domestic house-person, her current role, happily assumed.

"And you've not had any trouble here then?" asked Ulrika.

"No attack on me, if that's what you mean. In spite of the threat that I was next. Nothing. And that puzzles me."

"Yes," said Ulrika. "I can think of several reasons. None of which I like."

"I don't like anything about it," said Charmian. "It's giving me a bit of thought, I can tell you."

Kate suddenly realised they were talking over her head. Drat them, she thought, and drank some more coffee. "Coffee all right? Strong enough?" she asked hopefully, but got no answer. "Right," she said aloud. "You're enjoying it, Kate aren't you? Thank you, Kate." Sometimes she didn't mind being treated like a kid and sometimes she did.

Brian Gaynor returned to what was now his temporary home just as the last blast from the storm died away, and the clouds began to lift. There was still a sun out there somewhere, and soon it would begin to shine.

He looked into the sitting-room where

he found Tommy Bingham asleep in a chair; he did not disturb him. Instead he went into the kitchen hoping to see his wife and daughter. The boy, he knew, was at school for the week. 'And thank goodness,' he thought. 'At least he's out of it.' Mark always would escape, it was one of his skills, as his father dimly recognised.

Joanna and Annabel must be upstairs, he decided. He hesitated for a minute then went to the telephone on the wall. But before dialling he closed the kitchen door.

"Serena?" When talking privately, he did not call Mrs Justice Anstruther ma'am. "Are you on your own? Can I talk?"

Serena Anstruther said something tartly to the effect that he usually did, and she was in the habit of listening to him. They both got paid for it.

Brian's hand on the telephone trembled, he recognised that Serena Anstruther was still in the teaching mode, not to mention the punishing one as well.

"Serena, I have been thinking about what you told me to do, and I can't.

I can't do it. I know I should, but I cannot."

Serena gave him a stern speech about the wisdom of her advice. Hard to do, she said, but the best thing. Indeed, the only thing. And of course, he must speak to his wife first. This was her opinion. He had asked, and she had told him. It was Serena at her toughest.

"Don't give me up, Serena," he pleaded. "I am going to need you."

He knew his situation was parlous.

Your solicitor first, then your wife, was the command. Confess. She did not offer him a choice.

"I don't think I can do it, Serena. I know I should, but I can't. Give me time," he pleaded.

"Remember sex can be a killer," said Serena in a soft, quiet voice. "Don't let it kill you. You are worth saving."

He felt sick inside, unwilling to take Serena's advice while aware that he had asked for it and must follow it. He could see his face reflected in a mirror on the wall. "That's your face there," he told himself. "And that's you behind it, thinking all those thoughts you know about. Can you bear to look at you?"

The kitchen door moved in the wind, there was no one to be seen, a door to the garden must be open somewhere. He moved towards it. Whatever response he made to Serena Anstruther's demand, and he had an idea it was going to be No, he had better find Annabel. He thought she would rather die than have him do what he might have to do.

Brian stood at the door to the stable-yard and looked out. It was empty and rainswept, with only the sound of a television set, turned loud, coming across from the head lad's house where he lived with his wife. He could see the TV screen shining green and red through the uncurtained window.

Tommy touched his shoulder. "What's up, Brian? Sorry I was asleep when you got in. Meant to stay awake." He did a lot of sleeping lately which he resented since it seemed a waste of his life.

Brian swung round. "Nothing, Tommy," he said quickly. "Just looking out."

"Come and have a drink."

"Thanks, but I'd like to find Annabel first." By way of some explanation, he said, "We've got that policewoman and Dr Seeley coming tonight. I'd like to talk to Annabel before she comes."

"She was around," said Tommy vaguely. "Before I dropped off." He looked at his watch. "Been out some time."

"You go and have a drink, Tommy. I'll join you later. Perhaps Annabel would like one as well. Wherever she is."

"Looked upstairs?"

"No."

"Bound to be there."

But she was not. Nor was Joanna. There was no sign of either of them. Brian came down and stood in the hall, he didn't know where to look next. His imagination stopped there.

Slowly he went out into the stable-yard. The door to it had been open; that meant someone had gone that way.

Joanna first, then Annabel?

Or maybe Annabel and then Joanna after her, who knew?

He walked across the cobbles to the polo pit which was the only structure to attract his attention. It was there, that was why. The door opened to a touch, but it was empty. Which was about what he had expected. He had not expected Annabel to be there. She didn't like horses, they made her sneeze.

But it was possible she had been there. He thought he could smell her scent, an especially strong floral blend imported from America.

As he stood there considering, realising he was emotionally unbalanced and not thinking straight tonight, Tommy came out and joined him.

"She's not here, Brian. No point in standing looking. They've gone for a walk or something."

Some people might go for a walk in the situation in which the Gaynors found themselves, but not Annabel. And not with Joanna.

"Joanna might have gone off with one of the lads," said Tommy. "Very pally. Try Fred."

Tommy Bingham's head stable lads were always called Fred. But Fred, summoned from the television to his front door, denied any knowledge of Joanna.

"She didn't go off with the lads. They all piled into the car and went home."

Tommy pulled himself together, overrode his own pains, and took charge. It was, after all, his house.

"Come and have a drink. Give it half an hour, and if they haven't turned up by then, telephone that policewoman Daniels."

Brian Gaynor went white. "I think I'll just have a look round. They might be in the Great Park."

Tommy gripped his friend's arm firmly. "Inside with you. We'll have that drink."

He caught his stableman's eye, and as Brian went ahead into the house, gave a nod towards the Park. "Have a look round, Fred. See what you can find."

Brian sat for about fifteen minutes, clutching a glass of whisky, then stood up. "I'm going out to look for myself."

"Leave it to Fred. His father was a gamekeeper, he's marvellous at reading the signs in woodland, he'll know if anyone went that way." He added a reassuring tot to his friend's glass. "Drink up. I'm sure they just went for a walk, maybe to Ascot or down to Virginia Water to see the ducks. They'll be back soon."

Fred Walker, adept at marking all the small signs of passage through woodland and undergrowth, walked slowly forward scanning the trees, bushes and grass. Not many people came this way except on horseback, it was too far from the spots the average visitor wanted to see. He looked about him in his usual slow, quiet manner. He would rather have been watching his favourite television programme, but the boss had spoken and you did not ignore the boss.

Bruised leaves, broken twigs, he could see that one person had come this way. Possibly two, he was not an Indian scout and could not say for sure.

He moved on through a thicket: he was certainly following someone, but it might have been a large dog.

Charmian and Ulrika were just getting themselves ready to set out for Fletcher's Cottage, Brian Gaynor was resisting the nip of whisky, and Fred was plodding on.

Then he became aware he was looking down at a human foot.

12

THE telephone rang in the house in Maid of Honour Row just as Charmian and Ulrika Seeley were on the point of leaving for Fletcher's Cottage. Charmian paused on the threshold.

"Don't bother," said Kate. "Leave it."

Ulrika, who was behind Charmian, said, "Answer it. Coming just now, it has to be important one way or another." Sometimes she measured significance in ways Charmian did not fully comprehend, giving a kind of poetic or symbolic importance to things that Charmian rated unimportant or, at best, completely out of her control.

Charmian picked up the telephone. She listened quietly, her face looking more and more serious. "Yes, yes. Try and calm down, Mr Gaynor. Have you called a doctor? You must do that. Good. You must telephone Chief Inspector Merry at the Alexandria Road Station. If you haven't got the number, use the 999 code and let them cope. Dr Seeley and I will come right over."

Ulrika and Kate looked at her questioningly. "Well?" said Ulrika.

"I'll tell you on the way."

"What about me?" asked Kate.

"You can wait for the papers in the morning."

"Thanks."

As they got into Ulrika's old but speedy car, Ulrika said, "You were hard on her."

"She shouldn't ask questions."

"So what has happened?"

"Joanna Gaynor and her mother were missing. A search was made and a body found."

"Then you don't have to tell me whose body. It was the mother's."

"Yes," said Charmian. "They have found Annabel Gaynor." She said it evenly without inflexion.

As they were driving into the Great Park, she said, "How did you know? That it was the mother, I mean?"

Ulrika shrugged. "In the circumstances,

she was the most likely victim."

"What circumstances?"

"She was alone with her daughter. I would not have given much for her chances." Ulrika stopped the car outside Fletcher's Cottage. Tommy Bingham was at the door. "Don't you agree?"

"I didn't see it like that," said Charmian, rather sourly. "And we don't know yet what has happened." She felt muddled and confused.

"I think we do," said Ulrika, getting out and marching forward.

Tommy came down the path towards them. Even in his agitation his good manners did not desert him. "Miss Daniels, Dr Seeley, I am so glad you are here. Thank you for coming so quickly."

"Where is she? Show us, will you, please?"

"I left Brian there with his wife. He telephoned to you and to Alexandria Road while I stayed with her. And the doctor, and he's on his way."

"Let's take a look," said Ulrika. "I too am a doctor."

Tommy motioned them to the sitting-room. "In here." He opened the door.

"Wait a minute," said Charmian. "Where did you find Mrs Gaynor?"

"In a coppice in the Park, partly hidden. Fred saw her feet and found her lying there."

"And you moved her?"

"We couldn't leave her there," said Tommy simply. "We all three of us carried her in." He hadn't been physically strong enough to be much help himself, but he had held her limp hand, and pushed back the scratching branches from her face.

Brian Gaynor was sitting on the sofa with his wife's head in his lap. He was stroking the bloodstained fair hair. "Did you expect me to leave my wife out there in the rain and the mud?" he said.

But there was not as much blood as Charmian had expected. Annabel's jeans and shirt, although muddy and grass-stained were not torn or red with blood.

Ulrika knelt by Annabel and felt her pulse. "She's not dead." She looked up. Tommy answered:

"I told Brian that, but he wouldn't believe me."

The killer was interrupted, thought Charmian, before the job could be finished off. Or else Annabel had put up a fight.

She could see Annabel's left hand which was dangling towards the floor. Several beautiful nails were broken, and the back of the hands scratched. Yes, Annabel had fought her attacker.

"They heard the sound of a car stopping, a door banging. Tommy went out and then they heard his voice greeting his own doctor. Brisk footsteps in the hall and Tommy's voice talking again, with a strange man's voice interrupting. "Let me get in there, Tommy, and take a look for myself," they heard him say. Then more cars, the police had arrived.

Ulrika sat back on her heels. "I don't know. It's some time since I did general medicine, but I would say the blow on the head is relatively unimportant. But she is in a state of deep shock."

"Is she going to die?" said Brian Gaynor. He seemed in shock himself.

"Hospital is indicated."

"No chance of questioning her?" asked Charmian.

"Judge for yourself." Ulrika stood up as first the doctor, accompanied by Tommy, and then three policemen, one of them Wimpey, came into the room. Dr Killick at once gently pushed Brian aside and began to examine Annabel.

Charmian addressed herself to Brian Gaynor. "We have to find out what has happened to your wife."

"All I know is that I came home and found Tommy asleep and Annabel and Joanna gone."

Charmian looked round the room. "And where is Joanna now?"

Dr Killick was concluding his examination, speedily and neatly accomplished and accompanied by a soft mutter of comment to Ulrika, the only person present whom he seemed to recognise as worthy of comment. She nodded and he went to the telephone where he could be heard speaking to the hospital and ordering an ambulance. Yes, he would be coming with his patient.

So will the police, thought Charmian.

Two of the police officers had disappeared, led by Tommy to where Annabel had been found. He had left Fred on guard. Wimpey remained in the room with them. Charmian realised he was unobtrusively directing his attention at Annabel and Brian Gaynor.

Tommy came back into the room with the air of one sent away, dismissed. He felt homeless in his own home.

"Where is Joanna?" Charmian asked again.

"Joanna?"

"Come on, Mr Gaynor," said Charmian, in a falsely soft voice, since she felt quite tough. "Where is your daughter?"

Brian Gaynor turned his gaze back to his wife. Annabel had opened her eyes for a moment, but seemed to see nothing, then closed them again. He wanted to get back to her. Until this moment, he had not known how much he loved her. For the time being he could hardly remember the existence of Joanna. Yet she was always there, at the back of his mind, a silent accusing presence. "I don't know. I wish I did."

Tommy had been listening. "I think Joanna went out for a look at the stables, she went before I dropped off, I remember."

"Was Mrs Gaynor still with you in the house then?"

"Yes, she was here. She must have gone off after Joanna. Looking for her, I suppose."

"She may have found her."

Brian Gaynor spoke sharply: "Joanna didn't do this."

"Someone did, Mr Gaynor."

"I don't think I like this conversation very much," he said. "I am not going to continue it." Shock had pierced his self-control and loosened his tongue. He knew he would say something he regretted if they went on. Tell your wife, Mrs Justice Anstruther, had said, she hadn't said tell the world.

But no doubt she had had it in mind. There were, after all, some things that didn't stay quiet. And who knew that better than a barrister? And now he was awash in events that were about to sweep all control of the situation out of his power.

He went over to Annabel, took her hand, and spoke to her, although she showed no sign of hearing him. "We're going to look for Joanna, we've got to find her." It was necessary to find Joanna. He didn't say to lay his hands on her, although he both wished he could do that and yet vowed never to do it again.

"Do you think the girl has been attacked by whoever attacked Annabel," whispered Tommy Bingham to Charmian. "It looks like it, doesn't it? Perhaps Annabel was defending her."

So he too had noticed Annabel's torn hands, thought Charmian.

"Do you suppose the girl has been abducted? That's bad, isn't it?"

"I have no idea, Mr Bingham," said Charmian.

"Call me Tommy," he said mechanically. She was Humphrey Kent's girl, one must be friendly.

Dr Killick came over. "There's the ambulance now."

They watched as Annabel was lifted into the ambulance and driven away with the doctor and her husband.

Before he climbed into the ambulance, Brian Gaynor said, "Find Joanna. I don't know what's happened, but find her."

"We'll be trying."

Wimpey said, "I hope he knows what we might find."

Charmian said slowly, "I think he knows something we don't know. We've missed a bit of the picture, a fact, a fiction, or an emotion. There's a hole. He's hiding something."

Ulrika said, "I told you right at the beginning that the trouble was in the family, and the father is the obvious source."

"I don't see that," said Wimpey.

"He is an object of love and attraction to both mother and daughter."

Wimpey frowned.

"And possibly to other people as well," she went on.

"What does that mean?" said Charmian.

"I think he ought to be questioned."

"I was going to do that, anyway."

"He has something to say."

"Good," said Wimpey ironically.

"But he may not be willing to say it."

"Are you saying he has a guilty conscience?" asked Charmian.

"About the girl? I think so, don't you?"

"Yes," said Charmian. She introduced Wimpey and Ulrika. "Dr Seeley."

"We've met before," said Wimpey. He gave Ulrika a cool nod. "I know some of your clients. We have shared a common workload in some young delinquents that the courts didn't know what to do with."

"Old sparring partners," Ulrika was deliberately light. She knew Wimpey did not like her and had not enjoyed working with her. Also, he violently rejected her way of thinking.

"Well, I didn't always think them as lovable and innocent as you did."

"Not lovable," said Ulrika firmly. "Not that. I never said lovable. Horribly unattractive in most cases."

"And was that the trouble?" asked Charmian, interested in spite of herself.

"Oh no, just born to evil in most cases," said Ulrika. "Inherited it mostly. Not a chance in the world."

"But you try?"

"It's my job," said Ulrika.

"But not hopefully?"

Ulrika shrugged.

"Is that how you see Joanna?"

283

"I cannot answer that yet."

A uniformed constable appeared at the door and beckoned to Wimpey.

"They've found something." He led the way out. "In the area where Mrs Gaynor was found. Signs of a struggle there. The lady must have put up a fight. But you'd better see for yourself, sir." He gave Charmian a sideways look. "Ma'am," he added politely, remembering who she was and whom she knew. Her reputation had gone before her.

He led the way through the stable-yard and out through a white painted wicket-gate into the Great Park, then along a bridle-path between trees. In the distance a uniformed policeman stood talking to Fred.

The path was of hard beaten-down earth, marked with hoof-prints as if there was a constant traffic of horses from the stable and out into the Park. Even the recent heavy rain had not done more than make the path muddy, but here and there were great puddles through which first Fred and then Brian and Tommy carrying Annabel had trodden. The police had tried to avoid the tracks already made, stepping carefully onto the grass surrounds. They were anxious to avoid disturbing any evidence that might be left. But, as the constable now talking to Fred was just saying, unless you had wings, you could hardly avoid doing some damage. He was rather conscious of the mud on his own boots, messy testimony to the fact that he had tried and failed.

The path divided, one fork taking a sharp left-hand turn and the other dwindling away into a narrow path between the trees. It was here, in a thicket, where the bushes and undergrowth made a kind of natural hideaway, that Annabel had been found.

The constable stood aside and Wimpey pushed his way in. "I'm in charge," he said. "Chief Inspector Merry will be over later." This was not quite the case, the Chief Inspector was not going to leave the dinner which he was giving at home unless assured the attack on Annabel Gaynor related to the string of murders. At the moment, this was something no one knew.

You could guess, and Wimpey was

guessing it was so, but he had to have more than that to bring out Bert Merry.

He turned to the man who had brought them here. "What is it that you've got?"

"Mrs Gaynor was found here."

Fred nodded. "By me. I found her. The boss sent me out to look. I saw a foot sticking out from the bushes. She was in here, lying on her face. She had blood on her head and her hair looked as if she'd been hit with something like a bit of tree."

"And we think we've found the weapon." The policeman pointed to a small but thick piece of bough, shaped like a natural cudgel. "Someone pulled this down and used it to hit her. You can see where it came from that tree," he pointed. "The wound on the tree is still fresh."

Wimpey knelt down to study the lump of wood on which blood and hairs were clearly visible. "That's it, then. We'll have to get the forensics to take a look and make sure, but I don't think there's any doubt. Might not be any fingerprints, though, not on that bark."

"Could be. I've known them get them

off a piece of toast. Might be other traces, too," said Charmian. "Skin, blood, other than Annabel Gaynor's, shreds of clothing." She was used to the magic ways of the forensic scientists, producing evidence from what you could not see.

"Sure. We have to hope so."

Ulrika asked, "May I look?" She bent down and measured her fingers against the narrow waist of the bit of wood. "A small hand probably held this."

"Could have," said Wimpey cautiously.

"No, I'd put it stronger than that. He or she stood there clutching it and digging in the fingernails. You can see the marks where the nails went in, and they make it a small hand."

"You could be right. They could be nail-marks, but we'll have to see." He produced plastic gloves and a plastic bag into which he slid the branch. "So far, good."

But he still did not have enough to call Chief Inspector Merry from his brandy and port.

"And we found this hidden in a tree. A natural hollow with this in it. Come over and look. We left it where it was."

They had found a small travelling case, a light-weight affair of gaily striped canvas, complete with straps to throw over the shoulder.

Still using his plastic gloves, Wimpey drew it out carefully. "I think we'd better take it inside the house. The rain is beginning again. You two stay here."

Fred took his cue, and gratefully followed Wimpey and the two women back into the house, leaving the two uniformed men in the trees.

Outside, Charmian had kept in the background, letting Wimpey take charge, but now she wanted to study the case.

"Open it, please," she said.

The resourceful Wimpey produced yet another plastic bag, spread it out on the table in the sitting-room and pressed the lock. The bag sprang open.

Inside it was neatly packed with clothes, a pair of jeans, a jersey, several soft cotton shirts, and underclothes. A toilet bag held a toothbrush and some soap.

On top of everything was a model pony, made of wood with a flowing mane of real hair. The paint was wearing off where it had been handled over the years.

It was a treasured old toy, that its owner could not bear to leave behind.

"This case must belong to Joanna Gaynor," said Charmian. "She had it all packed, ready to be off."

Wimpey posed the obvious question: "And why did she leave it behind?"

"Who knows?"

Charmian covered her hand with a piece of tissue and slid it carefully into one of the side pockets and drew out a small purse, heavy with coins, and a packet of sanitary towels. She put them both on the table, without comment.

Then she felt in the bigger pocket in the lid and lifted out a blood-stained white T-shirt in which something was wrapped.

Inside, carefully covered with paper tissues was a knife.

Wimpey clicked his fingers. Now he had something with which to summon Chief Inspector Merry from his drinks.

13

THERE was no interviewing Annabel, whom the hospital had put into intensive care, not to mention the protective cordon set up by Brian Gaynor who was beginning to throw off his shock and act like a lawyer again. A policewoman sat by her bed, but no one was allowed to question her.

But the knife was public property for speculation. It was an impersonal, hard fact to digest.

What was it doing in Joanna's bag? There was a quick, easy answer to that one. She had it because she had used it, and she was hiding it for the same reason.

From this the argument could follow that she had been planning to run away, that Annabel had tried to prevent her and been attacked by her daughter.

There was, of course, another scenario which said that Annabel had attacked her daughter who had defended herself and then run away, leaving behind her case. The reasons for Annabel's attack, if it had happened, could only be speculated upon while she remained unquestioned, but it might have been connected with Joanna's obviously planned departure.

Chief Inspector Merry had arrived, smelling of cigar smoke and after-shave, neither customary fragrances with him, together with a team of assistants, and the full force of police activity had now moved from the Gaynors' house to Fletcher's Cottage. It had ceased to be Tommy Bingham's home and become the scene of a crime.

Merry had put his head round the door. "Talk to you later," he had said to Wimpey. Then remembering his manners, "If you don't mind waiting, Miss Daniels?" He had taken in the person of Ulrika Seeley, whom he knew, without pleasure. He had familiarised himself with her reason for being there, Merry always did his homework, but he found her an alien presence and would get rid of her as soon as he could. Charmian, of course, was another matter. No getting rid of her.

Tommy himself withdrew to a small, inner sanctum where he did his accounts and kept the stable papers. He was probably regretting having invited the Gaynors to stay.

"I'm sloping off," he said to Charmian. "Give me a call if you want me. I suppose you're staying around?"

"I intend to."

"Make yourself some coffee. You'll find everything there. Lesley keeps an eye on things for me. Gets things in. You know her, don't you?"

Charmian nodded. "Neighbours. I knew she worked with your ponies."

"More of a kind of housekeeper these days. Runs me a bit." He sounded not sure if he liked this. "Best of motives, of course. Anyway, help yourself to the coffee. Whisky in the cupboard. But I don't suppose you'll drink that on the job." He seemed to have an idealised view of coppers, Charmian thought. She knew plenty who would.

Presently, from the kitchen window where she was sitting with Wimpey and Ulrika Seeley, Charmian saw her neighbours, headed by Johnny and Lesley,

292

arrive as if they had swarmed in to protect their boss. They must love the man very much, she thought, and wondered if the Sunday lunch party with polo to follow would go ahead. Since Humphrey was a guest, she imagined it would. Things he wanted to happen had a way of doing so.

In a corner of the kitchen on a stand of its own was an Italian coffee machine, which both ground the bean, then delivered the drink. Charmian put in water, pressed a button and stood back. A row of bone china mugs with the initial B painted on them in gold, hung by the coffee machine, flanked by a tin of beans from Fortnum and Mason. A tin of chocolate Bath Olivers was underneath. Everything was polished and the spoons were silver. It was a bachelor's house with everything laid out for the owner's comfort. Tommy was a rich man, of course. A polo string was not run on nothing a year.

"I don't think Tommy would mind us having a chocolate biscuit, do you?" She got down the tin and put it on the table with their coffee.

Merry reappeared. "Oh coffee, good. I think I need some. Not sure I'm as sober as I ought to be." He was not a drinker, but liked his wine.

He seemed more cheerful. "Well, I've had a look at the hideaway and it's certainly where the attack took place." He took a chocolate biscuit. "We'll soon pick up the girl."

"Do you think so?" Ulrika sounded doubtful. "I hope so."

"Be surprised if we don't." Merry did not like Ulrika whom he regarded as a kind of witch doctor, dealing in spells and incantations which he did not understand. "I don't agree with you though, that the girl did the killings. I don't go along with that. No kid did them."

"I have never actually claimed that," observed Ulrika mildly.

"It's in the air, though."

"What about the knife?" Charmian asked.

It lay on the table between them.

"This is my first look at it." Merry did not touch it. "Good old kitchen knife, isn't it? Sure it's got blood on it?"

"Not sure of anything."

"It looks like blood on the T-shirt." Wimpey had kept silent until then.

Tommy Bingham put his head round the door. "Just had a 'phone call from the hospital. Mrs Gaynor has been X-rayed and so on. She has a contusion of the skull with lacerations — that was the message — and is coming out of the shock."

Merry thanked him for the information.

"Any news of Joanna?" asked Tommy anxiously.

"She's probably still in the Park; we'll pick her up in the morning."

Charmian turned to Tommy. "Are all the gates locked at night?"

"It's not quite night yet, is it?" Tommy looked out of the window. He saw that night was coming on fast, but there was still light in the sky. "But no, most gates are locked but the Bishopsgate entrance is always open. You can get out that way."

"But she'd be seen going through?"

Tommy shook his head. "Doubt it. Be lucky if she was. Not usually anyone around."

"I wonder about the railway stations?"

"Quite a walk, both of them. Could be done if she knew the way."

"Are there signposts?"

"Yes."

"Would she take a horse?"

"No, she'd never do that. She respects horses too much."

"Have you checked?" The question came out sharply, more sharply than she had intended.

Without a word, Tommy got up and left the room. Very soon, Charmian saw Lesley go running across the stableyard. Then he came back to stand by the door, waiting.

Presently Lesley hurried into the room. "Hoplite's gone."

"So much for that," said Tommy. He sat down heavily in the nearest chair. Lesley put a hand lightly, protectively on his shoulder, then removed it.

"You get back to the stables now, Lesley. Have a word with Fred. See what he knows. Not much, I don't suppose," Tommy added thoughtfully as the girl disappeared. He knew his Fred.

"We'd better get in touch with the

local railway station," said Charmian.

"Why?"

"She can't ride a pony all the way to London."

"She could have a damn good try," said Tommy, without pleasure. "And why London?"

Charmian shrugged. London was the place to hide in. It was where she would go herself if on the run.

"Yes, I agree about London," said Ulrika. "It is the place a girl of her age would think of, it is possible she has heard of somewhere there where she can stay. Word of mouth. Teen-age culture works that way. London, I think."

"And so do I." Merry stood up, his good humour gone. "I'll see about the local railway station. Better try Ascot as well, although it's more of a ride." He disappeared.

In a short time he was back, looking annoyed. "One railway station has no one in the ticket office because of shortage of staff. Passengers are buying tickets on the train. The next nearest station says it had two hundred young Italian tourists pouring through and couldn't tell one kid from another. She could have been there. And the third station claims to have seen no girl in jeans or any girl at all. In fact, they haven't seen anything. Professional non-witnesses to a man."

"That's probably the station she used," said Wimpey.

"If she used any station at all." Merry sat down heavily. He was a big man and in this hot weather he suffered from his weight. "I'll feel happier when we find her. Not that I necessarily go along with you lot in thinking she attacked her mother. Nor had anything to do with the killings. We've had three murders of a particularly nasty type: two adult women and one girl, and I don't see the kid doing them. It's a man, a Ripper-style serial killer, and I expect we'll be surprised when we see his face. Probably an ordinary looking bloke whose mates think he wouldn't say boo to a goose. Not the kid. In my book she's as likely to be a victim." For him it was a long speech, but the presence of Ulrika Seeley and Charmian Daniels in one room dragged it out of him. "I had to say it," he reported later to his wife. "I owed it to myself."

"There's the knife," said Charmian, who had been very quiet. "That means something."

"We'll have to see about that. I'm not speculating until we get the forensics. Or the girl. Whichever happens first." He stood up. "I'll have to stir my stumps."

Night was coming on, the sky was clear now, the storm was over, but there was no moon. It was getting hard to see into the corners of the kitchen. The tap was dripping with soft, regular persistence. Charmian went across to turn it off, then she reached out to the light switch and turned on the centre lamp. A hard cold glare filled the room.

Ulrika Seeley put her hand on the purse and the sanitary towels where they rested on the table-top.

"These two objects are interesting."

Charmian nodded. "Yes, I agree. She left the purse behind. So she has no money."

"She probably had a note or two tucked in her pocket," said Ulrika, who thought she knew just a touch more about young girls than Charmian.

"And the other?" asked Wimpey, he found the sanitary towels an embarrassing subject, one he usually tried to avoid.

"It means she is now half-way between a child and a woman, and she is probably frightened of the future she is embarking on."

There was something about the way Ulrika said this that silenced them.

Hoplite, a peaceful and wily animal, was tethered to a post in the field adjacent to the station. He was happily cropping the grass, but he had his eye on an interesting looking bush in a neighbouring garden. Supposedly he was tied up, but he had once shared a field with an elderly white donkey, put there as a companion, and he had learnt a trick or two worth knowing. Life seemed full of promise.

14

IN the morning a pony with a piece of wooden fencing pendant from his neck like a decorative frieze was discovered quietly grazing on the grassy slope hard by Fletcher's Cottage. Hoplite had come home. As well as teaching him guerrilla tactics, his donkey mentor had taught him to always learn the way home on the way out. You might not want the information, but it was better to have it. Hoplite, who was a conservative animal, had no intention of being a lost one. He was found by Freda who told Johnny who told Lesley. After a bit of thought, Lesley told Tommy. Hoplite's return was reported to the Alexandria Road police station where the call was received by Sergeant Wimpey, who passed it through all the correct channels, one of whom was Charmian Daniels.

Charmian received the news with her breakfast coffee. "Going to have to see the parents," she said to Wimpey. "I wonder how Annabel Gaynor is? I wonder if Brian Gaynor knows about the pony?"

"Knew before us, I expect," grunted Wimpey. "He's up there at Mr Bingham's."

Yes, Charmian would tell Ulrika. She would get her on the telephone this morning. They had not, as yet, located Joanna, alive or dead. Charmian and Ulrika thought she was still alive, Chief Inspector Merry suspected she was already dead. Either way, the search for her was becoming more anxious.

Charmian had got back late last night to Maid of Honour Row, having stayed talking to Wimpey and Ulrika in the former's office in Alexandria Road. Ulrika had then driven her home where the kitchen had showed evidence that Kate had been entertaining in her absence. Two wine glasses, two coffee cups, two plates with crumbs.

Probably Johnny had been the guest, Charmian decided, and wondered what, if anything, would come of that relationship. To her mind, they looked a dangerous combination, but perhaps that was what Kate wanted. It was what she usually got. Violence was spotted all over her past.

Someone might have to tell Johnny.

It was pleasant in her kitchen with the sun on her back, drinking coffee, eating toast and honey, and looking out over her own garden where she could see Muff strolling among the roses. She didn't remember letting the cat out, so it seemed likely that Muff had achieved her ambition and long-term aim of a whole night out.

A footstep on the stair made Charmian stir. "Kate, are you up?" It was early for Kate. Silence. She went to look.

Johnny was creeping quietly down the stairs. They stared at each other in silence. He didn't move, but did not speak, either. He looked bright, too bright for the early morning hour, and careful, he was waiting to see what she would do. Not the first time he had crept down a flight of stairs.

"I didn't see you," said Charmian. "This meeting did not take place."

"Thanks." He descended the last few steps. "Do I smell coffee?"

Yes, he was dangerous all right. He had that sort of charm that could get

303

away with murder. "You can have some if you like."

Murder, she thought. With my life, I ought not to use the word so lightly. Over their coffee and toast, they talked about the events of the last night, but in a detached, unemotional way. Johnny was sympathetic about the Gaynors, about his employer, most of all about the horses (Poor old Hoplite, he likes a quiet life, that one), but he was not prepared to break his heart.

As she closed the door behind him, Charmian asked herself if Kate would tell her about him? She was not a girl for secrets, but probably not.

But whoever tells anyone everything? Telling all could be therapeutic but it could also complicate life.

Yet persuading people to talk was part of her job, perhaps the most important part, and telling was what she was going to have to encourage the Gaynor family to do; and Ulrika had convinced her that there was much to tell. "Get them to turn over a few stones," Ulrika had said with gusto. "And watch what crawls out."

Annabel Gaynor had recovered conscious-
ness, her blood pressure had gone up to
something nearer to normal, she was out
of danger and so she was removed from
the Intensive Care Unit into a private
room. She would rather have been in an
ordinary ward because she felt the need
of company, but she was an object of
interest to everyone in the hospital and
to a good many people outside it.

Also, the police wanted to question
her. She was better on her own. So
she lay propped up on pillows on her
high hospital bed and stared out of the
window at the trees and roofs beyond.

Annabel recognised where she was,
both her babies had been born in the
Prince Albert Hospital, also in private
rooms. The private surgical wing was
on the top floor so tree-tops were all
she could see. Even in this way the
sight of others was denied her. But the
room itself was pleasant with blue and
white spotted curtains and a picture of
birds flying over the sea on the wall. She
had a bunch of flowers and a bottle of
mineral water, Evian, her favourite sort
on the table; she wondered who had

305

chosen the golden roses and who was paying the bill for this room. Perhaps her mother from her faraway hide-out in Corfu where she lived in the summer. Her mother wintered in Sloane Street where she maintained a small house. She disliked the rest of London, where she rarely left the neighbourhood of Knightsbridge because she said it was so changed. But she was good about sending flowers. They were her substitute for loving.

Brian sat by her side, but they were not talking. He was working on a brief with law books stacked in a pile on the floor. Annabel had noticed that he was only pretending to work, that his eyes did not shift from one spot on the page, but she was too far removed from reality to care. They told her she was better. She did not feel better, but she felt different.

Without turning her head, she said, "Why don't you ask me what happened?"

"Oh, you're awake."

"You know I'm awake."

"I didn't want to disturb you."

She was gravely disturbed already, probably permanently disturbed and she guessed he knew that too.

"So that's why you didn't ask me any questions?" No one had asked her any questions yet, but they were all there, hanging in the air above her waiting to fall, not like bombs, but more like ripe fruits that would squash on impact and stain her for ever. The doctors, the nurses, even the policewoman who had sat by her bed, had all been exceedingly gentle and kind, but she had felt the waves of their passionate interest washing all over her.

Her husband was silent.

"It's your job to ask questions, isn't it?"

"Oh Annabel."

"You're frightened to ask. Is Joanna home?"

He considered lying, but it wouldn't do. "No."

"So she got away? I thought she would do."

"She might have killed you."

"Oh no," said Annabel with conviction. "I might have killed her but she would never have killed me." Then she said, "But we might both have killed you."

Brian swallowed. "Aren't you worried about where Joanna is?"

Annabel looked out of the window. The trees were waving as if a wind had got up. "I think I would be more worried if she got back."

"You hit hard."

With a change of voice, Annabel said, "Of course I'm worried. I tried to stop her going. That's how this happened." She held out a tentative hand and he took it. It was the first real contact between them for weeks. "Who sent the flowers?"

"I did, of course."

"But you never send flowers." Even when she had the babies he had come in to the hospital carrying two books from the best-seller list, but not a flower, not even one rose.

"I did this time."

Before she left the house, Charmian had taken a call from Chief Inspector Merry. He sounded gruff. Never at his best early in the morning, he had had a bad night with indigestion. This had led to an irritable quarrel with his wife who blamed too much coffee, drunk too late, and not her excellently cooked dinner. This, in turn, had given him a bad headache. What with one thing and another he did not find it easy to be gracious to Chief Superintendent Charmian Daniels who he felt was an over-educated, over-promoted, over-active lady with powerful friends.

"I understand you and Dr Seeley are off to speak to Mrs Gaynor? I would have preferred to have had one of my lads do it, but I've had my arm twisted and I'm told you are likely to get more out of her."

Charmian was tactful. "I wouldn't put it quite like that, but we might just know more the sort of questions to ask."

"All right, I go along with that. You two are the experts." He paused. "But I want you to know that from my point of view this attack on Mrs Gaynor is a side-issue in a major investigation of three murders."

"I'm not sure if that is so."

"It's just how I see it. What's happened to her and the disappearance of the girl may have no relevance to what we are investigating. I've got three dead women, brutally slaughtered, and I don't see a twelve-year-old doing it."

He was a man of orthodox views who loved his wife and children in a straightforward way, and who, in spite of a wide experience of life gained in his police duties which had been tough and varied found it hard to believe, really believe (although he knew they existed) in paedophiles, incestuous relationships and parents who molested their children. Likewise he could not take on board the idea of a child as a multiple killer. But he was an honest man, who faced facts.

"There's no news of her?"

"No. But a railway worker whom we didn't see last night, says he thinks he saw a girl who fitted her description travelling on the six-fourteen train to Waterloo. The time would be about right. She could have caught that train. No one seems to have noticed the horse, but there's a broken fence in the field next to the station. Matches what the animal had round its neck. Seems to have eaten its way through half the apple crop on an overhanging tree. Wouldn't have thought a horse could do what that one did, but it did." There was a note of reluctant respect for the intelligence of the pony.

"Polo ponies are quite bright."

"Pity it couldn't talk."

If it could, it would probably be complaining of acute indigestion and comparing notes on the subject with him.

"Anything else?" You had to probe with Merry, he hated to disgorge information.

"As a matter of fact, yes."

As a matter of fact, yes, echoed Charmian in her head. God! Merry could be a bore sometimes. She felt she needed tweezers to pluck the facts out. Why couldn't he just say?

In the garden she could see Muff stalking something. She rapped on the window.

"What's that noise?"

"Just me. So what is it?"

"The blood on the shirt in the case does not belong to either Mrs Gaynor or the girl Joanna. They were both O, this is A."

"Well, that's interesting. And the victims, any match there?" Yes, she did need tweezers, sharp ones.

"Could be, just could be, Victim C."

The gay lady, the friend of Baby, Beryl Andrea Barker, the friend she called Maggie.

"But more tests are needed. You know how things are." Once they had got results in a matter of days, hours sometimes now, in the interests of precision, it could take weeks. "It could be Margery Fairlie."

So really Bert Merry had had something positive to impart, but how reluctant he had been to pass it on. Because it was on her side of the fence, this piece of evidence, and not his. It pointed to Joanna Gaynor as the killer.

Through the window she could see Muff emerging from a bush with a bird in her mouth, her eyes were bright, her tail bushy. This is the life, she was saying, never mind if it is someone else's death.

One more task before Charmian left for the hospital on the Datchet Road: she asked her secretary in London to call a garage and get her car repaired. Ulrika was about to drive her to the interview with the Gaynors, but it might be as well very gently to distance herself from Ulrika. She too had noticed a look in Ulrika's eyes, one or two gentle pressures on her arm and speculated; she was not as unaware as Kate had believed.

As she drove to the hospital, Ulrika said, "Am I just to sit in on this interview or am I allowed to talk, to ask questions?"

"Oh, you are allowed to talk, of course. Would anything stop you?"

"You mean I always interfere?"

"Something like that."

"But to a good end. You must admit it?"

Charmian said, "We're here. Don't overshoot the entrance. You can park under this tree."

"And I do come up with the answers." While talking, Ulrika was backing her car neatly into position.

"You seem sure of that."

"Mind, there are sometimes several answers." There was more than a hint of mockery in her voice. "I offer a choice." She locked the car. "Where do we go?"

The Prince Albert Hospital had undergone many changes since it had been built in the reign of Queen Victoria, after whose consort it was named. The original nineteenth-century building, a strong statement in Italianate red brick, had been deemed inadequate to modern medicine in the 1960s and doomed to destruction. There had then arisen a Victorian Preservation Society which had declared the building a gem of its kind. Local patriotism had taken hold, royal patronage invoked and the building was saved. It was now imbedded in a concrete and glass structure whose leaking roof and heat loss in winter, together with the intensity of the heat glare in summer, was a constant worry to the hospital administrator. The Victorian building, being the most comfortable, had been given over to the private patients, of which this prosperous district had a large number, and renamed the Armitage Wing after the original architect. An imposing staircase led to the main entrance.

"Up those stairs. She's in the Armitage Wing, that's where the private rooms are."

A nurse was at that moment coming down the steps. Since Florence Nightingale, the founder of modern nursing, had been influential in the setting up of the original hospital, the nurses at the 'Bertie', as it was locally called, still wore the pretty pleated caps and stiff aprons that she had devised, resisting the nylon dresses and paper hats of some other establishments. It was now recognised that this uniform, which was very fetching, pulled in the best student nurses and the richest patrons. The nurses looked so pretty in their lavender and white uniform that the marriage rate was high too. Many distinguished consultant doctors and surgeons, several bishops and a clutch of cabinet ministers had found their spouses while either working or being cured in the Prince Albert Hospital. Only by the young female doctors was this uniform resented as unfair competition.

The young nurse stopped them on the way up. "Can I help you?" They had all been instructed to watch out for journalists and sightseers. Mrs Gaynor was to be protected.

"Police," said Charmian, identifying

herself. "We are here to see Mrs Gaynor. Which room is she in?"

"Twenty-seven. I'm specialling her. I'll show you."

"How is she?"

"Coming along," said the nurse discreetly. "But you won't be staying long, will you? Not too long?"

Charmian smiled but did not answer.

Annabel Gaynor, in a pretty blue bedjacket, and with her hair brushed behind her ears, offered her visitors a nervous smile. Then she gave a quick look at her husband. Charmian did not fail to notice the look.

"Can I bring you some coffee?" asked the nurse from her position by the door.

Better take it. Relax the atmosphere. "Yes, please." Charmian smiled at Annabel. "Let's all have some."

"None for me." Brian Gaynor stood up, scattering his papers. "Damn."

There were only two chairs in the little room, one padded armchair and the upright chair by the bed on which Brian Gaynor had been sitting. He motioned to the chairs and took up his stance by the window, his whole bearing saying, "Let's get on with this, and not pretend it's a sociable visit."

"There's been a bit of news about Joanna," Charmian began. "It looks as though she did take a train to London. Waterloo Station. I don't know if you knew that?"

"No. Thanks for telling us." Brian looked at his wife. "Any news is welcome."

"Have you any idea where she might go? Any friends, family, that she might visit?"

"My mother has a place in London," said Annabel in a soft voice. "But she's in Greece. I don't think Joanna would go there."

"Can I have the address, just in case?" Charmian wrote it down, noting that Annabel's mother lived in a pretty classy area. "Mrs Porter, Two Arden Place?" Annabel nodded. "And you, Mr Gaynor, any family in London?"

"My parents are both dead. No one else."

The nurse appeared with a tray and three cups of coffee. "Let's leave that for a moment then." Charmian took her

317

cup and sat by Annabel's bed. Annabel gripped her cup, holding it in front of her as if it could protect her. "How do you feel now, Mrs Gaynor?"

"Better, thank you."

"And how did it happen, this attack on you? Can you tell me anything?"

From her armchair, Ulrika said gently, "Joanna hit you, didn't she?"

Annabel lowered her eyes. A pale skin was already forming on the top of the coffee. She wasn't going to be able to drink it, she hated skin. "Yes," she said suddenly.

"Why did she do that?"

"I was trying to stop her running away."

Charmian took a hand. "Why was she planning to do that? Was she in any trouble?"

Annabel fell silent. She avoided looking at anyone in the room. The only safe place to look was the coffee cup and she concentrated on the drink.

"It was a pretty violent thing to do, wasn't it?"

"We aren't on good terms. She doesn't like me."

"A family quarrel, is that it?"

"You could call it that," said Annabel, still not looking up. "There was something that happened that I didn't take her part over. Let her down. She thought so. Maybe it was so. I was angry, and I turned the anger on her."

It was hard to make out what she was saying, she was squeezing the words out.

"Has someone been hurting Joanna?" asked Charmian. "Something physical?"

Annabel made a small noise and spilt the coffee. With shaking hands, she tried to tidy herself up.

Ulrika looked at Charmian. "Leave this to me," the look ordered. "Mr Gaynor, tell me what your wife means. I think you know."

Brian Gaynor said roughly, "It was my fault. Something I did."

"To Joanna?"

"Yes." He had turned to face the window. "Something I shouldn't have done. I can't explain it. It happened."

"You molested your daughter? Sexually molested her? Is that what you are saying?"

319

Brian Gaynor covered his face with his hands.

"Come on now, Mr Gaynor. Let's have it."

"Nothing overt," he muttered hoarsely. "Just . . . touching. Once or twice."

There was a silence.

"She's been so full of violence ever since." Annabel was crying quietly. "And so have I, so have I. It tore us apart. We were a family torn apart with a great hole in the middle."

She might have been quoting Ulrika.

As the two women made their way out some time later, Charmian said, "Thanks for what you did in there."

"It wasn't so much."

"I think it was everything. Your presence there brought the whole thing right out."

"I believe they were getting ready to tell it. In fairness to Brian Gaynor, I have to say I think he was about to do so. I just gave him the chance."

"Poor kid . . . Could what happened, and after all, from what he says, and if we believe him, it wasn't a complete sexual invasion, could it provoke the reaction we think? Turn the child to killing?"

"There was a lot of anger in Joanna trying to get out," said Ulrika. "But I'm a psychiatrist, not a policewoman. The rest is up to you."

They both got into the car. At the entrance to the hospital they passed a big white Rolls coming in. Lesley was in the driving-seat, and Tommy Bingham was sitting beside her, carrying a big bunch of blood-red roses. He looked pinched and drawn as if death had given him a passing nod, but he waved at them cheerfully.

"It's a tragic business, however you look at it," said Charmian. "I can never take these family crimes. A family," she shook her head. "It ought to be a safe place, not a breeding-ground for murder."

"There's more than one sort of family," murmured Ulrika thoughtfully. "You ought to think about that."

In her office, later that day, Charmian had a telephone call from Sergeant Wimpey.

"First, Brian Gaynor came into the

station and made a statement. But I gather you know about that?"

"I do."

"Well, I won't comment. But second, a bit of news. No, not about Joanna, haven't found her yet. But we will. No, something else and I'm afraid it doesn't look good for the kid. The laboratories have had second thoughts on the hoof-prints. You remember the prints that were found?"

"I remember. So what?"

"At first, they said there was nothing much to learn, just prints. But then they showed them to someone who knows about nags. It's true enough, that as a rule in England, you can't tell one pony print from another. Just ordinary trammel ridges and a nail in the centre. But there are things called Polo plates. They have a higher, inner ridge. Came from the States. Some high-goal players are beginning to use them over here. Tommy Bingham is such a player and he has been using them. One of the few that does in Windsor. Apparently the casts made from the shoe prints suggest such a plate. The animal could

322

have come from his stable."

"Thanks," said Charmian. "Yes, that does fit in, doesn't it? What about the animal that came back this morning? Did he have these special plates on?"

"No. Apparently not all Bingham's ponies are shod that way. He's only just getting into using them. It's an experiment. But it ties in, doesn't it?"

Yes, it did. Poor Joanna.

15

THE garage returned Charmian's car in time for her to drive home that evening. The repair seemed minor, the bill large. She was more than a little worried about money. With the new house plus all the expenses that came with it, she knew she was spending more than she could afford. Inside her was an accurate little accountant that kept a tally and was now shouting Stop.

She had attended to her routine work, chaired a committee, and given lunch to a colleague who wanted advice. In addition she had received a flow of telephone calls from Wimpey, keeping her up to date on what the press was calling 'the Windsor murders'. Yes, he could tell her that more delicate tests could confirm that the blood on the shirt in Joanna's case was that of Margery Fairlie. And yes, the case was Joanna's. Annabel Gaynor had identified it. Said she knew nothing about the knife or shirt.

This might or might not be true. "Oh yes, and we called Brian Gaynor in to Alexandria Road again. He didn't want to come but we didn't see why we should make life easy for him. He's co-operating all right, though. He had something new to tell us."

"Not another confession?"

"No. But his son has told him that Joanna had some keys. She called them her secret keys. So maybe she did have a hideaway somewhere. Wouldn't put anything past that kid. And she's only twelve." There was something like respect in his voice. "Good job they aren't all like her."

"She's had things happen to her that made her grow up fast."

"But violence?" And such violence. He thought of his own child and felt sick. Could children have such strength inside them?

"It's a way out, isn't it? She's digging herself out of a hole." Ulrika had taught her to see it so.

"I have to tell you that Bert Merry doesn't see it our way. He's still looking for his serial killer. 'Wait and see', he says.

And he says we are making mountains out of molehills."

"He always had a gift for words."

But all the time, inside her, she was filled with a kind of practical anger at the situation within the Gaynor family. The first step towards resolving the anger was to find Joanna and then to help her, to break the destructive circle in which she was caught.

She was angry, angry, angry.

"No wonder I've got grey hairs." The bright summer sunlight seemed to show them up with greater clarity than usual. Some people had the luck to have a charming streak of silver, she seemed to be speckled. Not greatly speckled yet, but certainly going that way. Her mother had been white before she was forty; it was in the family. But there were things you could do about it. Possibly before the Sunday luncheon party?

On an impulse she telephoned Beryl Andrea Barker, whom she still thought of as Baby, at her hairdressing shop and asked for an appointment. "For a kind of tint." She knew better than to call it 'dye'. No one used that word any more. She had decided on an honest but cautious approach. "Nothing drastic. Could you do it?"

"Of course. Nothing easier. But, of course, red hair can be tricky. Unless you want to go really Titian? That would mean doing the whole head."

Baby, in her best professional mood, could be daunting. Charmian suspected she was enjoying it. Gave her a lift to be the one in charge of Charmian Daniels' hair-colouring.

"I'll stay with what I've got." A kind of rich carrot it had been once. "Just do a rinse or something."

"It's dulled down a lot lately, hasn't it?" said Baby with some satisfaction. "It does with age. I remember when I first knew you," when you were investigating the case for which I eventually went to prison, Baby meant, "it was quite bright."

"Thanks."

"Drop in tonight and I'll do you a quick job. Do it myself."

"Thanks," again. What else was there to say?

"Guess what?" Baby sounded quite

327

lively. "Maggie Fairlie left me a thousand pounds. I've just heard from her solicitor."

"Did she have that much to leave?"

Baby coughed. "I think she may have had a little bit salted away. I don't know who gets the rest. I wish she hadn't got herself killed, though. But I suppose she had it coming to her. She always was unlucky. Any word yet on who killed her?"

"We're looking."

"I reckon she knew the killer, because although she was unlucky, she was also careful. I reckon it was someone she thought she could trust. Wrong again, poor cow."

"You can't tell by looking," agreed Charmian.

"Hey," said Baby alertly. "You know something. You think you know who did it."

"Guessing and looking, Baby."

"Keep looking. I won't feel safe till you've found him. I don't fancy meeting Jack the Ripper in Windsor one dark night. And forget the Baby. Andrea, please. I asked."

Miss Barker put the telephone down feeling she had scored. She saw the relationship with Charmian as a kind of football match in which most of the goals had been achieved by Charmian. However, she acknowledged Charmian's tenacity and power for carrying things through. If Charmian said she was looking for the killer, then in Miss Barker's opinion that killer was as good as found.

From her seat by the telephone she could look through the large plate-glass window of her shop at the usual Windsor street-scene of shoppers, tourists, motor cars and cyclists, with beyond all this the River Thames.

The same river was in sight from Charmian's office where, high on the fifth floor, she could look down on the river and across London.

Somewhere in that city, she guessed, was Joanna.

A dangerous child to be on the loose.

The evening before, Joanna had climbed on the train to Waterloo in the middle of a crowd of Italian schoolchildren who were on a holiday trip. They were returning to their hostel in London after a day of heavy sightseeing. In her jeans and dark blue sweater, she did not stand out from them, and they were so busy shouting away and eating ice-cream that they themselves did not notice the cuckoo in their nest.

On arrival, the Italians swarmed around a bar selling hot chocolate and warmed-up croissants, so Joanna joined them there, too. She had a couple of fivers folded in her pocket, earnings from her work in the stable — Lesley had said that a labourer was worthy of her hire, and Tommy Bingham was not mean, although careful, so she was not without money at the moment. She had her Post Office Savings Bank book with her and that had plenty in it. She could survive financially for some time.

The Italians did not queue in an orderly fashion as a crowd of English schoolchildren would have done. Instead they pushed and jostled for position. Joanna shoved with them, taking care not to become too prominent.

Listening to what they said, she called,

"Quanto questo?" in her turn, pointing to what she wanted and then shovelling the money across. The woman behind the counter gave her a quizzical stare.

Joanna did not like that stare. She guessed it meant that, somehow, in some way, she did not look like the Italian crowd. Then she caught sight of her image in a big mirror at the back of the counter. Fair hair and blue eyes. Of course she was different from the brown-haired and sallow-skinned Italians. They were dark to a child. True, one of their teachers had red hair, but even Joanna could tell that it was dyed.

Thoughtfully, she carried her provender to a bench tucked away in a corner, where she sat eating. Another bunch of children sat there, English children, eating hamburgers and chips. But everyone ate hamburgers and chips, it was a safe meal. She might move on to those herself when she had finished her croissant, although to her mind it made the meal the wrong way round. Joanna was a slow, thoughtful and conventional feeder. She did not like surprises in what she ate.

The large W. H. Smith's bookstall was

still open, giving her the chance to buy a book (she chose a paperback horror story of a haunted house) to read with the hamburger and chips which she presently sat down to eat. In a different spot this time, on another discreetly placed bench, she was wary of being noticeable.

All the time she was thinking what to do. In a way, she knew. She had thought it all through weeks and weeks ago as a contingency plan if she had to make a run for it.

She knew where she was going, had been there with her mother and had the keys to open the door. But the timing was important. If someone saw her going in, she would be done for. They were a gossipy lot in that block, her grandmother had said so, and Joanna believed her. "I try to slip in and out without anyone noticing me," she had said. "Otherwise you are caught."

Joanna did not wish to be caught.

She patted the keys to her grandmother's maisonette where they rested in her pocket. Joanna fictionalised that her grandmother had given her the keys ('Have them, dear child, just in case.'), but in fact she had stolen them from Annabel who had come in for some grumbling for losing them, and had been put to a good deal of trouble to replace them. She sat there considering her plan of action.

If Annabel had seen her sitting there, hunched over her hamburger and book, she would have said, "She looks like my mother in one of her witchier moods."

Joanna finished her hamburger and read on. Without Joanna noticing it, the station had begun to empty. Soon it would quieten down into its night-time sleep. Already the small shops had closed and lights were dimming along the platforms where no trains ran.

As the travellers diminished, so some of the debris of the London streets drifted in to take their place. A woman who looked old but was not, carrying two plastic bags, wearing two overcoats and three pairs of stockings, appeared. She had emerged from the ladies' lavatory of which she had been dispossessed. She was turned out every night, always hopeful, for ever disappointed. She had the quiet persistence of a dripping tap.

Her path was crossed by an enemy, a dusty sexless lady who spat on her as she passed. They had never spoken, but some odd trifle picked up by one and lost to the other had set them for ever apart.

A man came to take the seat next to Joanna. She smelt him before she saw him. Acid, sour, and strong. A hand snaked out from a dirty sleeve and touched Joanna's thigh. The man did not look at her but stared straight ahead as if the hand had nothing to do with him.

Joanna reared upright, clutching her book. Without conscious volition, her foot delivered a powerful kick to his shin. Then she shot towards the Underground, and disappeared down its open mouth.

The escalators and platforms were busy with returning theatre-goers all talking with each other happily. Here and there an exhausted soul leant against the wall with closed eyes.

Joanna, who had done this journey often enough in her imagination, knew which Underground line to take and at which station to change. What she was not prepared for was the relative darkness and emptiness of the street into which she eventually emerged.

The ticket collector had looked at her oddly, but not spoken, so she had put on her most confident and boldest air as she walked past him. She was just a girl who happened to be out on her own. A young actress perhaps, with a part in the latest musical, who knew her way around. Or a ballet-dancer carrying her head proudly and high.

Thus protected, she walked at speed down the street to her grandmother's, mercifully empty, maisonette. She knew the set-up. There was a block of flats with a long hall, and through the glass door at the end of this you entered the quadrangle which was lined with the small houses. It was an expensive and sheltered domain. Part of the expense went to the wages of the porter who lived in a set of rooms by the street entrance and watched who came in and who went out.

That was the theory. But Joanna knew from listening to her grandmother's complaints ('We pay him a fortune so he can sleep in his armchair.') that his was not the all-seeing eye. She could get through.

There was no sign of the porter when she got there. Exactly as predicted. But a taxi drew up as she hovered about, from which stepped an elderly lady shrouded in pale mink (it was a warm night, too), who let herself in with her own key.

This allowed Joanna to observe which of the two keys on her ring was to be used, so she did not fumble a minute later, but unlocked the door smartly, walked through the lobby, used the same key for the second door, and marched out towards her grandmother's house. She was the lady of the house returning from a day in the country now, she had been studying wild flowers, on which she was a world expert, which accounted for her informal clothes.

Once inside the front door, however, she was conscious of an enormous fatigue. She took a long drink of water and collapsed onto the bed. At first, in spite of her longing for oblivion she could not find it. Sleep would not come.

Taking off her shoes, she padded into the bathroom and looked in the cabinet over the wash-basin. From what she knew of her grandmother, she would find something. A bottle of tablets ordered her to take no more than two a night, one hour before bedtime. She was to abstain from alcohol.

Joanna took three with a wineglass of the sherry from the kitchen. That ought to do it. Shortly after, she fell into a deep sleep.

She slept and slept.

So it came about that all the next day, while her parents were talking to each other in Annabel's room in the hospital, and while Charmian was looking out over London wondering where Joanna was, Joanna was falling from one restless sleep to another. In her sleep she occasionally shouted. Once she got up, not fully awake, and put on all the lights. With morning she woke up again and staggered around, drinking some more water and turning off all the lights. The drugs and the drink had been altogether too much, she needed help.

There was one person who would help her. Must. Also, as she suddenly remembered she had something she must tell.

It was still early morning, she could tell by the light and the quiet, although all the clocks in this place were stopped, but the place she wanted to telephone got to work early. A telephone call was probably safe if she worked it right.

Getting the number was not so easy. In her muddled state, she had a bit of difficulty with the dialling code, but the number rang at last.

"Hello?"

It was Johnny, she recognised his voice. She put the receiver down at once. In a little while she would try again. She knew his ways. He would not bother to answer the telephone twice in one short space of time. "One of you take it," he would shout. "Some lunatic there who won't answer." She had used this device in telephoning before. It was a kind of signal.

She tried again. This time Lesley answered as she had hoped.

"Lesley? It's me. Joanna."

A moment of dead silence.

"Don't go away. Please, Lesley. Help me."

"Where are you? Everyone's looking for you."

"Are they?" She both knew and did not know that they must be looking for her. Didn't want to know. She hated to be looked for, feared it. Had done since what she wouldn't talk about had happened. To be looked for was bad. "I'm at Gran's."

"Is she there with you?"

Silence from Joanna now, while she tried to think what to say.

"No, I'm on my own. I got in. I mean I had a key."

"Thank goodness you're safe."

Lesley really meant it. But how long for? The one thing that Joanna's life had taught her was that you couldn't trust anyone. People had shifting faces. "I've done something wrong."

"I know." Knocked your mother on the head, for one thing. What else? "Come on back. You'll be forgiven."

"No, I've got to say . . . I had my case packed. I left it behind . . . "

"Where did you leave it?"

"In some bushes. Tucked away."

Then the police probably had it, but Joanna wouldn't think of that, not in her present state.

"It was my running-away case. I left my purse in it. But I had a bit on me." Quite a lot really, but she was not going to say so. She wanted to bring Lesley to her.

"Is the case important?" Keep her talking and calm her down, Lesley was thinking, while you consider all this. There was so much to bear in mind.

"It had a knife in it."

"Oh dear." Could she believe this? She decided she could.

"Come and get me, Lesley. I'll feel safe with you."

But will I feel safe with you, thought Lesley. Is she leading me into a trap? But if the police had the knife . . . The knife was undeniably important.

"I'll come." She could take the group's old car. They would not be pleased, nor at her absence, but she would cover it up somehow. Say she had to go to her father. That had happened often enough in the past to be believable. "Tell me where."

There was a very long silence.

"I think someone is looking through the letter-box. I think I see a face."

"You're imagining it."

"I might be." Joanna did feel strange, as if the walls were coming in close and pressing down on her, shouting the while. Voices. She herself felt very very heavy.

"Where to come, Joanna?"

Sluggishly, Joanna said, "Arden Place, Sloane Street. Number Two, Arden Place. I think that's right."

"It'd better be."

"You come along. You're not to say anything."

Something she would have to say, but exactly what she would have to decide. "No," Lesley lied. It would really depend what she found when she got there, and how she managed the situation. She thought about that knife.

Joanna lay down on the sofa and closed her eyes. For a little while she slept. The flat was very hot and the walls seemed to be moving all about her. Above her the ceiling seemed to have a face embedded in it. Likewise a soft voice, which was calling her, but not by name. Just asking who was there. And the answer was No one. Had to be no one. She was now no one.

She got herself a glass of water, dropping the glass and breaking it. As she stumbled back to the sofa, she trod on a piece of glass, tearing her foot. No pain registered. Again she slept.

Even in her sleep her thoughts revolved painfully. She was walking through blood and her feet were sore. She deserved punishment because she was wicked. A bad girl. She knew it was all her fault. Evil had descended on her from she knew not where or why. But somehow or other she deserved what was happening to her. Inside her she knew this to be a fact. But another part of her wanted to deny it and to run away and avoid punishment. Whatever she did, she knew she was wrong. She groaned and shouted as she slept.

In the house next door, the neighbours heard it and complained. They had complained already to the porter that there was something going on next door in that house that should be empty.

Without realising it, Joanna had wreaked a certain amount of havoc in the place. She had opened cupboards and drawers in the kitchen without closing them again, she had knocked over a chair and broken a glass. A tap was running in the bathroom. Blood had dropped from her foot to the floor, now she was bleeding on the sofa.

She was awakened suddenly to find a man staring down at her. A small, stout man with a red face.

"Come on now, who are you? What are you doing here?" Joanna leapt up, she started to scream. There were no words in her scream, just the high piercing shouts of panic. The sounds tore through her throat, ripping out into the room, tearing the silence apart.

Fred, the porter, staggered back. He was almost as shocked as she was. He had responded to the complaints of the neighbours about strange noises coming from Mrs Porter's flat which should be empty.

He did not know what he had expected to find, but certainly not a screaming girl.

He looked nervously over his shoulder to the door which he had prudently left open.

He put his hand on her arm. Joanna looked down to see blood. Her screaming stopped. She threw a vase at him, then grabbed a chair and hit him with it. Then she tore into the kitchen and grabbed a knife from the open drawer.

She pointed it at him as he lumbered forward. The screaming began again. Fred desperately tried to fend her off. He was shouting himself now, as well as sweating profusely. He was bleeding too, they were both bleeding.

It was into this scene that Lesley walked through the opened door. She saw at once that the girl was beyond Fred's control, beyond her control, beyond her own control. Some boundary had been passed.

Lesley felt fear for herself. Anything could happen now.

This creature was no longer totally human. Evil had subsumed her.

Charmian was told the news about the finding of Joanna and of her state on the telephone in her office. Sergeant Wimpey was her informant. He sounded stunned.

"What's happened to her?"

"Temporarily under sedation in hospital. Poor kid."

"Yes, I suppose we do have to say that." Somehow it did not seem quite an adequate description. "Do her parents know?"

"They've been told."

"How are they taking it?"

"I think the mother more or less guessed where the girl could be. So she didn't act surprised. Perhaps she's not capable of surprise any more." For which, Wimpey implied, he would not blame her. "By the way, the porter of the building is in hospital, too. Same hospital, not the same ward. He got cut by a knife and then had a mild heart attack. He's not in any danger."

"I should like to see Joanna."

"I don't think it would do you much good at the moment. You could try." But he gave her the name of the hospital in south-west London. "I'd better tell you that Merry has in no way changed his mind. Glad the girl is found. Blames the parents."

"He could be right there."

"Agreed. But he still can't accept the girl as a multiple killer. Can't take it on board."

"In spite of the blood on the knife found in Joanna's case? In spite of the horseshoe? That ties the Bingham stables close in, doesn't it?"

"He's digesting all that."

"And you?"

"I don't know, I honestly don't know. Sometimes I think one thing, sometimes another." He was being honest. "What about you?"

After a pause, Charmian said, "I think I would say that her behaviour is, in a way, a kind of confession."

But she had a good deal of respect for the judgement of Chief Inspector Merry. Imaginative, he was not, a good straightforward policeman, he was. He kept on a straight path, but he very often got there in the end.

At the end of her day, Charmian drove home and submitted her hair to the ministrations of Andrea Barker. They were alone in the little salon.

"You're late." Andrea sat her client down and hovered accusingly. "I've been waiting."

"A busy day." Charmian shook out her hair. Yes, it needed attention, cutting as well as washing and tinting. Baby had trained her to call it 'tinting'. No one dyes any more, she had said. "A lot in it." She had gone to the hospital where Joanna was incarcerated to be told she was 'asleep'. If so, she was asleep with her eyes open. But it was impossible to talk to her, you could not get through.

Baby was drawing Charmian's hair through her fingers with a speculative look. "A bit out of condition. I can work on that. If you ever decide to go grey, I can do it for you beautifully."

"Thanks."

Miss Barker smiled; she had her own little techniques for levelling up with Miss Daniels. She needed it occasionally, otherwise there would be no doing anything with the woman. She'd walk all over you.

Charmian sat back while her hair was

washed. She had to admire the skill with which her friend put out a lazy paw and scratched her, Muff herself could not do it better. Reminded of Muff, she hoped that Kate had remembered to feed her, or an angry and hungry cat would await her when she got home.

Baby started on her job, brushing on a dark paste which would presently be washed out with shampoo. She hummed as she worked keeping a firm, restraining hand on Charmian's scalp as she did so. Thus may a surgeon or a torturer operate, with professional, pleasurable skill.

In a pause, she said, "Rumour's going around that the girl who's gone missing is the one that did the killings. Is there anything in it?"

"I wonder who started that story?"

Miss Barker shrugged. "You know how it is — Keep your head down, dear."

"Do you believe it?"

Another shrug. "Believe anything." She was towelling Charmian's hair with energy. "But it would explain why the women got caught: they wouldn't expect violence from a child." She wrapped a towel turban-style around Charmian. "Move over to here, dear. That's right, by the mirror. Want a magazine? We'll just have a wait before I give you a cut." She leaned against the basin and began to check on her own hair, teasing a strand of silver-blonde on to her cheek. "Mind you, nothing would have made Maggie Fairlie let down her guard. Miss Distrust in person. Of course, she might have known her killer."

Charmian tried a question at a tangent. "Keen on horses, was she?"

Andrea, she was definitely Andrea as she studied her face, laughed.

"Not her. Didn't know one end of a horse from another. Took a job when she first came out and was hired as barmaid when they had a big do in the Park for some American polo players, that'd be the nearest."

Charmian tried to nod her head, but found it caught in a vice-like grip.

Baby (she was back again, full of malice), gave a little scream. "Oh, horror! Something's gone wrong. You've come out bright green."

"What?" Charmian recoiled, staring at

her image in the mirror.

Baby reached for a cigarette and gave a giggle. "Joke. Just a joke."

Then she saw the look of fury in Charmian's eyes, remembered that she was teasing a high-ranking police officer whom it would be wiser not to offend and said hastily, "Silly me. I'll send you out looking lovely, you bet. And of course, it's all on the house."

16

HER hair immaculately coiffed (because, after all, she had this occasion in mind), wearing a new Italian silk dress, and accompanied by Kate, Charmian stood sipping champagne in Tommy Bingham's box. Box was a misnomer really since it was no more than a partitioned-off area of the main onlookers' stand with an awning at the back where luncheon was served. You could stand in it and hail friends in other boxes and this was what was happening on this highly social occasion.

Murder notwithstanding, the game of polo had to go on. This was an important international match against the Americans. Tommy would not be playing, of course, he had not done so since his illness but his ponies were there.

If one of those animals could talk, thought Charmian, we could solve this case on the spot.

"You're a dangerous lady," said Humphrey. "When I introduce you to my friends, death starts walking around."

"I don't think it's my fault. Just my job. Anyway, I rather think I have you to thank for involving me so closely in all this." The Gaynors were notable absentees at this Sunday lunch-party, although one felt their presence as a set of ghosts. "I think it was rather brave of Tommy to go ahead with this party, all things considered."

"He is a brave old boy. And I suppose it is one of the last occasions of this sort he may have: time is running out."

Charmian looked at him. "Oh?"

"He's got cancer. Terminally ill. I wonder he has lasted as long as he has. It's as if he keeps getting a boost of new life. Every so often you think, well, that's it, goodbye Tommy. Then he picks up again."

"I suppose that's the way it goes." Across the room, her eyes met Lesley's gaze, then flicked away. Neither of them wanted to be reminded of their meeting over Joanna's bed.

"It has with him."

Lesley and Johnny, together with Freda and Gillian, had been included in the party, but were not quite of it. They hung together in a group. A buffet lunch had been set out on a long table and they were tucking into that with enthusiasm. Charmian noticed a slight tendency on the part of Kate to edge towards them, but they were not encouraging her.

"Can I get you something to eat?" Humphrey nodded towards the food. "Chicken? Salmon? Tommy puts on a good spread."

They strolled towards the table. A girl in a crisp white overall was serving the food. She gave them a cheerful smile, as if she knew them. Or, as if even if she did not know them now, she would know them next time.

"Tommy always gets in local staff to serve," murmured Humphrey, "even if a lot of the grub comes down from London. Fortnum's, I think."

Charmian accepted chicken salad, taking it to a small table, with a good view of the party. There were a couple of dozen people present, a few of whom she knew. All present were noticeably well dressed and beautifully groomed. She had been right to get her hair cut.

It was the sort of occasion on which at least two of the murder victims might have worked behind the serving table. Perhaps they both had, it might be worth checking. But then, this was the sort of routine inquiry that Chief Inspector Merry's outfit did so well.

Humphrey put her glass of champagne beside her and sat down himself. "Kate's having a good time."

"She usually does, I fancy."

"You sound disapproving. You are a puritan." He wasn't quite joking.

"It's because of my Scottish blood," said Charmian, placidly forking up her chicken salad. She did not intend to get into an argument with Humphrey who had greater verbal dexterity than she had and always won. "You can't expect otherwise. As it happens, I don't disapprove of Kate, but I think she is a bit rash, that's all."

From across the room, Kate looked at her and smiled as if she had heard. Lesley and the other three had disappeared. Presumably to get back to work. Did all owners of a string of polo ponies let their stable lads come to drink champagne and eat smoked salmon? But Tommy Bingham seemed a special case.

Then she looked at him as he stood talking with one of his guests and realised that was exactly what he was. It was a farewell party he was giving. He had warded off death for a good while now, but his time was coming and he knew it. He was saying goodbye to his little family.

She wondered if Humphrey understood this, and guessed he did. About the others she was not so sure, they had looked so happy.

"Time we moved off," said Humphrey. "The first chukka will start in five minutes. They are always punctual when the Royals are here, especially if one of them is playing."

Charmian found she was able to take at least an intelligent interest in the game. Her diligent study of *An Introduction to Polo* by Marco had paid off. It had also given her some respect for the late Lord Mountbatten. As a young man he must have been very hard working to have been a naval officer, to have played polo as well as he did and to have written such a lucidly clever book about it. He was rich too, of course, and no doubt that helped. And those were leisured days.

But thanks to him, she now had some idea of the subtleties of 'striking', and of the skills involved in 'riding off' and the system of 'calling'. It still looked a rough, tough game, but she understood now that there were rules. But it was hard on ponies as well as men.

"Sturdy little beasts, aren't they?" murmured Humphrey at her elbow. "Tommy used to bring in ponies from the Argentine, they are much the strongest because of working with the cattle, but I don't know if he's been able to do that since the Falklands. Spoilt things a bit," he added reflectively.

"Spoilt a lot of things." And quite a few people's lives.

"Some Argentinians are coming back into the game here," said Humphrey seriously, as if this was all that mattered. What a man he was for concentrating on the matter in hand. No doubt a contributing factor in his success.

She still had little idea which side was winning when the interval came and was too proud to ask but, from the pleased murmurs all around her as they sallied out onto the pitch to tread in the sods, she guessed it was the side all her luncheon-party friends supported. Even on this point she could not be clear since it was a well mixed international group with a clutch of Americans, several Frenchmen and at least one German.

Without surprise she saw that Kate was walking by Tommy Bingham's side, her head bent towards him, her whole attitude one of graceful, affectionate support. Tommy was plainly enjoying her attentions. Kate could be a good girl sometimes, her godmother thought.

The soft turf was not doing the heels of her pretty, pale leather shoes any good and she would rather not have been trudging dutifully around grinding in her heels, but everyone else was. Suddenly a few feet away she saw the Trust twins, one on either side of Mr Pilgrim who was thus satisfactorily captured. The bridal party, she thought. For the first time the two women were not identically dressed.

Flora was in a flowered silk dress and the bride, if that was what she was, wore a thin chiffon in blue and white spots. The separation between them which she had foreseen was beginning.

She excused herself to Humphrey and made her way towards them. Both women looked pleased to see her. Flora smiled, but Emmy delivered herself of the first complete sentence that Charmian had heard from her.

"Miss Daniels, this is John Pilgrim, my husband-to-be."

Mr Pilgrim gave an uneasy smile. There was something in that smile that constituted a confession and convinced Charmian that he knew who she was, but before he could speak, Miriam Miller had forced her way through the crowd. "Flora, Emmy, dears, can I have a word?"

As Emmy and Flora turned to Miriam, Charmian took the chance to speak to the bridegroom of destiny. She had been learning things about Mr Pilgrim.

"Mr Pilgrim, or Joseph Archer or Eddie Turner, or whatever name you prefer, I hope you will make Emmy happy and go on making her happy. Since as far as I know you are not married to anyone else, your marriage to her will be legally binding whatever name you marry under."

"You don't need to worry, Miss Daniels," Mr Pilgrim gave a nervous cough. "I don't know what you know about me, but I'm done with all that. I want to retire, Miss Daniels, I assure you, I want to retire. I am marrying to retire. I mean to be a good husband to Emmy. She suits me down to the ground."

And so did her money, Charmian thought, but there was something about the new Emmy that made her think that she could look after herself. Perhaps she always could.

Miriam turned her attention to Charmian. "I've heard that Brian Gaynor has tried to kill himself." Her eyes were big and blue, demanding information.

"Not true as far as I know." Though he might feel like it or wish he could.

"But they haven't been seen, any of them, for days now."

"They've gone to stay in a house on the coast while things are sorted out."

"And Joanna? One has heard such things."

Charmian looked away. "No, Joanna is not with them. She is having . . . treatment."

"In hospital?"

Charmian was evasive. "Not quite a hospital."

"Is there anything one can do? I liked that child."

"If there is, I will tell you." Someone like Miriam, independent and clear-minded, might be a very good friend for Joanna eventually. She would need friends. "I will be seeing her one day soon."

"She's such a brave child. She was so brave about it when her brother hurt his leg, fell on a nasty piece of rusty iron, went in really deep, blood pouring out, and she coped beautifully. So good of her when she's terrified of blood."

Charmian considered Miriam's words as she walked back to the pavilion with a silent Humphrey. "You've got your thinking face on," he said. "I won't interrupt."

"I *am* thinking."

Blood again. Frightened of blood.

One of those little facts no one ever bothers to tell you about. A girl who didn't like the sight of blood, a girl who had just started menstruating and might well be sensitive about that too. Charmian guessed that this case was not wrapped up, ready to be put away.

Somehow it was not over, she had not seen the end of it.

Dacre Park was a sedate, decrepit country house, built by a war profiteer after the Battle of Waterloo and run down in two successive great wars, which had been bought up by a far-seeing local authority in the 1960s for no great sum and turned into a residential home for children too difficult and worrying to stow away anywhere else.

The Park had never been a place of great beauty since the original Dacre had wanted value for money in bricks and mortar rather than taste, but it had developed into a family house of some charm which had endeared itself to successive generations until the last Dacre had died in the Normandy landings. Now

361

it was imbedded in a cluster of modern buildings and had a sad air about it, like a good old dog somehow tethered to a mongrel puppy.

"Have you been to Dacre before?" Ulrika was doing the driving, negotiating the bends of the narrow Berkshire lane with skill.

"Heard of it. Never visited." Charmian was hanging onto the door nearest her, wondering what would happen if there was something parked round the next bend. They whizzed past a field of cows. "Is country air meant to be good for disturbed kids?"

"This looks like deepest country, but it isn't. There's an industrial belt dependent on Reading to the west," Ulrika nodded westward, taking her eyes dangerously off the road. "And a new town, Brinkley, growing up fast to the east."

Almost a week had passed since Joanna had attacked her mother, then run away. This visit by Charmian had not been easy to arrange. The doctors had advised against it, even now it was only set up under Ulrika's supervision. During this period there had been no more murders, nothing that came near to an attack on women, no threats. Even Chief Inspector Merry seemed to be coming round to the idea that all the trouble had emanated from Joanna after all. Proof he had not, acceptance he was beginning to admit to. "See what you can get," he had said to Charmian. "You could be right, after all. Get her to say something."

"Do you come often?" she asked Ulrika.

"As often as I have a patient here. It's a good place, does a good job, sheltering the children, offering various forms of therapy. Educating some of them."

"How long do they usually stay at the Park?"

Ulrika shrugged, again a risky manoeuvre considering the speed at which she drove. "As long as they need. A year. Until they are sixteen, anyway. After that date, they are either free or in prison."

"And what happens today?"

"I have the whole outfit lined up: Joanna, her parents, the brother if he wants to come, and her social worker. Oh, and her case worker at the Park. Then we talk. And talk. Something the

Gaynors have been conspicuously bad at."

"And yet he's a professional talker."

"I expect that is why."

"And if they don't talk?"

"Oh everyone does in the end. The Park somehow works it. It's a good place. Understaffed, underfunded and under threat, of course, like all these institutions." There was a small car park with several empty spaces, one marked Dr Seeley. "Oh by the way, I ought to warn you to protect yourself. I've seen evil popping out of the walls at these sessions sometimes."

"Protect myself, how?"

"Oh, I don't know. What do you usually do? Pray or think good thoughts."

Ulrika parked her car, locking it carefully, and led Charmian in to be introduced to the Principal and the Warden. The first, a man whom Charmian recognised as someone she had seen in court one day, arguing on behalf of some young offender. The Warden she had never met before, but she seemed a bright and aggressive young woman wearing the standard uniform of ragged jeans, buffed trainer boots and a thin sweater.

Ulrika might say that Dacre Park was understaffed, but there seemed plenty of people about. As far as she could judge there must be some six workers or so to every young inmate, which no doubt explained why these children seemed stronger and more aggressive than their protectors. They knew they were that important.

"Why are all the women dressed like men?" Charmian asked, as they sat in a great empty room, ringed with upright chairs, waiting for their party to arrive. "Jeans and boots?"

"Isn't it just practical working clothes?" Ulrika looked down at her own attire. She too wore the same clothing, her boots were newer and more expensive, her shirt prettier, otherwise it was the same.

"I think it's for self-protection. I believe I would be nervous myself if I worked here." The children who were meant to be so weak, seemed so strong. Strong in their indifference, strong in what was possibly wickedness. Power did not seem balanced the way she had expected at all. It might be an illusion, of course. In the end society probably had the stronger hand to play.

The clock struck and, promptly on the hour, their party filed in. Brian first, then Annabel who looked pale, Mark after them and finally Joanna with her social worker and her case worker from the Park.

Without a word, they sat down round the room, staring at Ulrika and Charmian. It might not be hostility, but it was not friendliness either.

With some dismay, Charmian observed that the two female Gaynors were now dressed in the penitential uniform of jeans and trainers and sweaters. It didn't augur well.

No one spoke. The minutes ticked by. One hour had been allotted to this interview and it looked like passing in silent communion.

Ulrika looked at Charmian. "You start," she said blandly.

Charmian heard her own voice say, "Mr Gaynor, the rumour is going round Merrywick that you have committed suicide. Do you want to comment on that?"

"I have committed suicide, I should think anyone could see that. Professional suicide, anyway. More than one way of doing it, you know. And what's more, I have taken the whole family with me."

"Not me," said the boy, Mark. He looked red and fearful. "I'm not dead, Daddy."

Annabel started to cry silently, but she put an arm round the boy and moved her chair so that she could take her husband's hand.

Brian removed his hand and went up and knelt before his daughter. "Joanna, forgive?"

Joanna did not answer. Presently she turned her chair to face the wall, then she walked slowly out of the room. The two social workers hurried after her. Presently one of them came back in and delivered her message.

"Joanna asks me to say that in less than three years she will be sixteen. Until then she wishes to stay here and she does not want to see any of you again."

They sat out the rest of the hour in silence.

At the end of it, Ulrika stood up and said briskly, "I think we may be able to do better than that next time. In spite of what you might think, we made a good start."

On the way home, Charmian said: "Did you really mean that about a good start?"

"Oh yes, I see a lot of hope there."

"I thought it was awful. Quite horrible."

"Oh well, I told you to protect yourself."

Joanna might begin to look a hopeful case, as if they would succeed in casting out her devil, but the trouble was once you let evil out of the bag, where did it fly to? Come to that, where had it already flown to?

"I suppose that hole, that conceptual hole, or real hole, as you think of it, that seemed so important — "

"Was indeed important," broke in Ulrika.

"Was really a hole in the family that she was trying to fill? Was she absolutely conscious of it, or was it a manifestation beyond her control that she could hardly put a name to? Family life is the devil," said Charmian. "Perhaps we'd all be better coming out of eggs."

Ulrika drove on in silence. Then she said, using words she had used before, "There's more than one sort of family, you know."

17

BUT Charmian was a sensible, practical police officer, with a long experience of crime. Behind delinquency — even serious crime — was poverty, bad housing, and unemployment, not evil. Surely she was not obliged to believe in evil? Even less must she believe it could reach out and touch her.

Nevertheless, she was glad of the presence of the healthy hedonist Muff in her house and of the lively company of Kate. All seemed to be going well with Kate at the moment. Her parents might, after all, not be divorcing and she was fascinated by Johnny.

"I'm persuading him to take a university course," she announced. "He says he's had enough of horses for the time being."

"Does he want to do this?"

"I can work it. He's very bright, you know. Anny thinks he's a good thing."

Briefly, Charmian wondered if Johnny

was a younger version of Mr Pilgrim because one only had to see Anny, her clothes, and the manner of her life, to know that there was money about. But she decided to give Johnny the benefit of the doubt.

"I'm glad they're not divorcing," she said of her friend Anny and her husband.

Kate gave a tolerant shrug. "It's the way they like to live. Couldn't stand it myself, but it suits them. Apart, together, fighting, making-up, that's how it's been for years. It's a way of life. Literally, I think. I mean, it saves them killing each other."

Charmian gave her a surprised look.

"Has it never occurred to you, godmother?"

"People don't kill each other as easily as that," said Charmian.

"Don't they? I think they do. Depends on the family. Something genetic, running in the blood." It was lightly said, but perhaps meant all the more for that. "And I never said easily, it would never be easy."

"And what about you? What about your blood?"

Kate laughed. "That's what I like about Johnny. I could never kill him. I'd be safe, he'd be safe."

"What makes you so sure?"

"It's just something I feel about Johnny. We match. Our genes would pool well. Making good blood, I suppose you could call it."

The opposite of making bad blood. "You are a funny girl," and Charmian touched her affectionately.

Good blood, bad blood, menstrual blood, equine blood.

"Blood is an interesting subject," she thought. "I'm sure it was the sight of her own blood coming from her cut leg that morning in her grandmother's flat that sent Joanna over the top." And waking up to a man's face peering down on her, of course. With her background that would be alarming enough.

But Kate was still talking. "By the way, Johnny says his boss is pretty bad. Had one remission after another. But now no more. They're all praying for him to get better or their jobs are gone. Not only that, they love the old boy."

"I didn't think them the praying sort."

"Well, whatever they do instead. Cast spells or something." She added casually, "Like another cup of coffee?"

In the county-police forensic science laboratory on the outskirts of the busy town of Slough, where the work on the 'forensic debris' collected in and around the three murder victims was being done, they were also interested in blood. Any trace of blood on anything was automatically tested and given a grouping. A careful cross-reference was being kept.

It so happened that Dr Stanley Easterborough, the principal scientific officer involved, had also been the man to whom had been entrusted the bundle of clothes worn by Charmian Daniels when she had been attacked.

At that time he had examined all the clothing for any blood that might have come from her attacker. He had been assured that Charmian herself had not bled. He had done his work, filed his report, trusting that someone of intelligence would read it, and pushed the clothes away in a drawer. It had been a busy day.

But now, a few weeks later, on that very morning when Charmian was drinking coffee in her kitchen, he found himself in a housekeeping mood. When he was feeling happy he liked to do some tidying up, and on this day he was in a splendid mood. An article he had written for a distinguished academic publication had been accepted for publication, which was the more satisfactory when he had also learned that one written by his enemy and rival for the top job had been turned down. That sort of thing cheered a chap up. What is more, he had made a very early start, coming in with the dawn chorus because he wanted a day off tomorrow. It was barely breakfast-time yet, and no one except the cleaners were around.

So he made himself a cup of tea (he did not drink coffee) and started to clear the drawers of his desk. In a plastic envelope were Charmian's clothes. He had not put them away as well as he might have done, so he drew them out to refold.

In the pocket of Charmian's shirt, he felt something. He withdrew a folded piece of stained tissue. It smelt a bit. That was blood on it, too. Untested blood.

A conscientious and scrupulous soul, he meditated for a short time about overlooking this trifle of paper, then turned to. He took a sample, shouldn't take him too long. Tidying up was tidying up, after all, mustn't sweep things under the carpet.

"That's interesting." He raised his head from the slide he was studying.

He realised that what he had found might be significant. He had read the newspapers. And if he hadn't, then his wife had done and kept him fully informed of what she considered interesting details.

All the same, he might not have passed on the information speedily if he had not been a friend of Sergeant Wimpey. He wanted to talk to him anyway, they were playing cricket together at the weekend and he needed to set up the arrangements for travel. Who would drive whom? Both wives were coming too.

He reached out for the telephone.

"Hello, Wimp," he said. "Are you interested in horses?"

Kate stood up. "If you want even more coffee, then the pot is keeping warm. I'm off to see someone I love."

"Johnny?"

"No, I don't love him yet, although it might come to it. I think it will." She smiled to herself. "It's been pretty physical so far, but I think the rest is there. I'm rather chuffed." She produced the piece of slang with conscious pleasure. "No, it's Dad. I'm going to help him pack to go back to Anny."

Charmian sat over her coffee, which seemed to taste the better for being made by Kate. It was getting late, she ought to be off, but a meditative mood kept her sitting there.

Without knowing the characters concerned but knowing the type of killings, what portrait of the killer would you make? She could hear Ulrika's voice advising her. Some things can't be put into words, she was saying, they are just emotions floating free. Bits of evil, slices of goodness, looking for somewhere to settle. This killer picked some up, or was offered them or stole them from family or friends. Probably family, because the family is the most notorious provider of such ingredients.

Nevertheless, Charmian could only think in words, so here she had to part company from her mentor.

She started to draw up a profile of the murderer.

First, because of the nature of the crimes, manifesting extreme aggression towards women, it was very likely that this killer had suffered abuse within a trusted circle, for example the family, possibly from a woman. Or anyway, blamed a woman, the woman defaulted in some way. The mother left the home perhaps?

Secondly, by the emphasis on the hole as manifested in the various notes and messages, this killer is saying he or she is filling a need in the family. Offering a death to fill a hole. The dead women are sacrifices. They are dying for something. That's how the killer sees it.

Thirdly (and this idea had only just

occurred to her), this killer may not be sure of his or her sex. So, if a woman or girl, they may have a name that could be masculine or feminine. Might blame this on the family too.

Joanna? It was possible. But, of course, there were other such names.

Lastly, but importantly, this killer knew the victims, knew enough about them to find them, attract their attention without causing alarm, and so get close enough to kill.

Charmian herself had been threatened and once followed. She had an idea that on another occasion she had come very close to an attack, but had been saved by a chance arrival.

Nearly everything she was thinking matched Joanna, although it was hardly what Chief Inspector Merry would regard as evidence. Valid after the event, he would say caustically. When you know who's done it, then you draw the picture.

The telephone rang, and she heard Wimpey speaking. "You remember the attack on you?"

"The one that happened, or the one that never was?"

"The man in the park."

"Oh that one. Had no connection with the murders."

"No, a chance attack. But you sent the clothes you were wearing off for forensic testing. Helped us identify your attacker. In the pocket of your shirt was a blood-stained tissue.

"That was his blood."

"No, or not only his blood. There was blood from a horse as well."

"At that time, I knew nothing about the slaughtered pony."

"No," said Wimpey seriously. "So where did it come from?"

Charmian did not answer, she put the telephone down on Wimpey in mid-sentence, without noticing that he was still talking.

She knew where the blood had come from. She saw that all the details in the picture she had been drawing fitted this person as well as Joanna. The name of this person had been in the frame every time, had cropped up in the life-style of each murdered woman.

She believed she even knew now why her own killing had not occurred after she had been appointed to the place of the next victim. She thought she could even see the motive for the killings. If you could call it a motive when it seemed more like a ritual act of sacrifice. Ulrika could get busy with her speculations here.

She understood now what Ulrika had meant when she pointed out that there was more than one kind of family.

The stables, with Tommy Bingham as father, that was a family. It had been Joanna's family too, in a crucial way, and she had been influenced by it and been loyal to it. Been loyal to the killer, taking a knife and shirt to London in her case to hide.

Poor Joanna, to find herself in the midst of two such dangerous families.

Charmian sat thinking, trying to fit all the facts together into a rational picture. There was a terrible rationality behind it, although not one the so-called real world would perhaps accept easily.

She could even blame herself. She found herself accepting that she had played her part. The killing of the pony had been a beginning from which nothing else might have followed, but for the attack on her. She could see now that that incident might have been inflammatory to a disturbed mind.

Charmian dressed herself and drove to the stables where she would find everyone she wanted to talk to. She wondered if she ought to warn Kate, but decided to leave it. She had gone off to see her father who might be no help in some things, but could certainly be counted upon to keep his daughter occupied for a whole morning.

She went right round to the stables, avoiding the house where Tommy himself would be resting.

Lesley, her bright auburn hair covered with a silk scarf, was crossing the stable-yard, carrying a bucket. She stopped as soon as she saw Charmian. "Hello, looking for anyone?"

"Yes, you."

Lesley looked thoughtful. "Are you sure? Johnny's around somewhere."

"I mean business, Lesley."

Lesley looked at her. "Not sure I know what you mean."

"I have a right to talk. You nearly

killed me. You would have done. I would have been victim number four if a car had not come down the road while I was looking down at the dead rabbit."

"Ah."

"I suppose it was always some trick like that you used to get close to your victims. 'Do come and look at this,' and then the knife in. They all knew you at least by sight. They worked or visited places you frequented." It suggested a kind of selection of the victims which would be interesting if it ever came to a trial. "Joanna loved you. Still does, I expect, in what she has left of her mind. You may not have meant to destroy her, but you did. She got infected."

Lesley stared in silence. Charmian knew she must pierce this calm, break it up.

"But tell me what the hole stood for, what did it mean? Because you did always leave that sign, didn't you? What hole were you filling?" She could almost hear Ulrika's voice asking that question. The only thing was that by now Ulrika would know the answer. She didn't.

Lesley started to walk across the

stable-yard to the tack-room. Charmian followed her. No risk, she thought. Bound to be plenty of people about, but she was on her guard.

"Come in," said Lesley. "It's starting to rain."

"We won't close the door."

The tack-room was warm and empty, it smelt of leather and horses.

"I don't know why you have come here."

"I've been asking myself that," said Charmian, "and it is not the way I usually go on, but I think I want you to confess. I want you to say Joanna is innocent. I think she deserves that from you. She's had a raw deal. Not least from me. I am going to do what I can for her, and talking to you now is one of the things. It might help her if you confessed. I think she needs your confession. So do I, because I feel I did a lot of wrong things."

"You mean you feel guilty?" Lesley sounded amused. "Well, good for you, Miss Daniels. Doesn't guilt get around?"

Charmian was silent, watching Lesley.

"Well, I can soon get you out of

that trouble. I need one more death. For Tommy, he has been more than a father to me, more than a mother. Especially my own, the bitch. I don't mind telling you, I'm proud of it. Those women, those animals, and there were more than you know about, died for Tommy. Every time one died, every time I got one, Tommy got stronger. Cause and effect. They were dying for him." She was reaching behind her for a length of rein. It didn't have to be a knife, strangling would do it. Might even be a more powerful prophylactic. "Now it's your turn."

"I am not in any danger," Charmian told herself. "I am a strong, trained woman and on my guard. She will not fill that hole she is seeking to fill with my body." Had there been other deaths than those she knew about? Or was Lesley fantasising? Other animals perhaps?

Charmian tried to step backwards. But she wasn't moving. Like a rabbit that the ferret had fixed with its eye, she seemed stuck. She made a strenuous effort to move backwards through the door. Her legs felt heavy.

From outside, someone was calling for Lesley.

The door was dragged open. "There you are, Lesley." It was Johnny. He looked surprised to see Charmian. "Glad to see you, Miss Daniels. We need help. Tommy's just had a haemorrhage. It's bad. Come and give us a hand, Lesley."

Saved by blood, Charmian thought, as she pulled herself together, and found her legs would move after all. "We'll both come," she said, taking Lesley by the arm. The arm felt limp. Lesley would not resist. She might want to, but she could not. Some life, some force had gone out of her.

Ulrika would have said, No, they never resist when faced with certainty, that's what they are like, not quite people like the rest of us.

An ambulance arrived to take Tommy Bingham away. From what she saw, Charmian guessed he was already dead. He would never know what he had been responsible for.

Very soon afterwards Chief Inspector

Merry and his team arrived. He was not pleased: events had taken over from him, which was not the way he liked it. An orderly progression of events leading to an arrest was the way he liked it. A team effort. This arrest had come about by what was almost an accident. He was inclined to blame Charmian Daniels, but did not feel able to say as much.

He would have got there, he implied, was getting there. The marks of the special polo-pony shoe had been a vital piece of evidence, indicating clearly that someone from the Bingham stables had been involved. The usual routine police work would have done the rest.

He did point out with quiet triumph that he had always said that the girl Joanna Gaynor was not the killer.

Kindly, and allowing himself to forget for the moment his rank and her rank, he suggested that Charmian went home.

There were already signs of police activity in the house next door to Charmian's in Maid of Honour Row. There was a police car outside the door and a uniformed man posted on the pavement outside.

A few spectators were already gathering to see what was going on. She was not surprised to see an interested Muff weaving her way around them.

Someone would have to see Lesley's father, she thought. She had better do it herself, if Merry agreed. Get Ulrika to help, she thought. She didn't know much about the girl's background except that her father was an invalid, but she suspected she would find a rejecting, probably cruel mother. Anyway, an absent mother. She knew that much.

Charmian grabbed Muff to her, she wanted the feel of that sane animal body smelling so sweetly of fur and sun. Muff purred loudly, flattered at being wanted, and hopeful of food. Must be hours since she had had a good meal.

While she had stewed rabbit, Charmian went through her address book, searching for a telephone number. She had not been strictly honest in saying she had forgotten this person, she remembered well enough, but it was a bit of the past she had tidied away.

"Professor Lamb, please." He was eminent now, and had a chair.

She had to wait for Professor Lamb to be located and dragged out of a seminar, but there were advantages to being a police officer. People did try to do what you asked.

"David? Charmian Daniels here."

"Good lord, a voice from the past. What do you want?" He knew what her career was, he was always well informed. "One of my students in trouble?" He'd never be in trouble himself, far too canny.

"Just wanted to ask you something. Might be a test of your memory, I don't know. Cast your mind back to our student days. Do you remember taking me round a museum and showing me some early Christian tombstones? Some of the effigies had beards. Frisian beards, you called them. Do you remember? Why did you call them that?"

"My goodness, did I say that?"

She could picture him sitting at his desk, holding the telephone and probably sucking on a pipe, if he still smoked. She remembered his red hair. One of the things (there hadn't been too many) that they had had in common.

Of course, it was the hair. From the first, her mind had made a connection between the 'hole' and red hair. It had been pointing her silently towards Lesley. She ought to have understood her own mind.

"A Frisian beard, eh?" She could hear him laughing. "I was joking, joking."

A case solved by a joke, Charmian thought. But it would not be one she would share with Chief Inspector Merry. Nor with Sergeant Wimpey, and certainly not with Humphrey Kent.

She might tell Ulrika Seeley though, and goodness knows what she would make of it. She had a way of illuminating a mystery.

Several days later Charmian was shopping for food in Windsor, choosing cheese from an array of some twenty or so different types spread out before her in Goodbody's, the large and splendid store where she did her shopping. Kate had been absent from under her roof for a few days — settling Dad in the family home was her explanation but she was expected back today. Charmian was planning a little celebratory dinner. To her surprise, she had greatly missed her god-daughter.

She had just ordered a slice of Brie and a chunk of Parmesan, because they were going to have pasta, when she saw Miriam Miller smiling at her from behind a foot or so of French bread.

"The Sesame Club is having a little supper party tomorrow. Do drop in if you can, Annabel Gaynor and I are doing the catering." She paused, waiting for Charmian's reaction, which was circumspect.

"I heard she was out of hospital."

"We decided that we had to grasp that particular nettle," said Miriam. "I put it to Annabel that she'd better get on a public face and come, and she agreed. Not easily, but she did. All of us in the Sesame Club think that the family is worth saving and we want to help. If that means helping Brian Gaynor, so be it. I'm not saying that we condone, or even understand, but we don't intend to sweep the whole affair and the Gaynors with it under a kind of mat."

"I think you're doing the right thing. I'll come."

"Annabel tells me she had a telephone call from Joanna yesterday. Didn't say much, asked after her pony and wants the little wooden horse she left behind, but it's a start. You have to start from somewhere." Displaying her usual acumen, Miriam said: "I suppose Joanna knew or guessed from the beginning who had killed the pony and then the women?"

Charmian nodded gravely. "I believe she has said as much to Dr Seeley. She knew from the moment the knife that killed the pony was found in her own bag. They were very close, those two girls. I think Joanna had confided a lot of her troubles to Lesley. She had certainly tried to protect Lesley by packing a knife and T-shirt used by Lesley in her case when she ran away."

Or had Joanna realised these objects might be used to accuse Lesley and prove her own innocence? Relations between the two had got very mixed by the end, with both love and hate entangled. It might be that Lesley would have killed

Joanna if necessary that day in London.

"There's a lot of strength and loyalty in Joanna," said Miriam. "And she's clever. I hope that when she's herself again someone will see she gets to a proper school, not that debby place she was in. Good boarding-school would do the trick. She needs a rest from family life, that girl. Of course, there won't be the money there was before," said Miriam. "No one's actually said, but reading between the lines we think it might be hard for Brian to go back to his practice as if nothing had happened. I mean men do forgive each other almost everything about sex, don't they, but perhaps not this. So we don't know what he's going to do, but Annabel is a very very clever girl and she used to hold down a good job of her own, and will again."

Charmian realised that in a gentle way Miriam was looking forward to a bit of role reversal in the Gaynor family. The Gaynors would have to sort themselves out, she thought as she walked on to buy some of that French bread, and would doubtless do it. There was stamina and brains in the family, and courage, as well as other things she did not admire so much. No one had asked what the boy Mark made of it all, she thought suddenly, and decided to ask Ulrika, that great mopper-up of life's problems, to see what she could do.

Cheese, French bread, Italian wine, fresh fish for Muff who was on a fish-eating kick, but not frozen, thank you. She gathered her purchases in her arms and walked home.

Kate's bags were in the hall and Kate herself was striding up and down the kitchen.

"Do you know what that man of yours has done?" Not my man, Charmian was protesting, but Kate marched on. "Did I or did I not, have Johnny lined up to take a degree in economics? And now what has happened? Humphrey Kent is taking over the Bingham stables and has asked Johnny to run them for him. And Johnny said Yes."

Charmian started to laugh. Kate would have to learn to put up with the quirkiness of life, the endless capacity of people to do something you didn't expect of them. The sheer muddle of it all. You accepted it, forgave them if you could, but anyway tried to help them, see them through their problems.

This was what Ulrika Seeley had taught her.

Even if their problem was murder.

She looked at her calendar hanging on the wall above the stove where Muffs fish was so delicately flavouring it and on which several dates were ringed.

On those days she would be seeing Lesley in her place of imprisonment. If she could help, she would.

This was the way to do it, a self-evident truth, but one to be learnt. Ulrika knew it, Miriam Miller knew it, she suspected that Emmy Pilgrim, born Trust, knew, and now she knew it. One day Kate would know it.

Talking, uncovering, conciliating, and with luck, mending, such was the process. Perhaps women could do it better than men.

CLOUD OVER MALVERTON
Nancy Buckingham

Dulcie soon realises that something is seriously wrong at Malverton, and when violence strikes she is horrified to find herself under suspicion of murder.

AFTER THOUGHTS
Max Bygraves

The Cockney entertainer tells stories of his East End childhood, of his RAF days, and his post-war showbusiness successes and friendships with fellow comedians.

MOONLIGHT AND MARCH ROSES
D. Y. Cameron

Lynn's search to trace a missing girl takes her to Spain, where she meets Clive Hendon. While untangling the situation, she untangles her emotions and decides on her own future.

NURSE ALICE IN LOVE
Theresa Charles

Accepting the post of nurse to little Fernie Sherrod, Alice Everton could not guess at the romance, suspense and danger which lay ahead at the Sherrod's isolated estate.

POIROT INVESTIGATES
Agatha Christie

Two things bind these eleven stories together — the brilliance and uncanny skill of the diminutive Belgian detective, and the stupidity of his Watson-like partner, Captain Hastings.

LET LOOSE THE TIGERS
Josephine Cox

Queenie promised to find the long-lost son of the frail, elderly murderess, Hannah Jason. But her enquiries threatened to unlock the cage where crucial secrets had long been held captive.

THE TWILIGHT MAN
Frank Gruber

Jim Rand lives alone in the California desert awaiting death. Into his hermit existence comes a teenage girl who blows both his past and his brief future wide open.

DOG IN THE DARK
Gerald Hammond

Jim Cunningham breeds and trains gun dogs, and his antagonism towards the devotees of show spaniels earns him many enemies. So when one of them is found murdered, the police are on his doorstep within hours.

THE RED KNIGHT
Geoffrey Moxon

When he finds himself a pawn on the chessboard of international espionage with his family in constant danger, Guy Trent becomes embroiled in moves and countermoves which may mean life or death for Western scientists.

TIGER TIGER
Frank Ryan

A young man involved in drugs is found murdered. This is the first event which will draw Detective Inspector Sandy Woodings into a whirlpool of murder and deceit.

CAROLINE MINUSCULE
Andrew Taylor

Caroline Minuscule, a medieval script, is the first clue to the whereabouts of a cache of diamonds. The search becomes a deadly kind of fairy story in which several murders have an other-worldly quality.

LONG CHAIN OF DEATH
Sarah Wolf

During the Second World War four American teenagers from the same town join the Army together. Forty-two years later, the son of one of the soldiers realises that someone is systematically wiping out the families of the four men.

THE LISTERDALE MYSTERY
Agatha Christie

Twelve short stories ranging from the light-hearted to the macabre, diverse mysteries ingeniously and plausibly contrived and convincingly unravelled.

TO BE LOVED
Lynne Collins

Andrew married the woman he had always loved despite the knowledge that Sarah married him for reasons of her own. So much heartache could have been avoided if only he had known how vital it was to be loved.

ACCUSED NURSE
Jane Converse

Paula found herself accused of a crime which could cost her her job, her nurse's reputation, and even the man she loved, unless the truth came to light.

A GREAT DELIVERANCE
Elizabeth George

Into the web of old houses and secrets of Keldale Valley comes Scotland Yard Inspector Thomas Lynley and his assistant to solve a particularly savage murder.

'E' IS FOR EVIDENCE
Sue Grafton

Kinsey Millhone was bogged down on a warehouse fire claim. It came as something of a shock when she was accused of being on the take. She'd been set up. Now she had a new client — herself.

A FAMILY OUTING IN AFRICA
Charles Hampton and Janie Hampton

A tale of a young family's journey through Central Africa by bus, train, river boat, lorry, wooden bicycle and foot.

THE PLEASURES OF AGE
Robert Morley

The author, British stage and screen star, now eighty, is enjoying the pleasures of age. He has drawn on his experiences to write this witty, entertaining and informative book.

THE VINEGAR SEED
Maureen Peters

The first book in a trilogy which follows the exploits of two sisters who leave Ireland in 1861 to seek their fortune in England.

A VERY PAROCHIAL MURDER
John Wainwright

A mugging in the genteel seaside town turned to murder when the victim died. Then the body of a young tearaway is washed ashore and Detective Inspector Lyle is determined that a second killing will not go unpunished.

DEATH ON A HOT SUMMER NIGHT
Anne Infante

Micky Douglas is either accident-prone or someone is trying to kill him. He finds himself caught in a desperate race to save his ex-wife and others from a ruthless gang.

HOLD DOWN A SHADOW
Geoffrey Jenkins

Maluti Rider, with the help of four of the world's most wanted men, is determined to destroy the Katse Dam and release a killer flood.

THAT NICE MISS SMITH
Nigel Morland

A reconstruction and reassessment of the trial in 1857 of Madeleine Smith, who was acquitted by a verdict of Not Proven of poisoning her lover, Emile L'Angelier.

SEASONS OF MY LIFE
Hannah Hauxwell
and Barry Cockcroft

The story of Hannah Hauxwell's struggle to survive on a desolate farm in the Yorkshire Dales with little money, no electricity and no running water.

TAKING OVER
Shirley Lowe and Angela Ince

A witty insight into what happens when women take over in the boardroom and their husbands take over chores, children and chickenpox.

AFTER MIDNIGHT STORIES,
The Fourth Book Of

A collection of sixteen of the best of today's ghost stories, all different in style and approach but all combining to give the reader that special midnight shiver.

DEATH TRAIN
Robert Byrne

The tale of a freight train out of control and leaking a paralytic nerve gas that turns America's West into a scene of chemical catastrophe in which whole towns are rendered helpless.

THE ADVENTURE OF THE CHRISTMAS PUDDING
Agatha Christie

In the introduction to this short story collection the author wrote "This book of Christmas fare may be described as 'The Chef's Selection'. I am the Chef!"

RETURN TO BALANDRA
Grace Driver

Returning to her Caribbean island home, Suzanne looks forward to being with her parents again, but most of all she longs to see Wim van Branden, a coffee planter she has known all her life.

SKINWALKERS
Tony Hillerman

The peace of the land between the sacred mountains is shattered by three murders. Is a 'skinwalker', one who has rejected the harmony of the Navajo way, the murderer?

A PARTICULAR PLACE
Mary Hocking

How is Michael Hoath, newly arrived vicar of St. Hilary's, to meet the demands of his flock and his strained marriage? Further complications follow when he falls hopelessly in love with a married parishioner.

A MATTER OF MISCHIEF
Evelyn Hood

A saga of the weaving folk in 18th century Scotland. Physician Gavin Knox was desperately seeking a cure for the pox that ravaged the slums of Glasgow and Paisley, but his adored wife, Margaret, stood in the way.

DEAD SPIT
Janet Edmonds

Government vet Linus Rintoul attempts to solve a mystery which plunges him into the esoteric world of pedigree dogs, murder and terrorism, and Crufts Dog Show proves to be far more exciting than he had bargained for . . .

A BARROW IN THE BROADWAY
Pamela Evans

Adopted by the Gordillo family, Rosie Goodson watched their business grow from a street barrow to a chain of supermarkets. But passion, bitterness and her unhappy marriage aliented her from them.

THE GOLD AND THE DROSS
Eleanor Farnes

Lorna found it hard to make ends meet for herself and her mother and then by chance she met two men — one a famous author and one a rich banker. But could she really expect to be happy with either man?